DAVID GRAHAM

INCITEMENT

ANDROMEDA PUBLISHING

First published in 2013 by
Andromeda Publishing
Dublin, Ireland

Paperback   ISBN: 978 1 909483 42 2
eBook – mobi format   ISBN: 978 1 909483 43 9
eBook – ePub format   ISBN: 978 1 909483 44 6
CreateSpace paperback   ISBN: 978 1 909483 45 3

Produced by Kazoo Independent Publishing Services Ltd.
222 Beech Park, Lucan, Co. Dublin
www.kazoopublishing.com

Kazoo Independent Publishing Services is not the publisher of this work. All rights and responsibilities pertaining to this work remain with Andromeda Publishing.

Kazoo offers independent authors a full range of publishing services. For further details visit www.kazoopublishing.com

Cover design by Andrew Brown
Printed in the United Kingdom

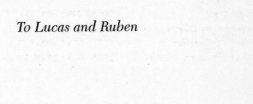

To Lucas and Ruben

acknowledgements

I'd like to thank: *The John Murray Show*, the *RTÉ Guide* and Kazoo Independent Publishing Services for running the competition and for providing all the authors with the opportunity.

The judges: Sarah Webb, Ferdia Mac Anna and Bob Johnston for reading the shortlisted entries.

Robert Doran for his brilliant editing and eye for detail. Chenile Keogh for running the project. Vanessa O'Loughlin for answering all my questions and for the invaluable advice.

Helene Graham and Jim Graham for the tireless proofreads. Deirdre McDermott and Brendan Kirwan for reading the drafts and providing encouragement.

And finally, Claire Wright for sharing her medical knowledge.

Any mistakes or inaccuracies are mine alone.

Incitement by David Graham is the winner of
The John Murray Show, RTÉ Radio 1/*RTÉ Guide*/
Kazoo Competition

THE JOHN MURRAY SHOW

RTÉ GUIDE

prologue

Eighty.

That was how many paces it took to patrol each side of the building. Two years of sentry duty meant he had walked the circuit thousands of times. There was a lot of time to think while working and, given his nature, that usually meant worrying about one thing or another. But even when his mind was otherwise occupied, he still subconsciously counted off the steps. He went over his checklist of current troubles. Maria had been unwell lately but she refused to visit the doctor, saying it was a waste of money. His eldest boy had been staying out later and later and he suspected his son was falling into bad company. More mundanely, as was usually the case, he was struggling financially. The younger children badly needed some new clothes and, once again, there was a problem with the starter motor on his truck.

Seventy-eight, seventy-nine, eighty. Turn the corner.

Roberto appreciated what he had. From his early days, scrabbling to make a living in the nearby Mexican border town of Conchillo, to the last couple of years working for El Cártel de Zaragosa, there had been many reminders of how hard life could be. Some of the things he had seen were better forgotten. Sentry duty might be tedious but it provided for him and his family. His wife did not like him working for the cartel. She had reluctantly agreed only after he had pledged to limit his participation to guarding the compound outside town. The truth, however, was that all of them had to sometimes participate in the punishment of those who crossed the cartel. He hated the deception but who could afford to pass up the chance of a steady wage?

Fifteen, sixteen, seventeen.

Patrol was the worst part of the nightshift. At least if you were inside, you had company and even the chance to catch up on some sleep. Outside, you spent most of the time alone, pacing your circuit. He didn't enjoy the violence; he never strutted around as some of the younger men did, infused with the sense of power that came with their brutality. Where he *did* find common ground with them was on the pointlessness of this monotonous work. Two pairs of men were assigned to each four-hour shift. One patrolled the perimeter fence while the other took care of the building. The extent of the security didn't take into account the absence of any threat to the cartel; the dual strategy of intimidation and corruption had worked. Night after night, all this wasted effort.

Twenty-eight, twenty-nine, thirty.

Of course, the amount of effort expended could be disputed. While Roberto's cautious outlook never allowed him to shirk work, others were less conscientious. Saul was on duty with him tonight. The traits that made him such a good drinking partner were not suited to the repetitive task at hand. He always tried to get by with the minimal amount of effort and, had it not been for an influential relative within the cartel, he wouldn't have lasted long. Saul felt his mission was to get drunk and to get laid as often as possible. Life's too short for worry, he said. Despite their basic differences, Roberto enjoyed his carefree co-worker's company.

Fifty-four, fifty-five, fifty-six.

Maybe he could get Goyo to come over tomorrow morning. His neighbour had worked as a mechanic briefly and might be able to resurrect the vehicle. As for Juan, he would sit down with the boy, talk to him as an equal and convince him that these friends were not the kind he should have. Maria, though, would be more difficult; her stubbornness was renowned but he would win her over.

Seventy-five, seventy-six, seventy-seven.

Roberto was almost at the corner when a patch of darkness detached from its surroundings and moved languidly towards him. "So how many beers did you have tonight?" he asked, laughing.

It happened slowly, like a dream where you are unable to wake up. He felt his head being pulled forward and could not muster the strength to resist. What was Saul doing? This kind of horseplay wasn't funny, the grip at the back of his neck hurt. A dull impact hit him just above the chest and he felt himself being dragged down as if by a heavy current. His legs buckled, and the figure followed him to the ground. He felt the hot breath on his face and caught the smell of mint. The strong grip slowed his descent, breaking his fall, for which he felt strangely grateful. He tried to speak but there was no sound except a soft rasping. That wasn't him, was it? The hand on his neck tightened, then he heard something being torn.

Larsen had watched the compound for three days. The men were eager to get on with it but he wouldn't be rushed. When they had arrived they already had a detailed plan of attack based on meticulously researched intelligence. They had drilled repeatedly at another location, preparing for the mission and gelling as a team. Despite this, he had insisted on waiting until he was totally satisfied that all of their objectives could be met. His involvement with this mission had started months earlier and he wasn't about to waste all that time because of some small oversight. Years of experience had taught him the value of patience.

Just before dusk on the fourth day, he saw the final component slot into place. Lowering his binoculars, he closed his eyes briefly and reminded himself of what he had learned about the green, yellow and red.

He signalled the men over and gave the order to go.

Two of the men moved down the hill, approaching the compound on opposite sides as closely as cover allowed. The last team member remained with Larsen, who was watching the sentries, waiting for them to hit their mark before giving the signal to fire. The snipers were equipped with M24 SWS Remingtons, which had mounted on them Litton Aquila X6 night-vision devices. The sentries, just inside the perimeter fence, were less than a hundred metres away, comfortably within the snipers' range. The subsonic ammunition ensured neither of the sentries closer to the building were alerted.

Once he had confirmed the kills, Larsen and the other man each moved to join the snipers and both pairs of men advanced towards the fence. Notwithstanding the limited range of the video surveillance cameras mounted on the building, there were other dangers. Occasionally, the guards assigned to building patrol would break with procedure and head out to the fence to talk with their co-workers. This random sloppiness unwittingly increased the difficulty of the attack. Powerful bolt cutters made short work of the fence and within seconds they had covered the open ground to the building. Larsen's companion watched as he dispatched the more dutiful guard on their side of the building while the other pair took care of his counterpart.

The remoteness of the location meant there were no fixed telephone lines to worry about, and activating the mobile jammer completely cut the building off from the outside world. Rather than use the traditional strip explosives on the two reinforced doors, they employed Simon Grenade Rifles. The doors were literally blasted from their hinges, becoming dangerous missiles as they flew inwards. The impact when they came to rest added to the panic and confusion of those inside. Two of the attackers headed straight for the video surveillance room. The only guard there, who had been slumped in front of the monitors, was wrenched from his slumber by the deafening explosions. Before he could gather his thoughts, a burst from a Micro Uzi 9 mm ripped through him.

Down the other end of the building, the remaining guards' state of readiness was no better. With the exception of one man at the sink, everyone had been lounging on easy-chairs drinking coffee, smoking cigarettes or playing cards when the explosions erupted. Their powerful assault rifles lay beyond reach and only the standing guard managed to get a shot off before they were cut down. When Larsen had confirmed his partner had not been hit they proceeded to the main refinery. The others were waiting there, standing over the bodies of the three workers responsible for purifying the morphine base.

"Surprises?" asked Larsen.

They shook their head and he instructed them to take up their positions.

They left the room without so much as a second glance

at its incredibly valuable contents. From raw gum through all its intermediate stages up to the final white powder, there was enough of the drug here to ensure several lifetimes of riches. Larsen removed his backpack and placed the explosives throughout the room.

Thirty minutes later, they were back at their base camp, loading their gear into the two waiting 4x4s. They had changed from their dark fatigues into T-shirts, jeans and trainers. None of them looked particularly remarkable. Larsen's Mediterranean skin tone had darkened after a few weeks' exposure to the sun and that, combined with his lean frame, meant he would be able to blend easily while he was in the country. Opening the door of one of the jeeps, he paused.

The rumble of the explosion from the distant compound washed over the hills. The other three turned back to look, able to make out the faint glow of fire, visible over the ridge of hills. When they managed to drag their gaze from the afterglow of the explosion Larsen was behind the wheel, the engine running.

"Good work. Follow the extraction route as planned. The contact channel will be operational for twenty-four hours, but only use it if absolutely necessary. The balance of your payment has just been lodged."

With that, he closed the door and swung the jeep out toward the highway.

one

She walked through the compound, not quite believing the scale of the devastation. Behind the tall red-haired woman, Campas was wrapping up the formalities of ejecting the local police, who were plainly out of their depth, from the bombsite. It had been more than twelve hours since the incident had been reported and yet some isolated clumps of wreckage continued to smoulder. The wind occasionally swirled and changed direction, causing the investigators to splutter as the thick black fumes assailed them.

Diane Mesi looked out beyond the perimeter fence at the arid landscape, still slightly bemused to find herself at the remote location. She had just about finished the second of her visits when news of the attack had crossed Campas's desk. When he had filled her in and invited her to accompany his team to the refinery, she had jumped at the chance. It was not the first time Campas's generosity had surprised her in the short time they had known each other. Her expectation had been that she would receive little cooperation or genuine sharing of information in Mexico but nothing could have been further from the truth. If things worked out, they could be working together on a regular basis, so this was a good sign.

Mesi had been appointed as head of a newly formed Drug Enforcement Agency department only seven weeks earlier. Christened the Trend and Alliance Intelligence Taskforce, or TAIT for short, their remit was to collate and process intelligence from a wide range of sources with a view to identifying possible current and future strategic initiatives by the major cartels. When news of the intention to form the taskforce had first been circulated throughout the administration it had been widely welcomed. The general feeling up to that point had been that the DEA had become too reactionary in its operations. New approaches were needed. This taskforce was seen as a first step in that process. The provisional budget was relatively modest but her seniors in the Agency stressed that they had to start somewhere. Mesi had been one of a large number of candidates who had applied for a variety of senior positions on the taskforce. She had been stunned when at the end of the second round of interviews she had been offered the team lead. Of course, some resentment had resulted when her appointment was announced. She had beaten a number of more senior candidates, something they found hard to accept given her lack of field experience.

Most of the seven years she had been with the DEA had been spent on financial analysis and predictive modelling, areas in which she excelled. She felt some of the criticism regarding fieldwork had been a bit unfair. She had joined the DEA after two unfulfilling years as an analyst with an investment bank following completion of her economics Ph.D. On completion of standard basic training, she had regularly requested assignments to active investigations but she had been turned down most of the time. Best to be assigned where you can do the most good was how it was put.

She was still waiting to be told when the remaining positions on the team would be filled and when office space was going to be allocated for the new team. Arthur

Marshall, the DEA director, had advised her that there were only one or two remaining glitches in finalising the funding and that these should be addressed any day now. In the meantime she had more than enough to occupy herself. Her first task had been to draw up a schedule for visiting the various other agencies, foreign and domestic, that she envisaged TAIT would be working with most closely. Mexico's Fuerza Antidrogas del Ministerio del Interior had been one of these. Her visit should only have been for three days but it had proven so productive, primarily due to Salvador Campas's accessibility, that she had extended it and then returned for another seven-day stay.

The two short visits had been invaluable. Not only because of what she had learnt concerning the Mexican and Central American drug scene but also because she heard about the obstacles the Mexican team had to overcome to get this far. In a way she learnt more from their mistakes than their many noteworthy successes.

She only hoped she could replicate Campas's achievements in her position. A twenty-year veteran of drug enforcement, he had been commissioned by Mexico's minister of the interior to set up their taskforce three years earlier. The move had been seen as an appeasement to the US State Department, which maintained that Mexico was not contributing sufficiently to the War on Drugs. They had specifically questioned the integrity of the previous minister, accusing him of collaborating with the cartels. These allegations had never been substantiated following the politician's assassination in a car bomb explosion, but a shadow had been cast. His successor had been determined not to leave himself open to similar accusations and he provided the impetus for the new taskforce. It had taken

Campas months to recruit his team and build up their own secure network. He had thrown up a veil of secrecy around them, sharing nothing with outsiders. Campas had confided to her how, after almost a year with no arrests, the minister had come close to disbanding the taskforce.

From then the team's impact had been dramatic. They had moved quickly to secure evidence and testimony on a scale previously thought impossible. Within a year of their first prosecutions, two of the largest heroin rings operating near the US border had been smashed and the ringleaders handed multiple life sentences. After this everyone, even the various US agencies with whom they liaised, realised the new force were the genuine article.

But it had not all been good news. Campas quickly became a marked man. He was now under twenty-four-hour protection. What probably rankled more was the fact that he and his team had become effectively exiled from all other branches of Mexican law-enforcement. Rather than taking pride in the arrests, the rank and file saw them as glory-hunting elitists.

If TAIT achieved its goals, it would not only provide invaluable assistance to their colleagues within the DEA but also enable foreign agencies like Campas's to achieve even greater degrees of success. Despite the months of anticipated backbreaking logistical and administrative work which lay ahead, Mesi could not wait to get started. With luck, she thought, looking around the wreckage, this would be a first step.

The Gulfstream V-SP taxied to a complete stop. Viewed from the terminals normally allotted for private charters, the plane looked like nothing more than another arrival on a routinely busy day.

The William M. Bridgeshaw Airport on the Caribbean island of Saint Kitts and Nevis was no stranger to flights like this and it facilitated their need for privacy. There was a bustle of activity as the door of the plane lowered to the tarmac. Four heavily built men armed with sub-machine guns moved quickly down the stairs, not encumbered in the slightest by the heavy flak jackets they wore. Two of the men took up positions twenty metres from the plane, scanning 360 degrees for anything out of the ordinary. The other two stood close to the foot of the stairs.

Everything appearing as it should, the remaining three passengers disembarked the aircraft. The owner of the plane stayed between two more bodyguards, the men who, if everything fell apart, would willingly take a bullet intended for him. Luis Madrigal and the close-quarter bodyguards walked swiftly to the middle of the three customised Mercedes S550s waiting beside the runway. Once the principal was safely in his car, the remaining guards moved to the others. Each of the vehicles was capable of withstanding a Magnum .44 shell at point-blank range and although nothing short of a well-placed anti-tank round constituted a threat, the convoy did not linger, speeding through the open gate.

It was always an inconvenience when Madrigal had to travel to these meetings but circumstances dictated the level of the precautions. The cars drove towards the hills, sweeping quickly along the dirt roads, the comfort of the ride compromised by the innumerable potholes. The further they drove, the more the heavy vegetation encroached on the trails, until soon only a thin strip of dirt marked the route. As they made their way, Madrigal reviewed his notes for the precursor to the forthcoming summit meeting.

He had arrived a couple of days early for the conference with the cartel heads. This was so he could be given a number of detailed presentations of the investment activities undertaken on behalf of the Alliance during the last quarter. Managing the fruits of their labour was a task that kept a horde of advisors and accountants fully employed. The financier he was meeting with today was typical of the professionals Madrigal selected. Educated at Stanford, he was on the fast track to a position as senior partner with a prestigious investment house before the Colombian had recruited him.

The cars arrived at a large estate, situated well away from the island's tourist areas. The main building was a squat structure built into the hillside, lacking in any aesthetic quality. No attempt had been made to conceal the building's function, which was essentially to act as a well-furnished bunker. The Alliance needed somewhere that could offer the best combination of protection and privacy for when they had to meet in person. Anti-surveillance devices were deployed throughout the house and it was scanned twice a day. The few windows were long, narrow affairs with specially designed glass capable of withstanding direct mortar fire. Lastly, if these defences and the well-stocked armoury were not enough, there were a dozen concealed exit routes which emerged at different locations around the hill.

Madrigal walked the long route through the central hallway of the fortress to the conference room. When he entered, the financier, a small dapper man named Wharton, practically bounded across the room towards him.

"Luis, how was the flight, not too tiresome I hope?"

Madrigal didn't bother to reply. Wharton had that most annoying of habit of asking a question and then not waiting for the answer.

Sure enough the hyperactive financier continued after only the briefest of pauses. "I'm sure regardless of how it was, you'll have forgotten it once we finish our review. It's been an outstanding Q2. You know about the investment bank in Slovenia and property deals in the UK already but there's so much more to cover."

Madrigal nodded and took a seat.

"Before we get into it, Luis, do you mind if I ask about these developments with Plan Coca? Any reason to worry that our projected cash flow will be compromised?"

Wharton was usually a bundle of energy, constantly moving or fidgeting. For the moment, though, he stood totally still, his tension obvious.

Madrigal was tempted to play on Wharton's anxiety and draw this out but he decided against it. "No, it's nothing to worry about. We've known about this raft of fumigation runs for some time. We know the area they'll concentrate on, how many missions they intend to fly and what their follow-up action will be. We're well prepared."

Madrigal could see the financier relax visibly as his desperate need for reassurance was met.

"Still, the State Department seems reasonably optimistic about the projected results?" said Wharton.

"And we'll give them every reason to believe the results are all they hoped for," came the calm reply. "We've already allocated specific crops for the fumigation. Ninety per cent of what they eradicate will have been specifically planted just so it can be destroyed. It's unfortunate that the growers will be out of pocket but isn't that always the way when a foreign colonial power moves against the downtrodden?"

Madrigal knew his comment would draw little response from Wharton who tended to ignore anything not directly related to finance.

"You're one hundred per cent confident, then, that last year's projections won't be affected?" he persisted.

"One hundred per cent. You can be certain that we will meet our projected levels for both cocaine and heroin to all our markets during Q3."

Wharton winced at the direct reference to the drugs. Despite having been employed by the Alliance for five years now, he still displayed a continued reluctance to mention the underlying source of their wealth, preferring instead references such as "the product" or "our resources".

"Superb! Okay let's get to that detailed breakdown of Q2. If you'll turn to page three here," the satisfied financier said, handing his employer a folder, "you'll see a rough agenda for the afternoon. We'll be spending some time on the peso brokerage scheme we set up a couple of months ago …"

Early next morning, a tired Diane Mesi looked around Campas's cramped hotel room. Pairs of bleary sleep-deprived eyes belonging to the other team members stared back. Everyone had worked through the night, trying to reconstruct the attack. The meeting was so they could share findings and decide the next steps. Through local intelligence they had known for months that the Madrigal-Zaragosa Alliance maintained a significant heroin refinery in the region but had never managed to locate it. When they had received news of the explosion there had been no doubt of the target. Before they arrived there had been conjecture that some opportunist, drawn by the large quantities of drugs, had carried out the raid. But once on site, questions started to crop up. Campas had remarked to Mesi that they could be looking at something new. The way he had said it left no doubt that he considered anything "new" in their business to be distinctly unwelcome.

Once the last team members had filed in, Campas called the meeting to order. He was not a physically imposing man: small with thinning hair and a hawkish nose. But he radiated such intensity and sense of purpose that he had no trouble getting the tired group to concentrate. "Antonio, the perimeter guards?" The enquiry was directed at a tall man leaning against the wardrobe.

"Both killed by shots to the head," said Antonio Guzman, a pathologist attached to the team. "We're doing some further work on the shell fragments but I'd say we're dealing with subsonic rounds fired over distance. Cause of death would have been a complete shut-down of the nervous system, almost certainly instantaneous."

"The nearest suitable cover to the compound is at least eighty metres, so we're dealing with a reasonably skilled sniper," somebody said.

"Snipers," interjected the SWAT officer Campas had temporarily seconded when he had first heard of the attack.

"Why more than one?" asked Mesi. Although she was there as a courtesy Campas had encouraged her not to be reluctant to ask questions. The way he saw it everything began with asking the right questions.

"Well, I can't be totally sure but I think it's more likely. Both guards were shot while they were the maximum distance apart," the SWAT officer replied, turning to a plan of the compound that had been stuck on the wall and indicating locations on opposite sides of the area. "For one man to do this, he would have had to kill the first guard then move at least two to three hundred metres across the hill behind to get into position for the second shot."

"Go on, Ruben," Campas prompted, seeing that he had more to say but was hesitant, unsure of the group dynamic and his new role.

"It doesn't seem that the building guards raised the alarm or left their posts. This indicates the attackers used rifles equipped with suppressors, consistent with the subsonic rounds mentioned."

"And to be confident of a headshot with a suppressor, an experienced shooter would have preferred to be within a certain minimum distance?" Campas guessed.

"Exactly, probably no more than a hundred metres. When the possibility of a long range kill was raised, I walked the compound perimeter and I couldn't find one suitable vantage point within a hundred metres of both guards."

"Anything else, Ruben? Don't be afraid to speculate."

"Stealth appears to have been a main objective of the initial phase of the attack, so I'm assuming speed was also important. The time between the first and last exterior guard being killed would have to have been as short as possible."

"Makes sense: the longer they took, the more chance of detection," Campas said.

"So, why would they take the risk of one man moving at speed across the hill to take the second shot?" Ruben asked. "It's not an easy thing to do, shoot, run over uneven terrain and then quickly shoot again with confidence. Also, while he's moving there's a chance he'd attract attention."

"I'll go with that," said Campas, nodding. "So, two snipers killing at a synchronised time?"

"Or at a signal, perhaps from a third party. One indisputable fact is the quality of the marksmanship; a head shot downhill from at least eighty metres with a suppressor."

Mesi sensed some uneasiness creeping into the room.

"It strikes me that detailed reconnaissance would be required to plan this kind of attack," Campas said. "Familiarity with the workings of the guards could only have come from time spent observing the compound, possibly over a number of days. Ruben, when we're finished start scouting the surrounding area, to see if you can find any evidence of their presence." He consulted a map of the area. "There's a lot of ground to cover. Will you need me to draft in more manpower?"

"I'd prefer to limit the number, at least initially, to minimise the chance of us destroying any evidence. If you could spare two or three people that I can give a quick run-through on how to proceed, that would be probably be best for now."

"Okay. Oscar, Carlos and ..." Campas turned to look at Mesi, smiling. "How about it Diane? Would you be willing to help Ruben with what's likely to be pain-in-the-ass drudge work?"

"Absolutely," she answered enthusiastically. She had shared with Campas how frustrated she had been at being continually assigned to back-office duties.

"Great, now what about the guards killed closer to the building?"

"One shot through the head at close range with a 9 mm," Guzman resumed. "The other had his throat cut. The killer struck him with tremendous force just above the clavicle using a heavy blade. The blow went through the carotid artery and was so severe that the spinal cord between the C5 and C6 vertebrae at the rear of his neck was severed. No defence wounds or signs of struggle. Total surprise, I'd say."

"Based on what we know so far about the attacks on the exterior guards, anyone want to say out loud what I suspect a number of us have been thinking?" Campas asked the room.

"Military training?" suggested one of the older members of the team. "It seems we're dealing with a professionally planned and executed operation. While we know that the cartels have used mercenaries in the past, I can't recall them being used in this fashion."

"I'm sorry, this may be a stupid question," Mesi said, "but what do we think the motive was for the attack? Robbery? What is the minimum quantity of drugs the attackers could have taken? Say, for argument's sake, they were on foot, how much heroin could they have taken with them?"

"We hear of soldiers carrying twenty to fifty kilo packs while force-marching over long distances," Guzman offered. "Even twenty kilos a man if there were just three or four is a substantial haul. They could have timed the bomb to allow them to escape on foot. Alternatively, they may have had transport standing close by, ready for an all-clear once the attack had been completed."

"True but if you have this capability in planning and firepower, is this the obvious place to strike? Once you have the heroin, you still have the risks associated with transporting it."

"Maybe they only had intelligence about this location, or perhaps the fact that it is an unlikely target was why they picked it."

"Perhaps, but I have to admit that, like Diane, I have some misgivings," Campas said. "The tactics employed and professionalism involved with this attack are without precedent. This refinery is significant because of one thing only: the amount of heroin on site at any one time, both raw and refined. We estimate at least 2,000 kilos. To execute the attack and remove that much heroin would have taken quite some time; very risky. Therefore, we can probably assume some of the heroin was destroyed in the explosion and if that's the case then, outlandish as it seems, why not all of it?"

It was clear to Diane that while some of the agents had considered this already, others had not. From the disbelieving expressions on some faces, it was not difficult to distinguish the two.

"So," Campas concluded. "We need to pursue both robbery and destruction as motives."

"Sal, do you think we might be dealing with a state-sponsored action here?" one of the younger agents asked.

"You mean, have the US extended the remit of Plan Coca without telling us?"

The Plan was a joint Colombian-US initiative to bring the drug war to the doorstep of the main producers in Colombia. The strategy involved applying military resources, in the form of fumigation runs from the air and troop movements on the ground, to forcibly eject the growers from their territorial strongholds. Unsurprisingly, it had no shortage of opponents including some of Colombia's neighbours who had complained that the Plan would push the struggle into their territories.

"Yes," said the agent, glancing at Mesi momentarily.

"No, I don't think so," came Campas's reply. "Plan Coca's

a highly politicised operation in a welcoming sovereign state. I think the most likely possibility is a serious falling out between two factions within the Alliance. What do you think, Diane? Any possibility this could be related to Plan Coca?"

"No, there's absolutely no way military action in Mexico would ever be countenanced, not even a covert attack like this," she said. "We've supported Colombia with military aid for years, so our involvement's welcome. Even though supporters of the Plan and other campaigners would like drugs to be a higher priority, at the moment it's not important enough to the US public for any politician or agency to even dream of risking the blowback of unsanctioned action in Mexico." Mesi could see that the men were at least a little happier with this explanation.

"Until we know more, let's hold off with further speculation on motive, we need to concentrate on the work we have in front of us." Campas paused and checked his notes. "I think we've covered everything we have so far. Here's how I suggest we proceed."

The limousine wound its way slowly down the gravel drive, leaving through the large wrought-iron gates. Lawrence Wallace turned briefly on the back seat and looked back at the sign on the estate's entrance bearing Elizabeth's name. It gave him some measure of contentment to know that the foundation represented a positive legacy to her brief life.

At the centre of the Illinois estate was a beautifully restored mansion in the Colonial Revival style, which would serve as the first of the foundation's rehabilitation clinics. The facilities there would provide comfortable in-house care for up to thirty patients at a time, and three times that number could be accommodated on an outpatient basis. Buildings in Seattle, New Jersey, Detroit, Los Angeles and Philadelphia had already been purchased and were being prepared to go into operation over the next twelve months. The idea for the foundation had come a few years earlier and the key to getting everything up-and-running had been to correctly identify the right people to oversee the operation. Through properly blending a team of people from the logistical side, such as accounting and management, with those who were specialists in therapy and research, he had maximised the foundation's chance of success.

Four years before, his daughter Carol had been mugged while returning from a shopping trip with Elizabeth, her four-year-old daughter. Whether Carol had resisted wasn't clear. The coroner's report indicated that she had been struck more than thirty times around her head and shoulders. Terrified, Elizabeth had bolted and run straight into heavy traffic, was struck by a car and died instantly.

The mugger had been picked up less than two miles from where the attack had occurred. He had been heading to a local crack house, desperate to feed his addiction, when he was arrested. He received the maximum sentence allowable but that had been no comfort to Wallace. Grief and anger consumed him. He learnt that Carol's had been the latest in a number of similar attacks in that neighbourhood, albeit the first one to end so brutally. For a long time he struggled unsuccessfully to find a way to deal with his loss, but now he hoped the clinics would give their deaths some small purpose.

Pulling his gaze from the view out the rear window, he removed a laptop from its case and powered it up. He opened the browser, logged on and accessed a free e-mail account, the name and password of which corresponded to the day's date. He found the message he was looking for, opened it and copied the text into the buffer. He then deleted the message and closed the browser. After firing up a specially written decryption program, Wallace pasted the text he had copied into the decryption editor and clicked on an icon. The gibberish was immediately translated into an intelligible message, which Wallace quickly scanned.

As he read, a smile spread across his face. The progress report could not have been more encouraging. After what had seemed an eternity spent on getting things up-and-running, it was now well on schedule. Again, this was a testament to identifying the best personnel and stopping at nothing to secure their services. When he had finished reading, he closed the decryption program and ran a custom-written program to delete all history files. After powering the laptop off, he ejected the disk-drive and, after removing a Swiss Army knife from his inside pocket, he opened the screwdriver tool and placed the head of it close to the spindle. Driving down hard he punctured a hole in the disk-drive and after repeating the manoeuvre twice, he reinserted the disk-drive and put the laptop back in its case.

After a few seconds mulling over what he had read, Wallace reached for the intercom and buzzed the chauffeur. "Greg, any word on the plane?"

"Fuelled up and waiting, Mr Wallace."

"Excellent. After you've dropped me off, there's a laptop that needs to be disposed of in the usual fashion."

"Very good, Mr Wallace."

Mesi had spent most of the day working in the sweltering heat and reckoned there was only a couple more hours of good light left. She and the others working on the search were hoping to find signs of the attackers' movements or ideally the site of a base camp. Over time, she had steadily worked her way further and further from the refinery. She stopped to take a drink from her canteen and tie back her hair from her face. Pulling out a handkerchief to wipe away some of the sweat, she turned to look back in the direction from which she had come. Her view of the refinery was now blocked by the hills she had walked over. A childhood memory sprang to mind, of being so absorbed in a treasure hunt at a friend's birthday party that the parents had to send out search parties when she had not returned.

Before they had split, Ruben had spent some time showing her and the other two team members how he conducted his search. He had explained what he was doing as he went and the logic he was using. As was often the case, it all seemed straightforward once it had been broken down. In the short time they had been with him, he had managed to identify three possible sniper points, two of which had almost certainly been the shooters' locations. Given her lack of experience she found herself doubting her ability to replicate his success but she was determined to give it her best shot.

Ruben had asked her to concentrate on a particular area, and rather than mechanically working her way over that entire section, she had decided to approach this as she would any other task. First, she needed a way to narrow the criteria. Studying a map of the area, she drew a circle with a seven-mile radius around the refinery. Given the terrain and the dangerous nature of the attack, this was surely the maximum reasonable distance the attackers would have wanted to march. Then she highlighted the part which fell into her search area. From there, she had tried to split the remainder into smaller parts, sorted in order of the security they would have afforded the attackers. She eliminated a section that lay toward Conchillo and another that lay alongside the compound's entrance route. This had left about fifteen degrees of the original circle, mostly to the north and west of the compound. Ruben had told them not to try to cover every square foot, to scan and look for disturbances, but even so, it was time-consuming work and she could see that she was unlikely to finish before dark. Putting the canteen away, she resumed the search.

While Mesi had been performing the repetitive work, she thought about what lay ahead in her new role. One of the things that impressed her most about Campas and his men was how well developed their sense of team spirit was. Individuals took pride in their abilities but there were no overbearing egos putting their own advancement before the larger objective. She had taken some courses in organisational behaviour at college and read quite a lot on motivational theory. The success of any team depended on more than just assembling a number of talented individuals. One of her primary tasks would be giving her team something they could be proud to belong to.

As the light started to dim, she began to question herself. Had she been wrong in her estimate of how far the soldiers could have marched? Had her process of elimination been flawed? Had she already missed the signs?

She was just about to stop when she saw the tyre tracks. There was no mistaking the relatively fresh imprints of the heavy tyre thread belonging to some kind of four-wheel-drive vehicle. It looked like more than one vehicle had intersected her search pattern. She decided to follow the tracks back towards the compound. After twenty minutes of tantalising pacing, the tracks converged near a slight rise. She was sure she had discovered the general location of the campsite. She quartered the area and began searching. Occasionally she would lie down close to the ground in a press-up position as Ruben had demonstrated and tried to spot any signs of an unnatural lie to the earth. She knew professionals would take care to cover any disturbance they made, but maybe … However, each time she thought she had something, she was disappointed.

The light had deteriorated significantly and while Mesi was confident that this was the campsite, she would have to return tomorrow with the others. She had just got out her walkie-talkie to radio back when something caught her eye. She walked toward it and as she got closer she realised there was more than one. She bent down and broke into a smile, before picking up one of the items with a tweezers and examining it. She placed it carefully in a zip-lock evidence bag.

While the noisy humming of the dilapidated air-conditioning units drove many of the hotel's guests to distraction, there was no complaint from this room. The occupant lay on top of the bedspread, clad in shorts with a damp towel draped across his face. He had expected the lethargy. For as long as he could remember, the aftermath of any operation or manoeuvre had always been accompanied by this strong feeling of anticlimax.

Larsen thought of his earliest days in the Corps, coming back after completing the diving to the wrecks scattered around the torpedo station at Kongsøre. The exercise involved the recruits being subjected to gunfire while explosives were set off all around. Most of them were elated to successfully negotiate it the first time. The adrenaline firing through their systems manifested in raised voices and boisterous horseplay. Larsen had smiled and played along with his comrades, joining them later for copious amounts of beer, but even then he had always felt somehow apart, removed.

He could understand what most other people went through before, during and after such an experience, the tension and release, but it was not like that for him. He had found that his release, his 'high', came during rather than afterwards. For a long time, the sense of purpose he felt during an operation had provided him with everything he needed. He trained to a fine edge and then applied that training. When the mission was over, the mood would recede rapidly and he would feel himself coming down. It was different now of course; action in itself had long ceased to be enough but the familiar descent afterwards still ensued.

A few hours passed before he removed the towel to stand and idly perform a series of gentle stretches as he assembled his thoughts. The refinery at Conchillo had constituted a major step up as far as the scale of target was concerned and everything was in place for the next phase. It was dangerous to linger in Mexico City after the attack but he wanted to monitor the cartel's reaction, to ensure it played out as predicted. Their targets should be aware of the incident by now and Larsen anticipated a flurry of activity; the early beginnings of a slow process of deterioration. Nothing too obvious yet, though. One attack, even one as significant as Conchillo, would not be enough to push them all the way. Moving through to the bathroom, he showered quickly then dressed. He grabbed the keys for the rental car and headed out.

"Cigarette butts?" Albert Sandoval repeated in puzzlement. "I don't understand."

Minister for the Interior Richard Mayorga expanded on exactly what had been found so that his chief political advisor might grasp the significance. "The ends of a particular brand of cigarette, Classic, manufactured by ..." Looking at the report in front of him, he mangled the pronunciation, "... by Duvanska Industrija Nis. It's a company based in the former Yugoslavia. The brand is popular in the region but rare elsewhere."

"So what, one of the gunmen smoked some foreign cigarettes?"

"Campas thinks it's relevant, based on a discussion he had at a conference in Europe a few months ago. He was told that Kosovar organised crime figures weren't happy that they were getting a fair share of the proceeds from their joint venture with the South Americans. That was the term that was used: South Americans. He didn't attach any significance to it at the time but with this ..."

"What would their unhappiness have to do with Conchillo?" Sandoval asked.

"The Alliance: Zaragosa and Madrigal, the Colombian, have been working together closely for the past few years. To hostile eyes, there might be no distinction between Mexican or Colombian targets."

"Has Campas got anything else?"

"The investigation indicates a mercenary-style attack, and mercenaries are in abundant supply in the Balkans. That's about it so far. Needless to say, this is speculative and highly confidential but we need to be prepared should more corroborating evidence be found."

"Surely no one's crazy enough to directly challenge the cartels or the Colombians? It would be suicide."

"My reaction exactly but according to Campas, the Kosovar mafia are an explosive cocktail of traditional gangsters, Islamic fundamentalists and ex-military. They've emerged as the dominant force in Europe, pushing out the Italian, Pakistani and Lebanese gangs. He says they're renowned for their savagery."

"Well, if he's correct, we'll certainly need to keep an eye on things." Sandoval rose from his chair. "Anyway, I think we've covered all of the topics on the agenda. Would it be okay if I finish a little early today? Millie's parents are coming over and I've been told to be home on time for once."

"Of course, please say hello from me and that I'm glad we can accommodate your in-laws."

Albert's laughter quickly disappeared once he had left the minister's office. He climbed into his car and, instead of heading home, pointed the car towards the upscale Colonia Roma area. Soon he was driving down the wide tree-lined streets, flanked on both sides by vast mansions. He pulled the car up outside the gates of a classic Barragán residence, pressed the intercom and announced himself, looking up into the closed circuit camera. The high gates swept open and a familiar feeling of unease suffused him.

After the frisking from the guards, he was shown into the drawing room where Caesar Rodriguez waited. Unease gave way to palpable discomfort when he came face-to-face with one of the most powerful figures of the Mexican drug scene. It was not just the man's position but also the coiled tension he exuded. After his meetings with Rodriguez, Albert would feel drained and grateful to have just gotten through. How he had come to be in the service of this barbarian tormented him. It was unfair that a few gambling debts should jeopardise the career he had worked so hard at for the past fifteen years. True, he continued to gamble and accept further credit, but now that he was committed anyway, who could fault him for making the best of a bad situation?

"Albert, you have news?" asked Rodriguez, whose physical characteristics – tall and powerfully built with a leonine head – complimented a naturally imperious manner.

"Yes, I think so … I mean maybe … if Campas is correct." He hated how he always lost his composure in Rodriguez's presence. Damn it, he had handled foreign heads of state better.

"Continue." Caesar indicated for Albert to take a seat on the deep leather couch, while he remained standing.

"They found cigarette butts at the campsite of the raiders, foreign cigarettes not sold here. Apparently they're a Balkan brand."

Rodriguez said nothing and when Albert lifted his gaze, it looked as if the drug lord had entered a trance. He stood frozen, gazing into mid-distance. The silence was uncomfortable and Albert was unsure whether he should break it, terrified that whatever he did would be wrong. One of the few times he had talked with Salvador Campas, the policeman had observed that being head of a cartel required intelligence, organisational skills and personal charisma. To think of their adversaries as mindless savages was to woefully underestimate them. Already in Rodriguez's grip at that point, Albert had enquired about his blackmailer specifically, wanting the investigator's opinion. Campas smiled and said Rodriguez was an exception, in that he was an equal blend of intelligence, charisma and mindless savagery.

"Albert, is there anything else?"

"Anything else?" he repeated, startled by Rodriguez's return to the land of the living.

"Regarding the raid?"

"No, no, nothing else."

"Okay," he said, nodding to the door.

Albert levered himself out of the deep couch onto unsteady legs and exited quickly.

They preferred to communicate using a dedicated secure satellite link, purchased and maintained at great cost. However, on rare occasions, when one of them felt it was warranted, they would meet face-to-face at Madrigal's island fortress. It was an assembly of the most powerful figures in the world of international narcotics production and trafficking. The meeting had been going on for an hour now and most of them were content to look on silently as the conversation between their leader and the agitated Rodriguez grew more heated. It had been difficult for Madrigal. Rodriguez, who was even more volatile than usual, was resisting all measured and logical argument.

"We can't let this attack go unanswered," the Mexican repeated. It was clear to Madrigal that he was trying to stir up the room and, in doing so, force Madrigal to change his position.

"Normally I'd agree but before we can retaliate, we need to be sure who to retaliate against."

Madrigal had to be careful; he wanted to be firm

without appearing dictatorial. Things ran more smoothly when there was the appearance of consensus.

"The report I received yesterday contains definitive fucking evidence. The Kosovars are behind the attack, and if we don't retaliate they'll be encouraged to go further. We have to act now to show them that this time they're not dealing with a bunch of putas." The veins on Rodriguez's temples distended while his voice rose.

"Cigarette butts are hardly justification to potentially start a war that could set us back years. Let's wait to see what else this policeman, whom you rate so highly, comes up with." Madrigal was well aware of Campas's pedigree but this was not the time to acknowledge it.

"We're not in a fucking courtroom, we only need to satisfy ourselves. I told you months ago that the Kosovars, whom you were so happy to approach with talk of closer partnership, represented our biggest fucking threat. Now they've done business with you and plainly evaluated you to be weak and vulnerable."

Madrigal was somewhat surprised. He knew Rodriguez harboured resentment at what he felt was the subordinate role of the Mexicans generally and himself specifically but he had never gone this far before. Clearly, his rage was directing him now.

"And you Caesar, do you agree that I'm weak and vulnerable?"

Something had changed in the shorter, stockier man's voice and those in the room began to shift uncomfortably in their chairs. Rodriguez, lost in his fury, ranted on obliviously. "You're vulnerable if you don't see the threat! When enemies perceive you to be weak then you are weak!"

Only when the last word had tumbled out did Rodriguez

appear to realise the implication of what he was saying. He glanced around the room. Madrigal had ruthlessly clawed his way to the top of Colombia's drugs elite then, against all the odds, pulled the many widely divergent Central and South American drugs cartels together to form the Alliance. It was suicide to challenge his strength so directly. "Luis, forgive me, I'm not expressing myself properly. There's no question that you're more than capable of dealing with any threat. It's just I appreciate the great number of demands made on you. A possible danger might be easily averted now with swift action but it will be more difficult if left to fester until later."

Madrigal took a moment, letting the silence underline Rodriguez's retreat for the others, before replying. "Here's what I think. The operation, as you pointed out, bore all the trademarks of a mercenary attack. Many mercenaries operate in Central and South America and, in recent years, some have probably gained employment in the Balkans. So, the cigarettes don't necessarily indicate someone in the employ of the Kosovars and can hardly justify an attack on an organisation that provides such a profitable sales channel."

"Luis, I agree that we should not rush to conclusions," interjected Cabieses, an elderly Peruvian. "Equally, we cannot just ignore the matter."

"No, Tomas, we will stay on top of it. I suggest that as well as monitoring the official investigation, we pursue one of our own. Our network runs throughout the continent. If mercenaries from this part of the world were used, we should be able to find out."

"Perhaps we could also extend our investigation to Europe?" suggested Cabieses.

"Of course, we can also use our sources there to make discreet enquiries," agreed Madrigal before adding a caution, "but we must be careful that the Kosovars get no inkling of this. If they are responsible, we do not want to put them on their guard. If they're not, then we don't want to risk offending them."

He could sense that some of them still had misgivings but knew they would not voice them. He warned himself not to become complacent on this issue and made a note to take time with some of them later, one-on-one, to smooth any ruffled feathers. No position was unassailable.

Later, when the meeting was over and the others had left to return home, Madrigal sat alone in the conference room with the lights dimmed, thinking about the meeting and its main topic. Something else bothered him about the attack but he was unable to put his finger on it. He put the matter from his mind, knowing that a little distance might help. He was used to this and could not remember a time when there was not a myriad of problems to contend with. Under his direction, the cartels had prospered beyond all reasonable forecasts. From assassination squads to investment houses and extremist militias halfway across the world, he had managed to blend divergent assets to create an impressive synergy with their core businesses. From his humble beginnings, begging and stealing on the streets of Bogotá, to where he was now, he had never experienced contentment. He felt that there must be a purpose to his single-minded pursuit of power and he was confident it would become clear someday. He remembered hearing once how a senior DEA official had said he was like Alexander in the breadth of the empire he had built. Apparently, the official had added that, unlike Alexander, he was unlikely to ever weep. He knew how his enemies, both internal and external, regarded him. He could hardly complain. Many times he had used their fear to his advantage. But it was not as simple as they believed.

He held the group he had met with earlier in secret contempt despite their perception of themselves as his peers. Greed was their only motivation. He had the same disdain for the agencies of the Western governments who lined up against him.

Plan Coca was just another exercise in US imperialism. The reports of widespread sickness after the fumigation runs proved they didn't care about the people of Putumayo. Coca and opium provided many people with the only way to break the cycle of poverty. These were downtrodden people. True, thousands suffered in the countries where the end product was consumed but these were weak, indulgent people whose hardships were self-inflicted. The suffering of these addicts was nothing compared to the struggles of the poor. Yes, it was sad to see lives wasted, but sometimes there was no alternative.

The camera homed in on a close-up of the captives. They were herded by, each stolidly refusing to acknowledge the presence of this intrusion. They walked wearily, hands behind their head, faces downcast. In stark contrast, the guards clearly enjoyed the camera's attention and barked commands incessantly. The picture panned to the right, focusing on Caroline Williams, an immaculately groomed reporter in a pressed khaki outfit.

"A resounding success for Plan Coca. Three days ago, a main stronghold of FARC was successfully overrun by the

Colombian army's Counter Narcotics Brigade. The Brigade has received extensive training from US experts and has been equipped by the US military under the direction of the MILGP." Williams' voice and body language were upbeat, matching the content of her report. "Despite strong resistance, they were able to take control of the FARC base, capturing many of the rebels. The Colombian government has been quick to stress the importance of this development, particularly in the face of recent criticisms that, up to now, the Plan had achieved nothing more than a series of ineffectual fumigation strikes."

While she continued her introduction, the shot moved out to take in the man who stood next to her.

"While there were no major coca crops close to the base, the government has identified it as a main distribution and coordination centre of the rebels, the loss of which will significantly hamper the drug traffickers. With me is Henry Maynard from the US State Department who was closely involved in planning this operation. Henry, is this only a short term blow to FARC or are we looking at something more?"

"No doubt about it, this is a major success for the Brigade," Maynard responded enthusiastically. "They've justified the time and effort we've committed to their training. This base was a prominent part of FARC's distribution network."

"And what will its loss mean to the rebels?"

"Without it, they need to rethink the distribution channels and replan future consignments. This doesn't win the war in itself but it shows that we're starting to get to grips with fighting the producers on their own turf."

"Some dissenting voices in Colombia have said this base had nothing to do with the drug trade and that the

Colombian government is using the resources earmarked for Plan Coca to crush the Marxist resistance?"

Maynard shook his head resignedly, leaving the viewers under no illusions regarding what he felt about this carping. "FARC is not a resistance movement, Marxist or otherwise. It exists solely for its own financial gain and has no real political platform. The sooner we recognise that we're battling criminals and not revolutionaries, the sooner we'll win."

"Critics have suggested those in charge of the plan could be more judicious in their target selection, concentrating solely on drug-related targets?"

"It's simplistic and self-defeating to assume that we can clearly distinguish resistance targets from those connected to drugs," explained Maynard. "No such distinction exists for FARC and if we're to defeat them we can't create one either. We need to dismantle FARC totally. I don't think anyone wants to see another instance where we state an objective and then seek to obstruct ourselves from realising it."

"The next step as you see it?"

"Continue what we've started here. Now that we've shown our ability to win what were previously thought to be strongholds of FARC, we've got to press on. I think if we can combine this kind of success with continued fumigation runs, we'll do permanent damage to the Colombian cartels' production capacity."

"Thank you. So, Plan Coca overcomes an embattled start and begins to gather momentum. This is Caroline Williams for IBNC in Putumayo region, Colombia."

two

The waves grew increasingly more powerful, sweeping the decks of the boats, which pitched wildly in the storm. The crew of the larger vessel were finding the footing difficult, constantly having to right themselves, but this was minor compared to what the four men who had just boarded the smaller yacht had to contend with. The line between the two boats had no sooner been released than a gap of forty feet appeared between the vessels. The men on board the yacht struggled through the violent throes as it was hurled one way then another, finally wrestling themselves to the boat's cabin. Once it was confirmed that they had all made it safely off-deck, the signal was given on the trawler to start transmitting.

Larsen and the other three men braced themselves in the yacht's cabin, nobody talking while they waited for what was to come. The forecast had warned that the storm was on its way but they had only one shot at this and had to go. The weather was beneficial in that it helped their gambit appear more authentic, but that was only if they didn't capsize. Despite all the rehearsals they had carried out, the storm had the potential to ruin everything. The boat rolled violently and Larsen caught himself just before he slid from the bench. He checked to confirm that the items secreted under his sweater were still in place and he visualised the expected sequence of events once more. Glancing at his companions, he searched for any hint of weakening resolve but found none.

He reminded himself again of the bigger picture, how much it mattered and the part this would play in the overall progression. The small handheld radio sheathed in plastic crackled into life, announcing that contact had been made. His thoughts returned once more to what he had learned of the green, yellow and red all those years before.

The *Spirit of Marseilles*, her decks heavily laden with cargo containers, made slow progress through the rough seas. The storm, however, was not the main source of the captain's worry. Circumstances had required that Christophe Chanet agree to carry more cargo than the coffee listed on the manifest. He was in an unenviable position. If the ship was intercepted by the US Coast Guard and its illicit load found, it would be impounded and he would face charges. If the cargo was successfully delivered, another mission would doubtless await. Even here, on his own bridge, he could not put the predicament from his mind and lose himself in the rudiments of negotiating the storm. The guard who stood at his shoulder was a constant reminder of what he had committed himself and the crew to.

Business had not been good in recent years. Chanet, as the owner-captain of the cargo ship, had handled affairs badly and fallen into debt. He had finally reached the point where it had been necessary to sell a share in the ship or face ruin. Surprisingly, an offer had materialised quickly once he had put out feelers. He knew that he should have questioned why a top-class legal firm, acting on behalf of a client, would have been interested in a share of the *Spirit*. At the time, though, he was in no position to examine any lifeline too closely. With the proceeds from the deal, he had been able to refit the ship in time to win a number of commissions on the Puerto Barrios-Miami route. It was obvious now that his new partner had been instrumental in arranging for the business to come his way and once again he cursed his stupidity.

The last time they had been in port, the lawyers had informed him he would be required to attend a meeting with their client. Over coffee in the plush downtown offices, he had learned the extent of his indenture. The man he met had explained how, on her next voyage, the *Spirit* would carry something more than was stated in the official contract. Three thousand kilos of heroin was to be hidden throughout the ship. To ensure there would be no difficulties, Customs in both ports had been taken care of. He had argued with the man until he was cut off and the consequences of refusal starkly spelt out to him. Chanet had enjoyed authority of some degree or other for almost twenty years but when it had come to dealing with this mystery man, he had been made feel completely inconsequential.

He had been informed that three men would be accompanying the voyage to ensure there were no problems. Any chance that the entire crew might not have realised the extent to which the *Spirit* had been compromised disappeared when these taciturn men had boarded. Once out of port, they made no attempt to conceal their automatic weapons and swaggered around the ship, daring anyone to challenge them. A number of times headstrong members of the crew had been barely talked out of accepting this challenge by their shipmates.

On the bridge the radio crackled. "… If anyone can respond, please acknowledge … We are adrift. Our engine's failed … last known coordinates … Repeat, this is the

Marlin ... four crew ... situation dire ... "

The first mate, Tiozzo, looked at Chanet who nodded to proceed. "*Marlin*, this is the *Spirit of Marseilles*. Please repeat those coordinates. Over."

After a couple of attempts the complete coordinates were communicated.

"We're in your vicinity and proceeding to your location. Standby to fire a flare on our signal," the first mate instructed.

The guard on the bridge stormed over angrily and wrenched the radio from Tiozzo's hands. "What the hell do you think you're doing, cabrón? You don't deviate from our course!"

"It's enough your people have commandeered my ship and undermined my command," said Chanet. "But if you think for a second that we're going to ignore a distress call in this storm then go ahead and pull the trigger." He stared impassively into the furious gunman's eyes. "Though you'd better be prepared to tackle the rest of the crew and then, if you should handle that successfully, you and your colleagues can look forward to crewing a thirty-man ship safely to our destination." For a moment the man looked like he was seriously considering the plausibility of such an action. "No doubt, you'll have a good explanation ready for the port authorities on arrival," Chanet added.

The gunman lowered the weapon with a petulant expression. "Okay, Captain fucking Samaritan, but you can be damn sure I'll be reporting this shit and then you better fucking believe it'll be you who'll have to do the explaining."

It took an hour and a half in the treacherous conditions before they arrived at the coordinates. No signal flare was released and with radio contact having ceased half an hour before, Chanet feared the worst. At last, just as he was about to call off the search, one of the crew spotted a blinking light off their port side. Changing course swiftly, they came upon the *Marlin*. She was a recreational vessel by all appearances, listing badly, her hull half-exposed and ready to go under at any moment. From the ship's rail, Chanet could just about distinguish four huddled figures perched precariously on the yacht's stern. He wondered at the lunatics who braved these seas for fun and adventure.

Despite the difficult conditions, they managed to get alongside and haul the men one by one off the stricken *Marlin*. Three of them appeared to be in their early thirties and the last, presumably their skipper, was a little older. Considering the ordeal they had endured, none of them looked too much the worse for wear. Chanet reckoned that, after some hot soup and rest, they would be fine. The skipper insisted on thanking him properly before he would excuse himself. In spite of all attempts to dissuade the man, he persisted and Chanet reluctantly agreed for him to come up to the bridge. Chanet was not happy about the armed guard there but figured that the yachtsmen would be with them until they reached Miami and were bound to see the gunmen at some stage anyway. He had not thought of the problems this might pose when answering the distress call but he would have to address it before they docked.

Chanet called for some brandy to be brought up and guided the man to a chair. While they waited, he studied the skipper. He was a lean man, perhaps five-eight or -nine and appeared to be recovering rapidly, his shivering subsiding noticeably as the seconds passed. Chanet could see his puzzlement at the presence of an armed guard on the bridge but there were no immediate questions.

"Are you sure you wouldn't rather go below?" he asked after the man had drained his mug.

"No, no, we owe you our lives, if you hadn't arrived … I'm responsible for endangering my crew and yours. I have an obligation." He spoke English with what sounded like an Eastern European accent.

"If you insist. May I ask, what in God's name were you doing so far from shore in a storm? Had you no warning of the weather?"

"We were –"

One of the crew from the *Marlin* appeared at the door, momentarily drawing their attention, and the skipper launched himself from his seat at the distracted guard. The gunman registered the movement and tried to react but before he could do anything, the skipper had grabbed him under the chin and pressed a knee into the small of his back. The skipper produced a knife and plunged it into the guard's exposed neck. Blood spurted from the deep wound over the floor of the bridge. Letting the body drop, the skipper straightened up and retrieved a small plastic package, secured by tape, from under his sweater. He opened the package and removed a handgun. He exchanged a few words with his crewmate, and although Chanet didn't recognise the language, the gist was clear. A progress report had been given and from the sounds of it things were going according to plan.

"Captain Chanet, you have been under duress for some time and I apologise that it must continue for just a little longer. If I may?"

The skipper took the radio, changed the frequency and began transmitting. In the same language as before, he issued instructions to whomever was at the other end.

"In a few minutes, a ship will pull alongside," he said, replacing the radio. "We'll relieve you of a portion of your cargo then dump the bodies of this one and his friends overboard."

"And after?"

"You'll be free to continue on your way. I realise you'll be facing a difficult situation with the owners of the cargo when you reach your destination." A smile touched the corners of his mouth. "If you prefer, I can sink your ship while you and the crew take to the lifeboats?"

"You're taking the drugs?" Chanet asked incredulously.

"Yes."

"And leaving us unharmed?"

"We've no quarrel with you. The abuse of the mayday signal was unavoidable and we regret any danger you were placed in."

Chanet could not take it in. With difficulty, he assembled his thoughts enough to ask another question.

"The ship, it won't explode after you depart, will it? I mean, we've seen your faces."

"Who would you describe us to?" he shrugged. "The authorities? I can't see it. As for the owners of the cargo, feel free to be as descriptive as you like."

A short time later, a smaller cargo ship pulled alongside and the crew of both vessels set about transferring the drugs. Within hours of the distress call being raised, no trace of the *Marlin* or its crew remained. Chanet could almost have convinced himself that he had dreamt it all.

After slamming the door then throwing her keys on the hall table, Mesi hurried through the apartment into the bathroom. She had hoped to return more relaxed from her

2,000 metres at the pool. She had been so nervous about what lay ahead today that she had hardly slept, and starting the day with some exercise to take the edge off had seemed a good idea. And it would have been if maintenance had fixed the showers in the workout area as the residents had repeatedly requested. Living in the well-appointed apartment complex involved sacrifices. Besides the steep rent there was a daily two-stage commute involving car and train. The only way she could justify these to herself was if all of the complex's amenities were working properly. Stepping hurriedly into the shower, she glanced at her watch again – fifteen minutes to get dressed and out the door. She would have some strong words for the building's service contractor the next time she spoke to him.

She lathered the shampoo through her hair while her mind raced. Director Marshall had come to her late afternoon the day before. In light of the latest incident, he had told her, they needed to revisit one of her earlier predictive reports. While he may have discounted it at the time, he thought it was prudent to take another look in light of the Miami incident. It had been gratifying to hear but then he had gone on to tell her about the meeting he had called for first thing the following day. He had invited an array of heavy hitters and he expected her to provide the main presentation. He had given her a rough outline on what she should and should not concentrate on and while it all sounded straightforward enough at the time, it had entailed an enormous amount of work.

The first thing she had done was call Jean, an old friend from college, to say she couldn't attend her dinner party that evening. That had not gone well at all. Despite the fact that ten others were expected, Jean's primary reason for the party had been as an excuse to get her together with one of the other guests. Jean had decided that Diane's total of just two serious relationships since the divorce eight years earlier was pitiful and that it was time for her to get her love life sorted before it was "too late". Diane wasn't opposed to the idea, quite the contrary, but for one reason or another their efforts had met with failure so far. Twenty minutes later, after having listened dutifully to the obligatory lecture about making time for a personal life, she had been able to concentrate on getting the material together.

The meeting was important for more than just the obvious reason of making a good impression on her boss. It had been more than ten months since she had taken the position as head of TAIT and the team had hardly progressed at all. By this stage, TAIT should have had a complement of fifteen agents and been on its way to establishing a profile throughout the DEA and beyond. Instead, the team consisted of just herself and two junior agents. She had raised the issue with Marshall often but never seemed to get anywhere. She would walk into his office, determined to get some straight answers regarding the reasons for the delay and a commitment for the future, but, somehow, he always managed to palm her off without providing either. Despite the plausible explanations about how long finalising the budget was taking, it had reached the stage where it was becoming a little demotivating. True, she had learnt a lot in the time since she had taken the job but unless she had the opportunity to apply it what was the point? As it was, the only function they served was as Marshall's private three-man research team. If today's meeting went well, she hoped all of this would change.

Marshall had indicated that one of her earlier reports

was the impetus behind the meeting; that was the first positive. Follow it up with a strong presentation and some momentum could begin to develop. Maybe enough to shake the bean counters from their indifference. It was imperative, though, not to incur the enmity of any of the attendees. Unfortunately, the content of her presentation had some potentially unpleasant implications for more than one of them. There was no avoiding that. The trick would be to ensure that her delivery was done in such a way to ensure that neither she nor TAIT were associated with the unpleasantness.

She finished drying her hair and got dressed. Normally, she would have considered the clothes she was wearing far too dressy for the office, but, given the audience she would have today, they were perfect. She checked the mirror one last time then took a deep breath and headed out the door.

The conference room was dominated by the large table at its centre. Its sheer size accentuated the fact that, as yet, only a handful of the expected attendees were present. Robert Allenby sat in his chair, drumming his fingers impatiently as the others drifted into the room in ones and twos. Given the full schedule he had planned for that Friday, the meeting had hardly come at an ideal time. The sooner they started, the sooner he could get away.

Allenby's role as advisor to the Plan Coca congressional subcommittee had been a godsend when he had accepted it two years earlier. Certainly, basking in the reflected glory of the Plan's recent successes had been gratifying and had done no harm at all to his prospects. He had decided, though, that he had gotten all he could reasonably expect from the association and that it was time to begin moving away from the Plan and on to other projects. Only fools pushed their luck; the Plan had served him well and even in the unlikely event it could sustain its current run, there was no point in being greedy. A fringe benefit of removing himself would be an end to incidents like today. The subcommittee chairwoman had been unable to attend and asked him to sit in for her. Given the lack of bearing whatever Marshall wanted to discuss would have on his career, he resented the imposition.

At last it looked as if everyone had assembled and the short, bullish DEA Director Marshall walked to the head of the room. Despite Allenby's annoyance at having to attend the meeting, part of him was intrigued as to why someone as senior as Marshall thought it necessary.

"Thank you everyone for coming at such short notice. I know some of you had to make significant changes to your calendars to make it to Arlington today," the director began. "We're here because of a report which crossed my desk yesterday morning. It related to a suspected act of piracy off the coast of Florida involving the theft of a large amount of heroin bound for our shores. In itself, it wouldn't have warranted dragging you here, so to explain why I felt that was necessary I'm going to hand you over to Diane Mesi. Diane's one of our senior specialists on cartel alliances and disputes."

Allenby watched Mesi stand and walk to the head of the table. One quick look was enough for him to sum her up. Tall and thin, she was attractive, he supposed, although the rectangular glasses and stern features didn't do anything for him. She had obviously traded on her looks to get this far and was sure to be hoping she could make the most of this chance in the spotlight. He looked at his watch and wondered how long he would be here.

Okay, she said to herself, take your time, it's a good presentation, just let it speak for itself.

She signalled for the lights to be dimmed then walked over to the projector screen and brought up the first slide. The photo was of an open-plan office in disarray. Desks were over-turned, tables and walls strewn with bullet holes. Amidst the chaos were the bodies of at least four men and one woman. The corpses were covered in blood and lay at unnatural angles; the woman's throat had clearly been slit. The picture's impact could be felt throughout the room.

"April twenty-fifth last year, the Guttierez family and associates. Originally they hailed from the Dominican Republic. This office is over a nightclub they owned in Chicago. The Guttierezes were renowned distributors and retailers for the Madrigal-Zaragosa Alliance. They dealt in everything. Heroin, cocaine, synthetics. Our sources tell us there should have been a large store of each when this attack took place. Next."

The image of the carnage-filled room disappeared and was replaced by another. The picture, taken from the quayside, showed a dark cloud of smoke billowing from a half-submerged cargo ship about 50 metres from shore.

"September twelfth, the *Mariner's Friend* sunk dockside in an explosion in Port of Spain. Maurice Jackson, one of the main drug traffickers in Trinidad and Tobago, and some of his senior lieutenants were on board at the time. We suspect the ship contained a substantial amount of cocaine and meta-amphetamines bound for the US. Next."

An aerial shot of the remains of a bombsite.

"February twenty-ninth this year, a major heroin

refinery just outside the small border town of Conchillo in Mexico. We believe the attack was perpetrated by a small team of well-trained, well-equipped hostiles. They killed the building's security personnel and virtually obliterated its structure. Next."

A split image. The left half of the screen showed a luxury speedboat, black and sleek in the water and at least thirty feet long; it was just possible to make out the bodies which were strewn around the cockpit. The other half was a closer view of the same cream leather cockpit, which contained a scene reminiscent of the Chicago nightclub. There were two bodies visible. The first had been raked with multiple gunshots to the torso, leaving it a blood-soaked mess, and the second, which lay half over the side of the boat, had its throat ripped open.

"July nineteenth. Rene Salazaar and one of his brothers. The boat was found by the Coast Guard. The coroner's report estimated it had been drifting for more than twenty-four hours before it was discovered. Salazaar's other brother and two more associates are missing. We think they were on the boat and either conducted the attack themselves or were killed and dumped overboard. Given the length of time since their last sighting, we favour the latter theory. Next."

A picture of a large container ship in port. Nothing was obviously wrong and there were puzzled looks around the room.

"November twelfth, the day before yesterday. The *Spirit of Marseilles* safely docked in Miami; no damage. Slight problem, though, for Rodolfo Dominguez, the largest wholesaler and distributor in the state since Salazaar's demise. A wiretap yesterday recorded him ranting on his main telephone line. Very out-of-character for the normally reserved Dominguez but the cause for his outburst soon became clear." She turned off the overhead projector and signalled for the lights. "As well as the coffee which was on the ship's manifest, there should have been 3,000-plus kilos of heroin on board. Someone boarded the ship and, in the middle of the night during a heavy storm, eliminated the cartel personnel on board and made off with the drugs."

"That's it, five incidents in just over eighteen months. Each a setback for the Madrigal-Zaragosa Alliance and we have no idea who's behind them. We don't know if these are it or if they're only part of a larger picture. What we've seen is enough to be of major concern but if there were more ..."

The attendees considered what they had seen and Mesi's closing remark. There was a lot to take in and the sense of people trying to get their bearings was evident.

Allenby was the first to assemble his thoughts. "You're obviously making a connection between them but ..." he hesitated, "couldn't they be a string of unrelated incidents?"

Mesi waited to see if Marshall wanted to take the question but he gestured for her to address it. "My team monitors cartel activity, trying to identify new trends or strategies as early as possible." She kept in mind the need to form her answer carefully. Allenby was a rising star in political circles and his profile had increased significantly in the wake of Plan Coca's positive press. Exactly the kind of person she did not want to antagonise but also, unfortunately, one of the people most likely to take issue with what was going to be discussed. "We try to discern what way the power structures are changing and use that to predict future developments. By definition, we're particularly interested in anything out of the ordinary. What you've just seen qualifies."

"I would have thought that in this environment, where violent criminals and enormous sums of money are not unusual, these type of episodes were quite common?" he remarked.

"There's more order than you might think. Most of it down to Luis Madrigal, whom I'm sure you're all familiar with. He's worked tirelessly to foster an atmosphere of stability among the various South and Central American cartels. Up to a few years ago, the Colombians and Mexicans particularly had gone their separate ways."

All of the attendees were riveted. The powerful presentation had set the stage and they wanted to know what the attacks signified. "Most of the division was as a result of the Mexicans bypassing the main Colombian cartels as a source of cocaine and their success in fostering their own indigenous heroin industry. Madrigal completely reversed the pattern by proving how everyone could benefit from cooperation. He's been very careful not to make the mistake of treating the Mexicans as subordinates."

"Just in case anyone here doesn't quite appreciate the breadth of Madrigal's organisation," Marshall added, "the Alliance he formed with Ernesto Zaragosa now comprises groups from more than ten different countries. A consequence of his work had been the reduction in the occurrence of events like you've just seen."

"But there's quite a long time frame involved here," Allenby commented. "Doesn't that reduce the likelihood of them being connected?"

Mesi knew Marshall had given no advance notice regarding the subject of the meeting. With no time to prepare, the attendees would be cautious in accepting any hypothesis put forward due to the possible implications for their individual agendas. That caution could manifest as either a direct challenge to what she was presenting or a subtler discrediting.

"I'd have to disagree with you there, sir," Mesi inwardly cursed herself for phrasing it so bluntly. "A year and a half in this context really isn't that long. Besides, there are too many common hallmarks to ignore the possibility that some of them are connected. If you consider the excellent intelligence regarding where and when to strike, and also the precision in their execution." She hesitated, aware of where the final observation might lead, before pushing on, "And, perhaps most worryingly of all, as far as we can determine, through all of our informants and wiretaps, none of the increasingly large quantities of drugs involved appear to have surfaced again. Ever."

The last statement caused Dan Schutterop from the FBI's Law Enforcement Coordination Office to look up from his folder quizzically. "If there were more incidents, say even ten more on a similar scale, and the drugs were being taken out of circulation, what would be the cumulative effect within the US?"

This was the question she had been dreading.

"Well," she replied warily. "Fifteen such episodes in total could be enough to affect availability." She knew the attempted vagueness of her answer would do no good.

"And that would impact prices, how?"

"They'd probably be pushed up," she replied.

"So, enough incidents could result in a drop in the availability of drugs and a general rise in prices, like what's been reported recently?" Schutterop persisted.

"Possibly."

The non-committal answer did nothing to dampen the apprehension that was creeping into the room. She recognised that some of the attendees would be delighted with what they were hearing while others would be displeased. Quite a few people had gone on the record as saying that little or no bottom-line impact should be expected from Plan Coca. As the Plan's successes had appeared to mount, criticism of them had grown and lately it had reached such a level that it looked like some people's positions might be in jeopardy. But if there were a variable of this magnitude at play, of which they had been unaware, then the apparently erroneous predictions would be mitigated, maybe even eliminated.

"Why are we only hearing about this now, if it's something which Agent Mesi contends has been brewing for more than eighteen months?" asked Allenby, no longer even attempting to hide his anger.

She tried to think of something to say that might defuse the atmosphere.

"Diane came to me immediately after the Mexican incident, warning me of the possibilities," Arthur Marshall boomed before she had a chance to reply. "I thought it was too early to jump to conclusions."

The message was clear; they were not there to find scapegoats and Allenby's attitude was not appreciated.

"Since the raid on the ship," Marshall continued, "I've had a rethink, mainly because we caught Dominguez mentioning that the captain of the ship thought the pirates may have been Eastern European. Diane, please explain the significance."

"As I mentioned, none of the investigations have made significant progress in finding out who was behind the attacks. The only lead was found during the Mexican investigation by Salvador Campas and his team of the attack on the heroin refinery." Given the mood, Mesi could not see any benefit in mentioning her participation in the investigation. "Based on physical evidence at the scene, they pursued the possibility of Balkan, specifically Kosovar, involvement in the attack. Add that to the captain's account and we might have something. Admittedly it's not much but –"

"If there's something to this then we'd be rightfully concerned, but before we get carried away, what's the basis for looking at the Kosovars? What was this physical evidence which led Campas to suspect them?" The question came from Will Samuels, whose shaven, bullet-shaped head matched his direct no-nonsense approach perfectly. Samuels was the DEA's chief of operations and de facto number two to Marshall.

"Cigarette butts found at the scene. They were a brand sold primarily in the Balkan region. The attack appeared to have military aspects in training and execution. The Mexicans suspected mercenary involvement from the outset."

"Anything else?"

"Subsequent checking of flights found that a number of Albanians had entered the country shortly before the attack. Enquiries with Europol revealed three of them had links to the Fifteen Families."

There was a pause before Samuels realised Mesi was finished.

"That's it, that's the basis for saying there was 'Kosovar involvement'?" asked Samuels incredulously.

"Campas did have serious reservations," she conceded.

"He pointed out that it wasn't guaranteed that these men were involved and even if they were, they could have been contracted by any number of third parties."

"Diane, I understand that it's your job to look for these tenuous connections but you have to agree this is very flimsy?" Samuels said.

"Can we afford to ignore it?" Schutterop piped up.

"But we're not ignoring it; this meeting is proof of that. We can't chase everything down. Sometimes we have to use judgement in regard to what we let go. In my opinion this is one of those cases."

So far, the meeting had not gone too badly. Other than Allenby no one had criticised her directly and she certainly didn't want to get on the wrong side of Samuels, but there was something she thought he was glossing over.

"I hope you're right and this is a groundless fear but whether we believe the Fifteen Families are targeting the Madrigal-Zaragosa Alliance isn't the only consideration. If the Alliance themselves believe it, they'll retaliate, and what happens then?"

Samuels pushed himself back from the table and stood up, clearly agitated.

"I don't like this!" he shook his head. "What reason could the Kosovars possibly have for engaging the Alliance? They don't have anything to gain."

"That's not strictly true," Schutterop offered.

"Excuse me?" said Samuels, sounding annoyed; he knew the FBI man's interest in stirring this up.

"It's just that they do have something to gain," Schutterop continued. "They're in direct competition with the Alliance, just like lots of others, exactly the same way as Chrysler and Toyota compete internationally."

"Can we get back to the matter at hand and leave the business news for some other time?" Samuels turned back to Mesi. "Do you believe the Kosovars are gunning for the Latin Americans?"

"I'm not sure."

"And what about the fact that you're saying the drugs disappeared. Wouldn't the Kosovars, if they had gone to this trouble, want to distribute them?"

"Maybe they did, maybe they redirected them to Europe," she replied, aware the answer sounded very weak. "Or maybe they destroyed them."

"And why would they do that? We're talking about a combined total of hundreds of millions of dollars."

"Which is still small potatoes in relation to the long-term value of the US market," pointed out Schutterop.

"I agree there's very little to go on but part of the reason for the meeting was to get people from different backgrounds together and see where the discussion goes," interjected Marshall. "Diane, for the benefit of those here unfamiliar with their history, can you tell us why it's reasonable to say the Fifteen Families are in competition with the Madrigal-Zaragosa Alliance?"

A quick look at Allenby and Samuels convinced Mesi that her hope of getting through the meeting without becoming dragged into the argument between the pro- and anti-Plan Coca camps was a lost cause. She took a deep sigh. "When the struggle in the Balkans exploded and Milosevic turned Sarajevo into a killing field, the plight of the Kosovars became widely known. The West, principally the US and NATO, rallied to support them and as a result the KLA came to prominence. What wasn't made widely known at the time was what the KLA had evolved from."

Her gaze drifted involuntarily to the representative from the State Department. "Their roots are in an armed brigade which has been maintained down through the years by the Kosovar Albanian traffickers. Many of the leaders of the KLA were the same people who had made a fortune smuggling heroin, weapons and illegal immigrants."

She paused to see if any of them wanted to ask any questions. Nobody did. "When the struggle escalated, the traffickers, sometimes collectively referred to as the Fifteen Families, boosted their activities. Some of you may remember a number of dramatic seizures by the European authorities during the mid nineties. This was a direct consequence of the Kosovars scaling up their operations. Just as many ordinary expatriate Kosovars donated money to the rebels, the traffickers too channelled their profits to help combat the Serbs. The difference here was in the amount; hundreds of millions of dollars worth of donations came from these crime lords."

"Where is all this going?" interrupted Allenby. "I went to considerable trouble today to attend this meeting. Had I known I'd be getting a history lesson, I wouldn't have bothered."

"I'm sorry, if you'll just bear with me a little longer. During this escalation period, the willingness of the Kosovars to resort to violence to gain a foothold in many countries' drug scenes meant that no one challenged them for too long. Ultimately, they became number one throughout Europe. It's estimated now that they handle at least eighty per cent of the heroin consumed there."

"Which is unfortunate but still a matter for Europol and not our concern –" Allenby began again before a warning look from Marshall silenced him.

"When the struggle in the Balkans subsided," she resumed, "the KLA came to power and debts had to be paid. There've been criticisms from some quarters that Kosovo will evolve into a virtual drug state with the primary mission of helping the Fifteen Families maximise their profits. One way to increase profits would be to start looking for fresh markets, and according to our statistics the amount of heroin in the US which originated from Golden Crescent has climbed steeply in recent years."

"What have relations between the Alliance and the Fifteen Families been like up to now?" asked Schutterop.

"We know that the Colombians and Kosovars have been working together to import and distribute South American cocaine to Europe," Mesi replied. "But on the heels of these attacks, there may be reason to wonder whether the Fifteen Families have grown tired of being a minor player in the US and essentially well-paid agents in the European cocaine business."

"The Kosovar regime is committed to supporting a growing number of armed struggles," agreed Schutterop, "many of which have served as familiar thorns in the side of Western Governments. To meet these obligations the Kosovars would need ever-increasing funds."

It was quite clear to Mesi and, she assumed, to everyone else in the room, that Schutterop, a Plan Coca sceptic, had identified that the stronger the case for a Kosovar campaign against the Alliance, the more his original assessment of the Plan's limited capabilities would be bolstered.

"You're saying their objective is to seize the US market from the Madrigal Alliance?" Samuels asked Mesi.

"It's just one of the possibilities, everyone agrees that the best time to strike is when your rival is otherwise occupied.

Maybe Plan Coca was the distraction they needed?" she replied, meeting Samuels' fierce stare. "Look, I'm not saying it's the only area we should be looking at."

"You're a specialist in trend detection and analysis. Of course you're going to advocate some outlandish global view," said Allenby, raising his voice. "And doubtless it'll have support at this meeting because it exonerates the inaccurate predictions of more than one of the attendees. But the truth is, ascribing Kosovar involvement for these incidents is questionable, bordering on irresponsible."

She tried to placate him but he continued, talking over her.

"For the record, I want to stress my objections. Any link between these attacks is pure speculation. I suggest what we have are a number of unrelated local rivalries that have flared up within a particular time span and which Agent Mesi then misinterpreted. All I can concede is that it's a coincidence that they all share common features." Allenby's tone was as dismissive as the look he levelled at her. "Incidents like this probably happen more regularly than we know. The fact that we caught these on our radar and that they coincided with Plan Coca kicking into top gear means they've been attributed more significance than they warrant. The shortages we've experienced were predicted by those of us who had a little more faith in Plan Coca."

"So you're one hundred per cent happy to dismiss the possibility of any escalation? You're recommending, for the record, that we drop this here?" Mesi asked, angry by this stage but trying not to show it.

"No, that isn't what I said. Of course we need to look into it," Allenby backtracked, realising that he could be exposing himself to future difficulties. "It's just that we need to keep things in perspective. We're under-resourced as it is and barely able to keep pace with real, concrete problems. I'm questioning the benefit of pouring too much effort into what's probably going to be a wild goose chase."

"There may be something to that view," conceded Marshall. Seeing that the meeting was deteriorating into argument, he stood up to signal its close. "I tend to agree with Will that the Kosovar link is a long shot but I also think it's unrealistic to say that none of these incidents are connected. I'm going to have Diane spend some time seeing if the Kosovar theory can be corroborated or dismissed. If in the course of her work she needs any assistance, I know I can count on each of you to give her total cooperation. I think that's it, there are dossiers for each of you to pick up on the way out."

The train doors closed and Mesi watched the platform slowly disappear. The combination of lack of sleep and nervous anticipation, followed by the events of the day, had taken their toll. Drained, she sank deeper into the seat and resolved to get an early night: something quick to eat when she got home then straight to bed. Although tomorrow was Saturday it made little difference; she would be working every weekend for the foreseeable future.

The events of the meeting were still playing on her mind. While her presentation had gone well, the rest of it had been mixed. Why had Marshall referred to her as a specialist rather than as the head of TAIT? Was there any significance in this omission in front of the external audience? Did it show a lack of commitment on his part to the team or was she simply reading too much into it? Marshall certainly had other things on his mind. While he may not have shown it outwardly he must be feeling some strain. After all, if the worst scenario came to pass and a conflict occurred, one that detracted from Plan Coca, it would have happened while he was at the DEA's helm. His professional legacy could be at stake, so perhaps the introduction had simply been a result of understandable preoccupation.

More significant had been her inability to avoid being pulled into the dispute. Even before she had begun her presentation, she could see the way the two camps had naturally aligned themselves on opposite sides of the table. She had known then that some clash was inevitable but she had hoped they would leave her out of it. Unfortunately, once Schutterop had forced her to speculate on the cumulative effect of the attacks, people like Allenby and Samuels tabbed her as anti-Plan. Thinking about it now, she was not so worried about Allenby. There was little chance of them crossing paths regularly; she was too low in the pecking order to justify his interest. Samuels, however, was another matter; as chief of operations, he could certainly influence her future in the DEA.

One positive she took away was the task Marshall had set her, to investigate further and establish one way or the other whether there was cause for concern. Yes, it meant seven-day weeks until she could offer something conclusive but it might help TAIT's cause. A good job might convince Marshall to break the budgetary deadlock.

The train stopped at a station and she watched some passengers leave. One woman stepped down, walked to a waiting man and together they headed off down the platform, arms interlinked. She would have to give Jean a call to see how last night's dinner had gone and check how annoyed her intended date had been. Lately she had found herself leading an increasingly solitary lifestyle, a trend she wanted to reverse. Being in her late thirties and having a demanding job made it difficult to meet new people. In college it had been easy; there had always been one party or other to go to and she had enjoyed the exhausting social schedule. Even during her brief time with the investment bank, building a full life outside work had been effortless. Most of her colleagues had been of a similar age and at the same stage in life, interested in making the most of life following the lean financial years of college. After the divorce, though, it had become harder. She had met Alan straight after college and they had been married just six months later, too quickly as it turned out. Less than two years later, when they had finally accepted their mistake, they split. A little time to herself afterwards to get her head together had stretched to months and had then been compounded by her radical career change.

During the first year with the DEA, she had lost touch with so many people, not all of it due to her being neglectful. The demands of the new job had played their part but by the time she had been ready to rekindle the friendships, a lot of the old crowd had moved on with their lives and, she had realised, so had she. Perhaps it would have been easier had she still shared the same professional background. But how many of them were interested in the street price of crack along the eastern seaboard and, for that matter, how much did she care anymore about the current rate of deficit spending?

Well, she knew she needed to make a concerted effort to reverse the trend in her personal life, and she would. Just not right now. When she had successfully completed

Marshall's assignment, the situation with TAIT would become clearer and things would get easier.

"… all the latest gossip from Hollywood."

"Okay, something to look forward to later in the bulletin, no doubt. Thanks for that, Mark."

Sandra Whittaker, the co-presenter of the evening news bulletin, swivelled away from the entertainment reporter to face the camera.

"Over the past months, the joint-initiative Plan Coca, the strategy designed to bring the struggle against the Colombian drug cartels to their own backyard, has intensified its operations. We have a report now from Caroline Williams, our correspondent in the Putumayo region of Colombia, on the campaign's latest success. Following this segment, we'll be talking to Senator Charles Dalton about the benefits the Plan is already demonstrating here in the US."

"In the early hours of this morning, Plan Coca experienced its most significant breakthrough to date." The picture opened with a close-up of the reporter's head and shoulders. *"For months, the authorities have been trying to locate a major cocaine processing plant in this part of Putumayo. Yesterday, they succeeded. Fierce ground fighting ensued between the army and the FARC rebels who until recently had undisputed control over this area. The battle raged for most of the day but, with the help of tactical air strikes, the army eventually forced the rebels' surrender."*

Footage was run of the interior of the large building. The pictures showed rough workbenches, primitive processing equipment and rows of palettes. Each palette was stacked high with large clear plastic bags and each of these bags was filled with white powder.

"We've learnt from the authorities that this victory exceeded even their most optimistic projections," Williams' voice resumed, in tandem with the images. "Given the size of the plant and the amount of cocaine seized, it's now thought that they've found the main production centre for the entire region. Although firm estimates are difficult at this stage, it's speculated that as much as forty per cent of the region's total processing capacity may have come from this plant."

The footage ended and Williams was joined by a short man dressed in green fatigues.

"I have Lieutenant Javier Blanco with me to discuss this latest success. Lieutenant, can you put this development into context?"

"We knew that the rebel forces had constructed a number of processing plants for the coca harvests of the region," the soldier replied. "The rebels guard these plants zealously; the revenues generated are their lifeblood and enable them to continue their campaign of terror. Initially we suspected that there would be many similarly sized plants, each capable of producing a small amount of processed cocaine."

"But that wasn't the case?"

"No, to our surprise, this plant was many times larger than anything we had envisaged. Based on our estimates of its peak capacity, it could account for ten per cent of Colombia's total annual production."

"Why the deviation from the practice of having many smaller plants?" the reporter asked. "Doesn't this maximise potential losses when they lose a plant?"

"I suspect that the rebels sought to benefit from the obvious economies of scale for production and distribution. This is not a political struggle we're dealing with but a criminal one." Blanco's disdain for the rebels shone through. "A movement truly committed to the advancement of legitimate political views would never have tied itself so closely to the proceeds of drugs."

"FARC's position has been that they're not directly involved in the narcotics trade but merely levy a tax on the cartels, just as they'd tax any multinational doing business in this area. You don't believe this?"

"Absolutely not. We and our colleagues in the US Administration consider the rebels and the cartels to be indivisible. To find where one stops and the other begins is impossible. The more success we have against FARC and the ELN, the closer we will be to eliminating the cartels."

"Thank you Lieutenant Blanco. So, another impressive success from Plan Coca and optimism that a drug-free Colombia is one step closer. This is Caroline Williams for IBNC in Putumayo, Colombia."

The report ended and the broadcast returned to the studio. A wider shot than before showed the distinguished figure of Senator Charles Dalton alongside Whittaker.

"Senator, before we talk about the broader aspects of the Plan, a question about your own role. You've been one of the biggest supporters of Plan Coca and, consequently, you've come in for strong criticism from some quarters. Do these mounting successes represent a personal vindication?"

"It's not a matter of vindication. This is far too important for anyone to be keeping a personal score sheet," the senator replied, looking aggrieved. "The reason I supported Plan Coca was its ability, beyond any other strategy, to deal with the crisis that's crippled our country."

"And your reaction to this latest report?"

"Developments such as those we've just seen are great

news. If we can defeat the drug producers and traffickers at source then we all benefit. From those spared addiction, to all of their families, friends and co-workers, not to mention the easing of the burden on over-stretched law enforcement and social services."

"And apparently the benefits are already being seen on the streets of some of our major cities?"

"Yes, Sandra, I thought it was vital to show end-to-end commitment to the Plan. With that in mind, my office established contacts with various police forces around the country, enabling us to receive direct feedback from the professionals who fight the war at street-level."

"Allowing the closest possible monitoring of the situation?"

"Precisely, no one is in a better position than our police. Some time ago we set a benchmark against which we could measure subsequent improvements."

"And you've started to see evidence of such improvements?"

"Indeed. In the past three months, the data clearly indicates that the availability of cocaine and heroin in key cities has declined and that the price has risen accordingly. This is the best news we could have hoped for. It's grass-roots confirmation of real progress."

"Can this progress be quantified?" she asked.

"Well, it's important to note that this is an informal study, by simple virtue of our limited resources. That said, I'm confident that the research is a reliable indicator. Our figures show street prices climbing an average of fifteen per cent across the board and by up to twenty-three per cent in some areas. Experts say this translates to a more than ten per cent drop in the availability of heroin and cocaine."

"And to those critics who dismissed your findings when you announced them earlier, maintaining that these price rises could be due to local fluctuations?"

"Rubbish!" Annoyance flickered then disappeared quickly as the senator's positive mood rallied. "An isolated price hike might be discountable but consistent rises in so many areas and of such significance? I don't think opponents can continue to begrudge Plan Coca the praise it rightfully deserves."

—

three

Madrigal sat on the veranda alone, looking out at the sunset. He had left instructions that he did not want to be disturbed while he considered what had happened and the appropriate response. The fact that it had been possible for the attackers to strike so surgically meant that they must have had access to inside information, but this was not his prime concern. He knew that any organisation as sprawling as theirs could not be totally protected from infiltration. What worried him most was the progression, the dangerous precedents that were set with each new incident. The Alliance needed to appear unassailable.

None of their enquiries in Europe had yielded any firm proof of Kosovar involvement. He had tried to ensure their investigation had been conducted discreetly. The Kosovars themselves had recently raised the subject of the attacks, mentioning that word of some disturbances had filtered back to them. One could infer that this demonstrated their innocence. Then again, maybe that was their intention.

He placed a call to Raul Cervantes and asked him to come over. Cervantes was the number two in the Colombian organisation and the only person he trusted. They had known each other since they were teenagers and he had learnt to rely on the big man's judgement. People often underestimated him because of an apparent slowness which he was only too happy to exaggerate, but Madrigal knew better. Even more valuable than Cervantes' capacity for violence and his unwavering loyalty was his well-developed intellect. When Cervantes arrived, he strode in casually and slumped in the other chair. Whereas other people would tread lightly around the drug lord, Cervantes had known him too long to stand on ceremony.

"We're going to have to move against the Fifteen Families," Madrigal began.

"Based on so little?" Cervantes asked. "We have no proof!"

"You know about the hijacking?"

"Yes, yes," the big man replied. "But there's only the captain's questionable assertions that the hijackers were Eastern European!"

"I know, but combined with the attack on the refinery in Mexico ..."

Cervantes shook his head.

"I can't believe we're ready to risk a war. Luis, can we even be sure we'd win?"

If it had been anyone else, Madrigal might have dismissed them as cowards, but he had seen Cervantes prove his bravery countless times over the years. "You think they can match us?"

"Maybe not financially." Cervantes shrugged. "But then they don't have to contend with a hostile state initiative backed by a foreign superpower. Not to mention some of the fucking lunatics they can call on."

Madrigal knew all about the Kosovars' ties to various fundamentalist groups but did not see what choice he had.

"If we don't move, the Alliance will fall apart."

"Why do you say that? Has that asshole Zaragosa demanded action?"

"No, but I can't afford to wait until he does. If I don't

take the initiative now, later it will look like I'm buckling to internal pressure. That would bring its own problems."

Cervantes knew he was right but had deep misgivings about the direction they were taking. They sat in silence for some time, the oppressive weight of Madrigal's decision hanging over them.

"Okay, then we need to decide what it is we want from the action," Cervantes said at last. "Are we aiming to wipe the Kosovars out?"

"Jesus, no. I just want them to back off, if they are behind the attacks. Even if we *could* take them off the board completely the cost would be too high and who knows how it would affect our access to Europe."

"Then we'll need to ensure that they can survive whatever we do."

"Yes but on the other hand, if our action is too weak, it might encourage them further."

"Not to mention providing Rodriguez and the others with something else to fucking stir things up."

"Exactly. Tell me, you've had some dealings with Lubomir Uka, how did he strike you?"

"Careful, a planner, someone who takes his time and tries to see the bigger picture. He balances out some of the other more impetuous leaders of the Fifteen Families."

"That was my impression as well which is why any targets we select should belong to him. If we were to move against one of the others there would be no subsequent opportunity to broker a truce, regardless of how much control we exercised."

"You're hoping Uka will see sense and convince the others to go along. It's a big fucking gamble, what if he can't do it, what if we've misread him?"

"Then we'll have to deal with it," he said matter-of-factly. "Any suggestions on what we should target?"

"I know Uka controls a number of heroin refineries and depots in Ankara. It should be possible to draw up a list of four or five of the less crucial ones."

"Perfect," the drug lord nodded, "the material loss would be minor but it would still make a statement. There's one more thing we need to consider however."

"What's that?"

"After the attacks, someone will have to approach Uka, explain the restraint we showed and stress that this should be seen as a conclusion to matters."

The two men locked eyes.

"I'll do it," Cervantes said.

"You're sure?"

"Who else can we trust?"

Madrigal leaned forward and tapped Raul's knee.

"Listen, I want you to be careful, you're not to participate directly in the raids. Conduct the meeting with Uka and then get back here."

"He'll see sense, don't worry," Cervantes replied, pushing the doubts from his mind.

"Okay, start preparations and let me know when we're ready to review."

Larsen watched the three bodyguards get out of the car and scan the immediate vicinity. Once Bajo, the enormous bodyguard, was satisfied he leant back into the rear of the car to give the all-clear to Dobroshi. The four men entered the lobby of the apartment building and left the driver to start circling the district until the appointed time. Larsen was satisfied after two weeks of surveillance that the information had been solid.

The traffickers lived like kings, enjoying the very best Prague had to offer. The judiciary were in their pocket. They flaunted their extravagant lifestyle, secure in the knowledge that no one could threaten them. It hadn't been difficult to find a disillusioned narcotics officer who had finally had enough. A generous supplement to a modest salary was all it had taken. Detailed reports of the main traffickers' movements were produced and, based on them, Larsen had chosen Nisret Dobroshi as the target.

Dobroshi kept a beautiful young Czech girl in the upmarket apartment building and got away to visit her as often as work and domestic arrangements permitted. The two subordinate bodyguards always waited in the lobby while Bajo ascended the stairs with his charge. Larsen knew from previous reconnaissance that Bajo waited in the hallway outside the apartment. He took a deep breath and exhaled, finding a calm centre. In many ways this was the pivotal operation, more risky than anything that had gone before, but if he succeeded it would tip the scales. He focused, moving himself to a place where he would be able to do what was required.

"We will train you, harder than you ever believed possible and teach you all there is to know about weaponry and tactics," the drill sergeant told them.

The sixteen new recruits stood on the tarmac at Flyvestation Aalborg as the driving rain beat down on them and the incessant wind howled. Although the sergeant spoke loudly they had to strain to hear him as the gusts whipped his words away. "Many of you have had extensive training already. We will add our experience to help mould you," he continued. "But all of this will count for nothing, if you lack one thing."

The recruits stood rock-steady, eyes firmly locked straight ahead.

"Can you tell me what this thing is?" he asked one of them.

An uncomfortable pause then the nervous attempt at an answer. "Courage?"

The sergeant snorted dismissively and turned on his heel, pacing away from them. Coming around to face them he delivered the answer. "Willingness." The sergeant let it sink in before continuing. "Most individuals will split every challenge they are faced with into three categories. Things they're happy to do, things they do not want to do but are willing to suffer and finally those things they would never consider," he explained. "Like a traffic-light, green, yellow and red. If a person is willing to attempt something, really attempt it, with every fibre concentrated on success, this is green. But if he perceives it to be too dangerous, too far beyond his capabilities or if he merely makes a half-assed attempt to save face, he is in the red zone." He scanned the line, examining individual recruits.

"Many people will say with total conviction they could not kill another human being. Put these same people in a position where someone is threatening their child and watch what happens. What's changed? Their willingness to act! Circumstances have conspired to push their green zone far beyond its perceived limits."

A smile broke across his craggy features.

"We will repeatedly put you in situations where you will become accustomed to diminishing that red zone. We will challenge you, again and again. Most of you will not last. Those that do will understand all about willingness." He

nodded, almost to himself. "Those that do will be Jægere."

This was green.

Using the key he had obtained, Larsen entered the basement's laundry room via an exterior door. The internal door to the laundry led to the rear stairway, which converged with the main staircase between the lobby and the first floor. To protect Dobroshi properly, one of the bodyguards should have been positioned on this landing while the other watched the elevator. But months of the same routine, in a city that held no surprises, had bred complacency.

Once he got to the second level, he pressed for the elevator to climb the last couple of floors. The lift door was an old trellised affair that ran up the centre of the staircase, allowing people on the stairs to see in. He assumed a stooped posture and coughed hoarsely. Combined with the threadbare clothing, white wig and pale make-up, he looked like one of the many callers to the retired jeweller living across from Dobroshi's mistress – elderly, decrepit and unthreatening. Bajo stared intently at the lift's occupant through the grille while it ascended. Unlike his subordinates downstairs, he was a veteran with years of hard-earned experience and could not be easily circumvented. Everything depended on overcoming him without alerting Dobroshi. The intelligence Larsen had been given did not specify Bajo's proficiency with arms, although Larsen assumed he was a rated marksman. What Larsen was aware of, though, was the man's ability in unarmed combat, enhanced by his prodigious size and strength. He was perfectly suited to the role of close-quarter protection. His gaze never left the old man who stepped from the elevator, wrestled to close the door and, still struggling to regain his breath from the effort, shuffled down the hall.

Larsen focused totally on his laboured progress and it took him ten seconds just to cover the short distance to the bodyguard. Once Larsen passed him, he sensed the big man relax ever so slightly, letting some of the tension ease from his frame. The surprise was total when the bent-over figure twisted back fluidly and drove the knife up towards his throat. Years of combat drills enabled Bajo to react quickly enough to prevent a fatal strike and he managed to deflect the knife's arc with his extended forearm. The blade lodged painfully in his shoulder inches from his neck. Normally, in this kind of confrontation, he would have drawn the assailant close where he could use his natural advantages to quickly end matters but the risk of the attacker worsening the injury was too great. He struck out at his assailant's chest with the heel of his left hand in an attempt to drive him back and create some distance between them. Larsen managed to turn his torso enough to prevent the blow from landing with full impact and was only knocked back a half step. Even so, the effect of the partial blow was enough to convince him that he could not survive a protracted struggle in such a confined area. Bringing his left knee up to waist height he struck out and down with his foot, driving it in viciously just above the bodyguard's right knee. Bajo's leg collapsed and he crumpled forwards towards the floor. As he fell Larsen grasped the hilt of the knife with both hands and with all the strength he could muster drove the blade through the heavy muscle across the throat. The blade sliced through the larynx, severing his opponent's air supply abruptly.

The dead bodyguard tumbled to the floor and Larsen sagged against the wall, battling to control his breathing. He pushed himself up, aware that time was short. Removing the suppressor-fitted Glock from his coat, he used a second key to quietly enter the apartment. Any concerns that the struggle might have disturbed the apartment's occupants were put to rest by the sounds emanating from the bedroom off the hallway. He pulled the dead bodyguard's heavy bulk inside the apartment before slowly opening the bedroom door to reveal the sight of Dobroshi, a million miles away, eyes closed, lost in pleasure as the girl straddling him worked industriously. Though her back was to him, she must have sensed his presence because she stiffened in mid-motion, disturbing her lover's bliss. The trafficker opened his eyes and looked as if he had trouble believing what he saw. Before he could command himself to move, Larsen shot him twice, once in the head and once in the chest. The girl shrieked and tried to push herself off the bucking corpse but her hands slipped on the blood-slicked torso. She inhaled sharply, gathering herself for a powerful scream. Larsen quickly grabbed her and placed a hand over her mouth. Stepping close, he applied pressure to the base of her throat. Once she slipped into unconsciousness, he bound and gagged her, leaving him free to complete his work undisturbed.

Cervantes was quite satisfied with how well things had gone. Three attacks in four days, all carried out faultlessly, creating exactly the effect Madrigal had wished for. The effort involved in exercising such control would not have been wasted on Lubomir Uka, whom he had travelled to the Macedonian city of Skopje to meet. He didn't think his optimism about reaching a settlement was misplaced; while there was no doubting the Kosovar's ability to use violence when it was needed, it had taken more than mere bloodlust to get him to where he was today. Uka kept a close eye on all areas of their operations and stamped out any activity he viewed as inconsistent with the long-term goals he had defined. While he may have been willing to approve some speculative forays against the Alliance, Cervantes could not see him pursuing it any further. The Kosovar chief had to see that a continuation down the road they were on would be disastrous for everyone. This was not to say he wasn't nervous; a certain amount of negotiation and diplomacy were still required.

He was relieved of his firearm before being granted access. His companions were instructed to wait in the courtyard outside while he headed in alone. Regardless of his confidence concerning his task, he felt quite vulnerable when he was led into the darkened study. Uka, seemingly oblivious to his arrival, sat behind a large desk studying a photograph under a lamp, which provided the sole source of illumination. Guards stood around the perimeter of the room as motionless as statues. He yearned to get this over with and his discomfort grew as the silence dragged on. Finally, Uka placed the photograph face down on the desk and looked up at him. In his late forties with dark skin and a slightly receding hairline, he possessed a natural air of authority.

"I've been told that you want to deliver a postscript to your actions?"

Cervantes found something in the casual tone of the question off-putting but there was no time to dwell on it. "Lubomir, we regret the action we've been forced to take but we had no alternative. We want to put this dispute behind us and resume working together for mutual prosperity. I hope you'll see how sincere we are from the restraint we exercised." He had mentally rehearsed what he wanted to say again and again but now, that the time had come, he was annoyed with himself. Rather than the calm measured delivery he had hoped for, the words had tumbled out.

"Restraint? Please elaborate, so that I'm sure I can draw full comfort from this control you exercised."

He recognised that Uka was determined to make him spell it out and in the process make it as uncomfortable as possible. He was obviously put out over the targets they had hit and would not admit their relative unimportance. He hadn't expected such petulant behaviour; the Kosovar had always struck him as a wholly pragmatic man. Still, if a satisfactory resolution required his dignity to be slightly compromised, he could deal with that.

"We know that the attacks caused some financial injury and unavoidable bloodshed. It was the last thing we wished for and we want to stress that we don't see any need for further action. We want this to end here. You must see that if we truly sought to do real injury there were other targets and …" Raul hesitated, "… personnel we could have singled out."

"So you targeted only what you felt was necessary to make a point? Am I to infer from this that the victims of the attacks were considered token and that I should be grateful it wasn't much worse?"

He wondered why Uka was putting such an emphasis on the elimination of some hired guns. He was all for the use of diplomacy to smooth ruffled feathers but the Kosovar was being churlish. He had agreed with Madrigal that the meeting might get fairly heated at some stage, harsh words might be exchanged, but they had anticipated that any rancour would focus on more substantive issues like the damaged supply lines or lost inventory. Perhaps this was a negotiating tactic. If he complained strongly about the loss of contracted labour, he might think he was building a case for compensation on the material loss. If that was it, Cervantes realised he needed to adopt a stronger stance to illustrate that Madrigal's desire to be reasonable had its limits. Uka was aware of Cervantes', position and closeness to Madrigal; this awareness provided Raul with a degree of protection. Emboldened by this, he decided to be more direct in the hopes of getting the conversation back where he wanted it.

"Lubomir, let's be honest with each other, this could indeed have been much worse," Cervantes said. "You know some of the people Luis has to deal with and their tendencies. Believe me, it's a good thing that only Luis and I were involved in deciding what to target. It's unfortunate anyone had to die but, frankly, these men can be easily replaced."

Uka's nostrils flared and his face trembled. He threw the photograph he had been studying down to land at Cervantes' feet. The Colombian looked questioningly at Uka whose stare bore through him. Stooping over, Cervantes picked up the photograph.

"Tell me again, how I should be grateful for your restraint. I must be stupid or blind because no matter how long I look at this and the others, I can't see it at all."

Cervantes was so riveted by the image in his hands that he barely heard Uka. A feeling of dread overcame him as he realised that Uka blamed him for what it contained. He had seen many dead bodies and more than a few had died at his own hand but the scene contained in the photograph was beyond anything he had ever witnessed.

"Who … ?" he began.

"It's clear to see what your intention was. You believed your visit, so close on the heels of Nisret's torture, would have us cowering in fear." The Kosovar shook with rage as he uttered the words but then, with a noticeable effort, quelled all outward signs of emotion. "The calculation was that the brutal slaughter would be terrifying. We would gratefully accept whatever subordinate role you've envisaged for us and be thankful that you stopped where you did. After all, if my cousin meant so little to you … well, the object lesson hasn't been wasted."

He nodded his head and two of the guards drew their guns and fired. The bullets shattered Cervantes' shinbones and he collapsed. The pain was unbelievable and he struggled to retain consciousness as wave after wave of agony assailed him. Uka walked around the desk and looked down at the writhing Colombian.

"Please, this wasn't us. You must see that?"

Uka was not listening. "I'm saddened but not totally surprised. Madrigal obviously believes himself beyond our reach, unaccountable for his actions. Well, we'll see."

A second nod from Uka was accompanied by another explosion of pain as both of his knees disintegrated under the impact of the soft-nosed rounds. This time he did lose consciousness.

When he was revived, his suffering lingered for what seemed an eternity, before the next, final, release.

four

Mesi was looking forward to the evening that lay ahead. The bath had just been drawn and she had rented two classic movies, *The Awful Truth* and *Arsenic and Old Lace*, for later. She lit three scented candles, placed them around the bathroom and turned on the CD player, smiling as the first strains of *Rusalka* permeated the apartment. Now, all she needed to do was get the stack of magazines and newspaper supplements from the living room and everything was set. At last, a work-free evening. It had been flat out since the meeting in Arlington nine weeks earlier. Sleep and leisure time had both been sacrificed. She knew, though, that she could only work so hard before a break was required and tonight, she had decided, was going to be just that.

She had placed a lot of the pressure on herself to either substantiate or dismiss the link between the attacks and the Kosovars. As she found herself unwilling to trust her subordinates to make decisions on whether data was pertinent or not that left her to sift through innumerable reports alone. The vast majority of it ended up being discounted but to even establish its lack of significance took time.

She had decided to err on the side of caution and focus on a reasonably long time period, starting from six months before the first suspected incident right up to the present. Besides searching for signs of incidents that may not have been spotted up to that point, she was also interested in trends that could constitute secondary effects of a campaign against the Madrigal-Zaragosa Alliance. All of these she entered in a specifically designed database. If there had been any reported change in street prices for various drugs, it might tie in to an underlying shortage. If a geographic analysis of a drugs seizure had thrown up unexpected results, it was entered as a possible indication of alternative sources moving in to fill gaps in the normal supply. If there had been a rise in figures for particular types of crime that had proven correlations to drug dependency, these too were logged.

In parallel with the data analysis, she had also contacted overseas colleagues. Some were law enforcement, others academics, some were just people with whom the DEA had developed a relationship at some point, such as a tour guide in Thailand who smuggled funds and medicine over the border into Burma. The theory was that if a fundamental shift was occurring in the global drug economy, someone might have started to see some localised manifestations. And no matter what she was working on or whom she was talking to, she always had to factor in Plan Coca. Regardless of whether it had been unjustly lauded up to now, the irony was that it could still have a major impact, if applied to a market already weakened by something else.

The result of all of this analysis?

Nothing. At least nothing definitive.

Oh, she could make what seemed like a plausible case for a secret war being waged but she could just as easily discredit the theory.

Lately, as the sum of her findings proved more and more ambiguous, she found herself straying in a different direction. She could not remember precisely why she had started – it might have been frustration or just some tangential thought. She had made a copy of the original database and begun modelling projections based on the worst-case scenario she could envisage, socially and financially. She wanted to know what the end result might be if there was a full-on, no-holds-barred war between the drug superpowers. As a backdrop to the model, she had created as many interdependencies as possible between the drugs trade and mainstream society, some of which were admittedly arguable. The model had grown to become a kind of doomsday scenario. It had predicted a complete breakdown in social order; spiralling crime, looting, high absenteeism, companies going bust, rehabilitation facilities overwhelmed by demand, disintegration of family units, financial markets tumbling and even declarations of martial law. She had gotten so caught up in it at one point, so frightened by the results, that she almost forgot it was just a hypothetical exercise. When she had caught what she was doing, she admonished herself for being like a child who deliberately asks for a horror story in the sure knowledge that they will be scared witless.

As a result of her failure to develop anything solid, she knew that she would be told to abandon the investigation soon and TAIT would have lost an opportunity. Since the meeting there had been just one incident that seemed consistent with a drug war. An attack on a haulage depot in Ankara resulting in five men being killed and 150 kilos of heroin being seized by authorities. Despite the investigation by the Turkish police, nothing more had materialised. Her last outstanding task involved flying up to New York tomorrow to meet the director of a methadone programme, to discuss a recent surge in the demand for places.

Clutching at straws.

She was testing the bath water when the phone rang. On the verge of letting it go to the machine, she changed her mind at the last minute and ran into the living room to pick up.

"Diane, sorry to disturb you so late," Arthur Marshall began. "There's been a significant development. I think you'd better come into the office."

The tone of his voice was worrying.

"What's happened?"

"I've just received reports of two incidents, which I think confirm our fears. The first happened in downtown Vienna. A prominent local figure with documented ties to the Fifteen Families was attacked in one of the city's upmarket restaurants. At least five men entered the building and opened up with automatic weapons. Some of those at the table managed to return fire. Busiest time of the evening and the place was turned into a shooting gallery. It was all over very quickly and reports are that all the attackers got away."

"Casualties?"

"In addition to the presumed target and his party of ten, at least nine bystanders are dead; more injured, some critically."

"Christ! You said two incidents?"

"Madrid, an unconfirmed number of hit squads systematically moved through an area well known for street dealing. They appeared to be targeting pushers and their customers but weren't too choosy about who they hit. Any congregation of two or three was fair game. Most of the victims were just residents of the area going about their normal business."

"How many dead there?"

"Not sure yet. What we have so far is less clear than Vienna. The authorities are just getting to grips with it. I've got to go; there's a call waiting. We'll talk when you get here."

She returned the phone to its cradle and went into the bathroom to blow out the candles.

Mesi and Will Samuels sat across the desk from Marshall waiting for him to finish the latest call. She had read what reports they had but everything was still very sketchy. The footage of the news report from Vienna on the muted TV in Marshall's office was terrible. She felt guilty for all the times she had wished an opportunity would arise to prove her suspicions.

Marshall put the phone down and looked over at them, the anger clearly visible on his face. "Typical! Most of these calls are from people who didn't want to know when we called the initial meeting. That jerk Allenby is a prime example," he growled. "All I've heard for the past two months is how he's been bitching about us trying to undermine the State Department's initiative. Now he's burning up the telephone line trying to find out what all this means. Do you know what they're most worried about?"

"Similar incidents on our soil?" Marshall guessed.

"No, surprisingly enough. They're afraid of the media fallout when someone figures out what's behind this. It's bound to happen, sooner rather than later. I guess we should be worried too; we'll be crucified."

"You mean if we knew incidents like this might be likely, why didn't we do something? If we didn't know, why not?"

"Exactly. The only silver lining is that we never aligned

ourselves as strongly with Plan Coca as some others. All it's going to take is some reporter asking how long the dispute's been going on."

"Maybe they won't," offered Samuels.

Marshall shook his head. "If no one thinks of it themselves, there are plenty of critics of the Plan who'll be happy to help them. The Plan will either be painted as responsible for the dispute because it was such a destabilising factor or ..." He looked at Mesi.

"Or some commentators might come to the conclusion that the success attributed to Plan Coca was really a by-product of this dispute," she said. "Either way, all those people who couldn't wait to jump on the Plan Coca bandwagon and take a little of the credit are screwed."

"Fuck it, we need to focus on what's within our control," Marshall declared. "Here's what's going to happen with the investigation. Will, I want you to draft a preliminary plan on what role the different departments need to play in tackling this situation. Also, assign a dedicated liaison to the various European agencies." He looked at her. "Diane, you and your guys will be under Will's direction for the duration. Make sure that he's up to speed with everything you've found so far, then continue with the analysis, giving updates as appropriate. So, based on the escalation we've seen tonight, what do you think is next?" he asked her.

"Well, first order of business for the Kosovars is to retaliate against whoever carried out the attacks."

"What do you mean?" Samuels asked. "It was obviously the Madrigal-Zaragosa Alliance?"

"Only indirectly. I'm assuming twenty Latin Americans didn't fly over to Spain and Austria, smuggle an arsenal with them and carry out the attacks personally. They would have gotten others to act for them," she replied. "The logical candidate is one of the Kosovars' local rivals. The Fifteen Families probably won't be too particular about finding out which one it was; they'll target everyone indiscriminately. We might see a lot of people getting sucked in. Over time, new disputes, totally independent of the current one, will develop." She realised she had just recited portions of the doomsday scenario she had worked on.

"Then there's the issue of what offensive action the Kosovars will take against the Alliance here and in Latin America," Samuels added.

"Can the Fifteen Families match the Alliance head-to-head?" Marshall asked him.

"If not, they can go damn close. Diane's right, of course: Madrigal employed subcontractors for tonight's attacks and the Kosovars will probably follow the same tactic. They could either contract in firepower or offer a partnership, a share of what they take from the Alliance for any of the other major players willing to throw in with them."

"They might also try to have the Alliance crumble from within," Mesi added. "There are lots of internal rivalries and there's nothing to say one of the affiliates wouldn't defect, if the enticement is great enough. Factions like the Dominicans, who operate almost exclusively as distributors, are prime candidates."

Marshall's phone started ringing again. He sighed heavily and picked up the receiver.

five

The men's progress to the ridge of the tall dune was slow, the heavy sand providing little traction. The taller man was struggling to keep up, his breathing laboured due to the hard pace. Larsen had insisted that they move away from the busy areas of the beach before beginning their discussion. Finally, after forty minutes marching without a word passing between the two, the trailing man was grateful to see his companion stop on the crest of the dune, apparently happy with the location. He wearily trudged up the last few steps.

Andrew Brewer bent over, placing his hands on his thighs, and stifled an oath. Scrambling around on windswept beaches like this was ludicrous. Normally a man who took pride in his appearance, as evidenced by his carefully coordinated wardrobe, coiffed silver hair and neatly trimmed goatee, he did not appreciate his linen shirt being soaked with sweat or his handmade loafers being filled with sand. While he waited for his breath to return, he studied his companion out of the corner of his eye. The lean, spare frame betrayed no sign of expended effort and the Dane, clad only in a T-shirt and jeans, seemed oblivious to the cold wind sweeping in from the surf.

Brewer was used to other people making the running in conversations and waited for Larsen to speak. And waited. It soon became obvious that nothing would be forthcoming, that he could stand there for ever while his companion gazed out over the waves.

"Is it always necessary to make these meetings so difficult?" he asked. "I've told you before I can't be expected to drop everything at short notice, to head off on another mystery tour. One of these days, you might find yourself out here alone." He tried to inject a laugh at the end, hoping to make it one of those half-serious, half-joking remarks, satisfying his own ego without forcing a direct confrontation.

Larsen turned to look at him and the cold stare made him happy he had not used more forceful language.

"I take the precautions I think are necessary. We both share the same paymaster and both know you'll be at every meeting, regardless of inconvenience."

That was it. Never any attempt at diplomacy or cordiality. Larsen just said what he thought, take it or leave it. The apparent lack of malice in the remark only added to the insult.

As CEO of Spartan Personnel, one of the ascendant companies in the lucrative field of military contracting, Brewer was used to being shown more deference. Before he had joined the private sector, he had been with the CIA, responsible for various operations throughout Central and South America. It was during that time that he had seen the growing opportunities for commercial entities who could provide military and law enforcement personnel to fill government contracts. Fortunes could be made if someone could provide the politicians with a way to pursue their interests on foreign soil while maintaining a safe distance from any controversy. It was far easier if a contract company was the one suffering casualties or becoming embroiled in local controversies. The economics of it actually made sense as well. Customised manpower could be applied, and once a job was finished the contract was simply terminated. There was no need to involve unwieldy and expensive command structures. A combination of the strong growth in the market and his personal contacts had ensured Brewer had no difficulty raising the start-up capital he had needed.

Spartan offered a comprehensive range of services. They participated in eradication missions, training and drug interdiction. They also provided air transport, reconnaissance, search and rescue and airborne medical evacuation missions. When filling contracts for the State Department, the aircrafts were provided by the Department but all of the pilots and technicians were provided by Spartan. In the last couple of years, they had branched into infantry and counter-insurgency training for approved foreign governments and he couldn't have been more pleased with the way this had gone. While their "trainers" had strict guidelines forbidding participation in live missions, everyone knew the score. There had been occasional casualties but generous settlements combined with strict non-disclosure terms in the contracts ensured these brought a minimum amount of publicity.

In the decade since its inception, Spartan had grown to more than 200 permanent employees scattered throughout fifteen countries, with three times that number on short-term contracts. Over the previous year, they had billed $45 million with a $110 million contract backlog, and analysts were bullish about their prospects.

Brewer enjoyed the influence and celebrity Spartan had brought him. People as powerful as four-star generals and US senators listened carefully to what he had to say. So it rankled when he was reminded that he still had clear limitations, that there were still those who were far higher up on the food chain. It was even more galling when the reminder came from a lowly gun-for-hire like Larsen. He hated having to deal with the Dane who always gave him the impression that he viewed Brewer as nothing more than an expedient tool.

"Does everything have to be so confrontational with you?" he asked. "We have to work together and it wouldn't hurt to show a little cooperation."

There was no response to the remark and he decided the sooner they dealt with their business the better. "It seems Prague was enough to finally spur Madrigal into action. There were four attacks on the Fifteen Families' assets last night. Two of them were significant enough to have been picked up by the international news services." He smiled. "It's going exactly to plan. These simpletons are going to tear each other apart."

"You don't have a high opinion of them?" Larsen asked.

"Of course not. They're a bunch of peasants who were lucky enough to find themselves sitting on a gold mine. Whether it's South America, the Golden Triangle or the Balkans, most of these guys are just common thugs elevated by massive firepower," Brewer said contemptuously. "They rely on intimidation and bribery to overwhelm inadequately funded police forces. Now, they're going to see what it's like in the big leagues."

"All we've accomplished is the initial phase of the project and, even so, we've been fortunate," Larsen said.

"Nonsense, we've had meticulous planning and the success of the operations is a testament to that."

Larsen just stared at him, and Brewer felt as if his opinion was being summarily dismissed.

"You have the information?" Larsen asked.

"Yes, it's first-class stuff. Here, I've added my own summary to it," said Brewer, handing him a data stick. "We used contacts in Mexico, as well as a couple of proven freelancers in California, hired through a blind cover. There's no doubt about it, Zaragosa runs their West Coast distribution. From San Diego to Seattle, if you're shooting or snorting, it's likely your money is heading back to Mexico via Francisco's pockets." Watching Larsen pocket the stick without any comment, he added, "You've got information there about his movements, the organisational structure beneath him and his two main residences. It's surprising how freely he's been able to operate without incurring any serious media or police scrutiny. My guess is that a lot of people's incomes are going to suffer when he's eliminated."

"Fine," Larsen said. "One more thing; I'll need another transfer of funds to the same five accounts. Two million, evenly spread."

This was another source of irritation for Brewer. The level of autonomy enjoyed by Larsen should never have been approved. He had argued that he should control all finances, releasing funds when operational plans submitted in advance met with his approval. After all, he compiled the shortlists of personnel from which the teams were selected and organised all of the intelligence on the targets. Larsen had objected, saying he would not accept the contract under those conditions, and that had been that. It was not the money itself that annoyed Brewer, although he was sure there was some skimming going on, it was the erosion of his role in favour of someone like the mercenary.

"It must be good to have unlimited access to funds. You know, you've gone through quite a sum already. My offer to help you with the planning still stands. Honestly, for what you've spent, I could have organised the same operations three or four times over."

"With the same degree of competence that you showed in that Nicaraguan hit before you left the Agency no doubt."

Brewer was stung by the remark. Larsen's casual attitude was one thing but this! It was infuriating that he would have had the audacity to do a background check on him and even more so to make such an arrogant judgement based on it. Who the hell did he think he was? For a moment he fought the urge to lash out physically. He soothed himself with the thought that there would be a reckoning down the line.

"Is that it?" he asked.

Larsen nodded, turning away without another word. Brewer stared at the back of his head for a few seconds, feeling his temper rising, before leaving for the long walk to the car park.

Larsen watched the waves rolling in. The coastline here was reminiscent of Hanstholm, where he undertook training exercises more than fifteen years earlier. Young eager recruits going through a variety of exercises, throwing themselves from helicopters into the water. The pure joy and exhilaration was as fresh in his memory as if it had been yesterday.

Despite the planning Brewer had crowed about, the odds had been strongly against them achieving the one hundred per cent success rate they had enjoyed to date. In contrast to Brewer, he had a healthy respect for the abilities of their targets' senior personnel, particularly Madrigal, whom he had studied in detail. His greatest fear was that the Colombian would somehow identify the provocateurs.

In many ways Brewer typified everything that had come to repulse him about the world he had descended into. The contract executive viewed himself as some kind of captain of industry, a mover and shaker; all Larsen could see was another pig, gorging himself at the trough while others paid in blood. The episodes that had made Brewer's reputation at the Agency represented many of the organisation's most shameful moments.

He pushed the thoughts from his mind and reminded himself to concentrate on the objective.

"Tim, ignore them – they're nothing: anonymous suits who've never had a creative thought in their life. You're the reason this project exists. You're the talent; remind them of that. They keep whining on about the shooting going over budget. Disappear again; they'll soon see sense."

Francisco Zaragosa was seated at an intricately carved nineteenth century Louis XV fruitwood table with breche d'alep marble top. He was speaking into a gold antique Stromberg Carlson phone, telling one of Hollywood's biggest stars to walk off the set of a $125-million movie. Looking out through the glass doors over the veranda, he watched the sprinklers burst into life and begin dousing the beautifully manicured lawns. Beyond the perfect sea of green, the rest of the impeccably landscaped gardens stretched majestically. It did not get any better than this.

"They're busting my balls, saying I can't just go to Acapulco for a week in the middle of shooting. They don't seem to appreciate the pressure I'm under. I don't know, I want to tell them to, you know, go fuck themselves but …" Tim Mitchell, star of countless action movies, known far and wide as a no-nonsense tough guy, wavered.

"Tim, there is no 'but'. Don't you see this is what they want. First you start second-guessing yourself and then, before you know it, you need their permission to breathe. Someone like you shouldn't have to put up with this. Stay in your trailer; refuse to see them."

"They're hovering outside like vultures."

"I'll ask Joanne to go over with a little something to help pass the afternoon," he reassured the fretful actor. "Let these guys stew. They'll soon see all their power trip has resulted in is the loss of another precious day's shooting. They'll get the message. Later."

Francisco put the phone down and thought about Mitchell. He was sure he liked the actor but was faintly aware of a small degree of contempt mixed in somewhere. He knew his advice had been good but was not about to lose sleep over it one way or the other. It was amusing to see what passed for a crisis in the actor's life. Spending so much time with people like Mitchell caused him to sometimes see them as his peers but nothing could be further from the truth. He wondered how his pampered acquaintances would fare if they were asked to fill his shoes, for even a week.

Looking at his watch to see how long it was before his next appointment, he decided to take a walk around the grounds. Whenever possible, he made a point of enjoying his beautiful gardens – a leisurely stroll around the tree-lined paths and he felt completely restored. Whether he was uptight about some business-related matter or just burnt out from an all night partying session, his worries and fatigue melted away.

When the opportunity to purchase the estate had arisen five years earlier he had decided he would use it to create something as close to a perfect environment as possible. He had overseen all aspects of the transformation, whether it was restoring the architecture, furnishing the interior or landscaping the gardens. Nothing had been done without his approval and more than once he had changed his mind about some small detail or other, requiring huge amounts of work to be scrapped. He appreciated the perfection of form wherever it could be found and had an encyclopaedic knowledge on all aspects of classic and contemporary art and design. He could talk at length about subjects as diverse as a painting by Caravaggio or a Le Corbusier chaise longue. He had been determined that concerns of time and expense would not compromise his labour of love. Because every facet of the project had to wait until he had time to address it, the transformation of the estate, formerly owned by an actress from Hollywood's golden age, had been painfully slow. The long wait had merely meant he would never take it for granted.

The estate, like everything else in his life, was a tribute to hard work and a testament to his unspoken conviction that he was different. His spectacular successes had vindicated his uncle's patronage. Even more remarkable than his material wealth was the social position he had attained. He had arrived from Mexico seven years earlier, a virtual nobody. Today his circle of friends included the most celebrated and powerful in California. The only restriction placed on him was the care he had to take not to be caught directly in the spotlight himself. Being the nephew of Esteban Zaragosa, a man who dominated the Mexican drug scene, had definitely been a blessing but it brought with it certain limitations. He had been determined, though, that his observation of these limitations would not mean spending all of his time skulking in an illicit world. Someone as special as he was should have a special life and, as he had proven to himself and others, when he felt he should have something, nothing prevented him obtaining it.

When he had been forced to come to the States, his uncle had left him with no illusions of how important it was that he make the most of this chance. Esteban had no children of his own and as a result doted on him. Growing up, Francisco had never had to recognise the boundaries of acceptable behaviour most people had to observe. When difficulties arose, they quickly disappeared once it was made known whose nephew he was. When his striking good looks had matured as a young man, they had only accentuated his proclivity for trouble. Other young people from privileged backgrounds gravitated towards his company and were willing to go to any lengths to win his favour. He revelled in the attention and did nothing to discourage them. It wasn't long before the spoiled group developed quite a reputation. They became fixtures around the exclusive haunts of Mexico City, a king and his court engaging in all night drinking sprees before finally collapsing into any available bed.

Something was bound to happen, and it finally did one night at a packed nightclub. An off-duty policeman partying with his friends had inadvertently pushed into Francisco, causing the young man to lash out angrily. The ensuing altercation had quickly degenerated into a melee between the two groups. One member of Francisco's group, most likely as a result of his exhortations, got carried away. A gun was produced and the policeman was shot dead. The entire incident had been captured on the nightclub's closed circuit TV and the story ran in all the dailies the next day. Editorials called for the guilty parties to face the same consequences as anyone else would have to. Esteban moved swiftly to protect his nephew. Within days no copies of the tape could be found, the youth who had fired the shot had committed suicide and key figures in the police force had been mollified with some generous "donations". The press was taught to keep their fervour under check in the future as well. Two of the most outspoken editors were gunned down before the charges had even been dismissed.

When everything had died down, Francisco was summoned by Esteban and for the first time in his life subjected to his uncle's anger. He sat through the long tirade during which the man, who had never so much as raised his voice to him before, poured out his frustration at his nephew's behaviour. It ended with Esteban telling him it was time for them to map out his future. Despite the fact that the shooting seemed to have been resolved satisfactorily, he had decided that it would be better for everyone if Francisco started over somewhere new. Esteban told him that he was going to take an enormous gamble. He had impressed on his nephew how a failure to validate his faith would have consequences for both of them.

It had been arranged for him to go to California and to work under Enrique Montoya. Montoya was an old man and one of Esteban's most loyal allies in the cartel. Francisco stayed in the background, assisting the old man in long-term planning, mostly learning but also offering the benefit of his fresh perspective. He was never involved in the day-to-day running of the business and only interacted with a very limited number of key personnel. It did not take long, however, for him to make his mark. Voraciously reading books on a wide range of topics from marketing to terrorist tactics, he realised he had a skill for gleaning what was relevant and applying it to the cartel's situation. As a result of his suggestions, the sales of drugs to teens rocketed. Schools, rock concerts, nightclubs and even youth clubs were all targeted with specific promotional drives. Attractive, exciting brand names were introduced, helping to build product loyalty. Every six or nine months, they phased out products that were struggling and replaced them with new ones. Using a cell structure, they recruited their sales force exclusively from the ranks of the young and attractive, a resource California had no shortage of. These recruits, encouraged by generous bonus incentives, built up their own teams in turn. This pattern repeated endlessly and resulted in the market size growing and their share increasing exponentially. Occasional setbacks were easily handled as the recruitment mechanism ensured that key personnel were so far removed from the retail transactions that they were unknown to the authorities.

Francisco also formulated strategies that allowed them to systematically out-flank the competition. Starting with their weakest competitors and working upwards, they concentrated on geographic areas of strategic importance to their rivals and began flooding them with large amounts of highly subsidised drugs. They would pursue this to the point where only one outcome was possible. Lacking the revenue to continue, the competition was forced to abandon the marketplace. Twice, when the process was taking longer than projected, he had advised sudden shows of force so savage in nature that they had immediately resolved the matter. These displays had required not only the murder of specific individuals in the rival organisations but also the elimination of their entire families. He had hated being forced to act so brutally and had derived no pleasure from the slaughter. Indeed, he had agonised long and hard before he had advised the second action. Subsequently he had tried to ensure that others could recognise without his help when such a response was required.

In parallel with his advancement of the cartel's business, he had set about his social advancement. Initially a stranger in town, it had not been long before his natural charisma, not to mention his wealth and unlimited access to high-quality drugs, began to attract a new retinue. The constantly growing circle of friends included people from many walks of life, although close inspection revealed a few common traits. First was their desire for his company; second, they were invariably either wealthy, attractive or both. No one with a tendency for violence or a history of serious brushes with the law found a way in. He had learned well from his experience in Mexico. The cartel's business satisfied any thirst for adventure that he might have and this other life remained totally untouched by strife. In time the most exclusive sections of society opened up to him. Whether they were politicians, celebrities or even select members of the judiciary, he had complete access. Between his plausible cover of property speculator, considered contributions to political campaigns and shunning of direct publicity, he avoided any unwelcome scrutiny.

As difficult and demanding as this double life was, he knew he needed both aspects for total fulfilment. When his uncle had recently suggested that he withdraw more from the cartel's dealings, he had rejected the idea. Nothing matched the thrill of outmanoeuvring rivals and operating beyond the sphere of the law. Perhaps in a few years his appetite for such dark excitement would be sated, but not yet.

He stopped on his walk and took a moment to look around. It would be difficult to feel further away from the daily stresses. Unable to even see the house from this part of the path, it was as if he had been transported to another place and time. In order to preserve this atmosphere, he had left strict instructions that no one, not security, not friends, no one but the trained staff who tended the garden, were allowed to enter these areas. And so his surprise was all the greater when a figure emerged from the bushes and moved swiftly towards him. Surprise briefly gave way to outrage and by the time fear surfaced, the black-clad interloper had closed the distance. The intruder struck him viciously, driving a fist up into his solar plexus, followed swiftly with a knee to his groin. As Francisco fell, the attacker wrapped one of his arms tightly around his victim's neck and prevented his pain-wracked body from crumpling to the ground. Francisco fought to retain consciousness but the pressure of the hold combined with his own dead weight was too much and darkness overtook him.

Larsen bound Zaragosa's hands and feet during the brief time he was unconscious. When the drug lord came to he immediately recognised his plight. He attempted to cry out but the thick handkerchief that had been stuffed in his mouth muted his attempts. As the cry evaporated, Larsen saw something leave his captive's frame.

Francisco began to murmur, the tone plain even if the words were not, all of his customary poise and style deserting him. His captor did not acknowledge the sounds and turned to his backpack, taking out a small leather pouch. He tried to calm himself, thinking this must be a mistake, which was bound to be resolved. Looking down he realised he had lost control of his bladder and the indignity added to the feeling of unfairness, causing his last shred of reserve to crumble. His assailant, distracted by the uncontrollable sobbing, stopped what he was doing for a moment and looked him in the eye. Somewhere in the dark gaze, Francisco was certain he detected a trace of hesitancy.

Even with Larsen's knowledge of Zaragosa's history, the look of terror in his eyes combined with the knowledge of what lay in store for his captive were enough to stir feelings of pity. He told himself that the Mexican deserved no sympathy, that he had never shown it to the legions whose lives he had ruined. In fact Zaragosa had displayed a heightened ability to divorce himself from the pain of his actions. The incidence of teenage drug-dependency on the West Coast had risen over two hundred per cent since his arrival in California. Larsen had decided something special was required at this juncture but, now that he was here, doubts rushed to the surface. The pharmacists had explained it in detail and their words had sent a chill through him. The main ingredient induced a form of paranoia in the subject, causing him to enter an extreme state of withdrawal, losing any ability to trust what his body told him was happening. The second constituent impaired most of the main motor skills, meaning even the simplest physical functions were beyond the victim. The combination effectively created a prisoner in his own body, which was in turn imprisoned in a harsh, hostile world. The two experts had disagreed about its permanence but even the one who had argued its toxicological effects were reversible agreed it could take years. By that stage, the subject would be so traumatised by the experience, it would be academic anyway.

The intruder took out a small jar and drew its contents up into a syringe, quickly flicking the hypodermic a few times to eliminate any air bubbles. Francisco began to plead even more frantically for the ordeal to stop. Strong hands gripped his shirtsleeve and ripped it open. The tightness of the bonds had made his veins protrude and the needle went in immediately. He watched the hypodermic being pressed and felt his reason desert him.

Larsen removed the needle, gathered his things and left quickly without another glance at the convulsing form.

Caesar Rodriguez waited for his guest in the massive drawing room. He believed the size of the room helped to increase the discomfort of his visitors. Not as much as the reputation he cultivated for bouts of explosive rage but it was important to exploit every advantage. Tales of his legendary temper were well founded, but over the years exaggeration had crept in and he had been quick to see the benefits. Even the best-prepared arguments from seasoned debaters could melt when faced with an enraged Rodriguez. Occasionally the outrage was genuine but most of the time he was simply performing.

Today's meeting, however, would be different. Unlike almost everyone else he dealt with, Esteban Zaragosa was immune to intimidation and held enough power to influence Rodriguez's future. Indeed, it was Zaragosa who was currently in need of careful handling. Rodriguez knew about the recent episode in California and was in no doubt as to what the subject for discussion would be. He knew the next few minutes could take him a significant step closer to his dream. He reminded himself not to become overexcited; caution was the watchword. Esteban was a veteran, possessing instincts honed over many years.

One of the men escorted the bull-like Zaragosa into the room and Rodriguez nodded for them to be left alone. The toll recent events had taken on the older man was clearly visible, even before he had completely closed the distance between them. Zaragosa, known for his strong constitution and active lifestyle, looked tired and worn. He guessed Zaragosa's demise was imminent, regardless of anything agreed today. He embraced his guest then stepped back and looked at him sorrowfully.

"Esteban, I don't have the words to express my grief, what kind of evil is this?"

This close, he caught the whiff of alcohol. Things were definitely unravelling, he thought. He motioned for Zaragosa to sit but the older man shook his head, so they both remained standing.

"You warned him!" Zaragosa said.

"Francisco?" he asked, knowing full well who Zaragosa had meant.

"No, that gutless bitch Madrigal. He waited so long to move against our enemies, and then acted so ineffectually. He encouraged them to believe they could get away with anything." The emotion carried in the words showed a fury barely held in check.

"Please, have a drink; it'll settle you. It's not good to be so agitated." Rodriguez moved to the drinks cabinet, poured a generous glass and handed it to Zaragosa, who had sunk into a chair.

"How is Francisco? I have only heard a little." Rodriguez

knew the details of Francisco's condition intimately but the screw had to be turned.

"My fine, beautiful boy is no longer. He was a prince among men, a king, loved and adored by everyone. Now ..." Zaragosa's eyes welled up, "we don't even know if he recognises us. Nothing intelligible comes from him. He has seizures constantly and has no control over his body. He shrinks from our every word or gesture."

"Terrible! What have the doctors said?" he asked, dragging it out.

"Those fools, they're useless. They can't even say what's wrong with him. Maybe he'll recover within a month, maybe a year, perhaps more. I suspect they fear the worst but are too weak to say it to my face." He shook his head. "It doesn't matter what they think anyway, they don't know Francisco's fortitude. He'll recover."

Based on the reports he had heard Rodriguez doubted this.

"I know it's a secondary consideration but there must be some retribution. Do we know anything about the attackers? Francisco's men must have seen something?"

Zaragosa drained his glass and held it out to be refilled. "They saw nothing. I've spoken directly to them more than once. I told them, regardless of how difficult Francisco made it, their first duty was to protect him at all times. I stressed this when the troubles began. Instead of doing their work, they grew soft, indulging themselves and taking advantage of Francisco's good nature. They've been dealt with."

Zaragosa fixed him with a firm stare, providing a timely reminder not to let his guard slip and consign the old man to the scrap heap prematurely. He had heard of the brutal execution of Francisco's bodyguards.

"We must do something. The moment I heard of Francisco's plight my heart cried out for justice. I've thought of little else but it's difficult to know which course to take."

There it was, the perfect invitation for Zaragosa to speak his mind.

"You are absolutely correct. Something must be done and it's something that has been crying out to be done for months. Not just because of poor Francisco but to redress the many unpunished transgressions that have been committed against us. Madrigal has to be removed. He let this situation develop." He put his hand up to stop Rodriguez's protests. "Believe me it's necessary. I've already garnered significant support and if you'll join us, the outcome is assured."

"Oust Madrigal, are you sure this is the way? It's well known we've had our differences but –"

Zaragosa reached forward, grasping his hands. "We don't need him. He elevates the Colombians, belittling our contribution. With him out of the way, a fairer balance could be struck. What are the Colombians when you get right down to it? A bunch of savages controlling some crops. It's our distribution and trafficking that have been the real success."

Rodriguez tried to look as if he was having difficulty digesting what he was hearing, as if he did not know where to begin. "Esteban, I see some truth in what you say but the fact remains that the Colombians do control production, and without product everything else is irrelevant."

"Don't worry about control of production," Zaragosa replied, becoming animated, his lethargy fading away. "I've talked to factions in Bolivia and Peru, they're ready to resume their former levels of production and they see us as a way of ensuring the Colombians don't interfere. We would hold the power in that relationship."

He had already known of Zaragosa's approaches to these but he needed to be sure there was nothing else. "Esteban, your years of experience speak for themselves but are we risking a two-fronted battle?" Rodriguez asked, trying to elicit greater detail. "In addition to the Kosovars, we'll also have those loyal to Madrigal targeting us. Even if we could remove Madrigal, won't another Colombian emerge to fill the void? The successor won't trust us. He'll probably try to cut us out entirely."

"No, that won't happen. There's no Colombian strong enough to step in. For all of his weaknesses, when it comes to organisational ability and personal leadership, Madrigal is far superior to any of his compatriots," Zaragosa reassured him. "With him out of the way, a group of evenly matched rivals with bitter histories will seek to gain control. We only need to position ourselves to back a few key players I've already enlisted. The men I've picked have limited ambition, they'll be only too happy to work with us."

This only convinced Rodriguez more that he had decided on the correct course. Was Zaragosa's mind so addled with age and grief that he thought Madrigal captained such a loose ship? No doubt these "key players" had run scurrying back to him at the first opportunity.

"Madrigal's security is exceptional. Are you sure we could succeed?"

"Never underestimate a man's greed or overestimate his loyalty. I know Madrigal's planned movements and he'll provide us with our opportunity in the next couple of weeks. Final preparations for the hit are being made now."

This was the first piece of news that surprised Rodriguez.

Not the absurd notion that Zaragosa had co-opted people close to Madrigal but that he had moved so quickly. It showed the deficiencies in Rodriguez's sources.

"How can I help? You seem to have thought of everything, what's left for me?"

"I'd never have approached you this directly if I had not known you shared my feelings about him. I've no need for direct action from you. I want only two things. The first is your endorsement."

"You have it. I can't think of a better future than you assuming control. What else?"

"I'm not a young man and I have no successor, not anymore. I'll need your strong support and for you, over time, to take the reins."

"I can't say how proud this makes me. Of course I'll agree to help in any way I can, but if this meeting has proven anything, it's that you're far from retirement."

Zaragosa shook his head. "No Caesar, today's business represents my final effort. Francisco's plight has left me with little appetite to continue. I'm only undertaking this because there must be consequences for my nephew's condition. I feel as if everything I've striven for was worthless and each day takes its toll."

With that, he got to his feet, drained his drink and started towards the door. On the way, Rodriguez gripped his elbow lightly and gently guided him out.

Left alone, he wondered if he should feel guilty about what he was going to do. Zaragosa seemed sincere in his desire to have him as a successor. The simple fact of the matter, though, was that he could not afford for Zaragosa's gambit to upset his own plans. Better for the moment to remain loyal to Madrigal. He had no doubt that the

Colombian knew of today's meeting. If he did not contact Madrigal, it would be interpreted as a hostile move.

There might be a silver lining to this development. He would warn Madrigal of what the Colombian already knew and in the process he might gain some kudos. In any case, even if Madrigal recognised the self-interest of the warning, there was no one else he could choose to take over Zaragosa's operations in Mexico and California. Only Rodriguez had the personnel and resources to keep the money rolling in. The larger strategy was still on course but, if it went awry, at least he had positioned himself optimally. No matter what happened, his time was coming.

Despite the coldness of the room, Larsen, clothed only in a thin T-shirt and loose cotton trousers, moved easily. Back and forward across the large workout mat, he performed sequence after sequence of strikes and holds. He knew the benefits physical exertion could bring to a troubled mind and he searched for these now. Earlier, he had worked through a long set of floor exercises for the better part of two hours. Sweat poured to the floor as he pushed himself harder and harder. Still the uncertainties lingered.

There had been a time when doubt would not have existed. Not that he had always been convinced of the righteousness of his actions; hardly. Issues of right and wrong had just never entered the equation. He could not identify the exact moment when that had changed, or the cause for that matter. It could not be ascribed to a religious conversion; he had started life as an atheist and nothing the world offered had shaken these convictions. He was not in the least sentimental, conventions and traditions that were of great importance to others had made little impression on him.

Ready to commence, he gestured to the instructor who exploded from his corner of the hall, hurling himself at the client who had paid handsomely for this session. Closing the distance rapidly, the larger attacker launched a series of low kicks and foot swipes which forced him to the edge of the mat. With nowhere left to retreat, Larsen was forced to step inside in an attempt to smother the attacks. The instructor kneed him to the top of his right leg, deadening the limb, and sought to follow it up with an elbow to the temple. Managing to duck under this second strike just in time, Larsen grabbed the instructor around the neck and tried to trip him to the floor, the intention being to use their combined bodyweight to wind his opponent. He found himself turned effortlessly and thrown back across the mat. Having gauged his strength and found it wanting, the instructor launched another, stronger attack.

All through military service, the mission had been sacrosanct. You did not question orders, you obeyed them. You belonged to something and you gave back to this thing that succoured you. Excelling in your duty made you ... what? Useful? Worthwhile? He had known the answer once. Later, selling his skills to the highest bidder, there was less sureness but still there was the mission. He no longer gave allegiance to unit, army or country and was despised by those comrades who were once closest, but the mission endured. Finally, interest from different quarters, proposals of a different kind. Assassinations, kidnappings, blackmail; it didn't matter, as long as there was an objective to achieve. The descent continued – questionable causes, glimpses of curious allegiances and, always, innocent suffering. Then, finally, the doubts began to undermine the tenets of a lifetime. Things he thought to be immutable were thrown into question.

This time the instructor feinted with a kick to his knee. When Larsen took the feint and moved to the left, his opponent was ready. His T-shirt was gripped and he was pulled on to a powerful right elbow which struck his cheekbone. He felt himself sag and, as his head swam, he realised a chokehold was being attempted, which would settle the encounter. Letting himself go, he relaxed totally and the sudden looseness of his frame allowed him to slip from the instructor's grasp. He staggered backward.

It had gotten so bad that he had abandoned a crucial assignment before completion, not caring to consider the consequences. Word of his actions filtered out and his reputation suffered. He had gained nothing from his action, in fact he had been lucky to escape with his life. At that point, he had decided to take himself off the board, at least temporarily, before someone else took the decision.

He had to go on the offensive despite his rapidly dwindling resources and his opponent's indefatigable zeal for combat. He stepped in and threw a knee intended only to distract. When the instructor stepped back a half step to avoid the blow he attempted an eye-gouge. His strike was easily evaded and his wrist caught in a powerful grip. He felt his bodyweight being turned back around the outstretched hand and pressure applied to the back of his shoulder forcing him to the ground.

During his sabbatical he pondered his actions. Was it attrition? Had he burnt out, lost his edge or had he been infected by some other malaise? Notions of morality? He wasn't sure he wanted to know the answers. Then he had been offered this assignment. He researched those behind it meticulously. All of the normal criteria were there: commitment, ability to pay, exploitable weaknesses to dissuade treachery. But there was something more to this. An opportunity. The more he looked at the proposal and its goals, the more he realised how much he needed it.

Just before his face struck the mat, he managed to tuck his head and roll forward. Grabbing hold of the instructor's tunic with his free hand, he used the momentum to pull the opponent down. He scrambled to apply a chokehold before a defence could be mounted. Whatever he tried was countered, and as hold after hold was defeated, it took a much greater toll on him than the larger man. He could not break free from the grip on his right wrist and constant movement was necessary to prevent it surrendering a conclusive advantage. Eventually a chop aimed at the instructor's chest was deflected to strike under the arm and broke the grip. As he rolled backward to his feet, battling for his breath now, the opponent bounced up and, with a confident grin, came on once more.

A series of operations. Their brutality calculated by him, seen as vital to achieve the goal, not at all wanton. Each step of the way, *he* had decided what was necessary to progress the conflict and had seen to it personally. But as events had progressed, his actions began to sit less easily. The latest of these had been the attack on the young Mexican, Zaragosa. There could be no doubt of the suffering Zaragosa had caused and that he deserved little sympathy. The drug lord should have been aware that there might be consequences for his choice of life. Why then, did he keep coming back to those final moments before the injection? Did Zaragosa warrant this degree of soul-searching? In Larsen's mind, the

Mexican's worst offence had been his ability to disassociate himself from his actions. If Larsen couldn't examine his own actions, he would be guilty of the same transgression. The fact that this scrutiny brought so many doubts was immaterial.

He was tiring quickly now, blows rained down. Kicks and knees to his legs, elbows and palm strikes to his body. The room was beginning to swim. The instructor grabbed his T-shirt, ignoring his feeble attempts at counters and lashed out with a head-butt. Just in time, he pulled his head back and avoided the brunt of the blow. Despite this, his cheekbone, which had been struck earlier, cried out from the impact. He tried to break free but his remaining strength was ineffectual. Knees from his opponent bombarded him, striking his upper legs as he twisted to block against a decisive groin strike. There was no way he could escape from the grip, he had no option but to surrender to it. Let it happen; some pain and then it would be over. Larsen stopped struggling, as he knew he must.

He knew that the doubts would only grow but he had committed to this assignment, he needed to see it through to the end. Its successful completion would be a final testament to his … career? Life? One of these. It was not about redemption – he had slid too far for that – but there would be some measure of redress. This would make a difference. He knew he had to force a culmination quickly. His growing uncertainty could not be allowed to ruin everything. If he was to have any hope of achieving the peace he had recently glimpsed, he needed to see this through. This time, his last, he would determine how it played out. This time, he would determine what his work accomplished.

———

Sensing the change, the instructor released his grip to make room for the finish. Pushing back with one palm against the exhausted mass, he threw his whole body into an elbow aimed to strike upwards under his defeated foe's chin. There was no question of hesitation, this was a place for the elite only. Full-blooded combat had been requested and paid for, all necessary waivers signed. Standards had to be maintained; the reputation of the gym among its exacting clientele was the issue. His blow never made impact, sailing past the intended point with no resistance. The instructor felt a blow to his face and his vision clouded with blood. Strikes, too quick to count, assailed his ribs and his defences deserted him. He felt his feet leave the floor, swept from beneath him. Falling heavily, he landed on his back with bone-shaking impact. The momentum whipped his head into the mat. His sternum groaned under a tremendous blow and consciousness danced in and out of reach. The pressure around his neck mounted and there was nothing he could do to stop it. Darkness engulfed him, and then receded.

The client smiled and reached down to pull the instructor to his feet.

The opening graphics disappeared and a distinguished face filled the screen. Leonard Boswell had been the presenter of Behind the Headlines, *IBNC's flagship current affairs magazine, for the past ten years.*

"Good evening, everyone. Let's get straight to it," *he began in an introduction that played to his no-fuss reputation. "First up tonight we're going to be looking*

at Plan Coca, and we'll start by going over directly to Colombia to speak with Caroline Williams about the deaths earlier today of five US civilians."

The picture split to show a tired looking Williams, reporting from a small village in Putumayo, on the right side of the screen.

"Caroline, earlier reports were that the US contractors died during a scheduled fumigation mission, has this been confirmed?" asked Boswell.

"Yes Leonard. Our latest information confirms the initial report and gives us a more detailed account of what occurred. So far, though, no comment from the US embassy in Bogotá or the State Department."

The first reports had come in thirteen hours earlier and competition to be first to give the full story had been fierce between the news stations. Williams had been growing more desperate when it appeared a number of her rivals had pulled off surprising coups by convincing individual contractors to go on the record. She had been ready to admit defeat when help arrived from an unlikely source. A contractor she had met only a couple of times and had always found to be particularly uncommunicative had approached her, saying he wanted to talk. With the clock ticking she didn't have time to dwell too much on his change of attitude. She had only finished talking to him thirty minutes before this live link-up to Atlanta. With no time to verify what he had told her, she had decided to gamble, and use it as the basis for her report, rather than allow her competitors to steal the march on her. Taking a deep breath, she started to read from her hand-written notes.

"We've learnt that three aircraft were brought down during the exercise. There were four in total taking part in the mission, three HUEY II helicopters and a fixed-wing fumigation craft. Two of the helicopters were heavily armed escort aircrafts whose function is to act as a deterrent to any anti-aircraft artillery. One of these was hit by a shell and the pilot quickly lost the battle to stay airborne, crashing down into the forest. The third helicopter, which had search-and-rescue responsibilities, flew over the crash site to determine if there were any survivors. Subsequently this aircraft was also hit. The attack appears to have been carefully planned with the onslaught coming simultaneously from multiple locations. There were literally only seconds between each aircraft being downed."

She stopped for a moment, having to search her notes briefly before finding what she wanted. "The next bit is sketchy but it seems the remaining escort helicopter then split from the fumigation aircraft which, now totally unguarded, abandoned the mission and returned immediately to base. Additional support aircraft had been scrambled once the first reports came in, but by the time they reached the area the wreckage from the three helicopters was plainly visible. A check confirmed that there were no survivors."

A group of children had congregated in the background, shouting and jostling for the camera's attention, and Caroline tried to move away a little while continuing her report.

"I'm sure a lot of people will be surprised at the involvement of US civilians in this kind of operation on foreign soil. How did they come to be there?" enquired Boswell.

Williams had known about the heavy presence of foreign contractors from the little research she had done even before arriving in Colombia. They had been there for *years in steadily increasing numbers. In fact the foreign journalists and contractors often socialised together when off-duty. There was an unwritten agreement that their presence here would never constitute a significant part of any of the news reports. She had once raised this curious omission with one of the main news editors. All he had said was that some feathers should not be ruffled and to leave things as they were. Well, all that was about to change. The death of their colleagues and the downing of the helicopters had struck a chord with many of the contractors and convinced them to talk to the media. They could not be ignored and consequently the disastrous mission was set to become a major news story.*

"Well, although the State Department has yet to comment officially, some people have been at pains to point out that the involvement of US civilians here significantly pre-dates the Plan. These civilians typically work for large companies and are ostensibly here only to provide training."

"But surely training wouldn't extend to participation in actual missions?" the host of the current affairs programme probed sceptically.

"It's a grey area. There've been repeated categorical statements that the US military will not be directly involved in any engagements down here. Special Forces instructors work closely with the counter-narcotics battalions of the Colombian army but they maintain that this is in an advisory capacity only."

"But we're talking about civilians here," interjected Boswell, "civilians who certainly can't be classified as advisors."

"Exactly," agreed Williams, feeling rushed by the host's habit of interrupting her planned presentation of the

situation. "In the case of civilian contractors, the policy isn't as clear-cut. Guidelines are implied rather than spelt out and may vary from company to company. In relation to Plan Coca, the intention has always been to reduce the high incidence of contractors but that's not an easy thing to do."

"Because?"

"Well for the simple reason that the Colombians rely on their expertise. According to the contractors themselves, it's been a common occurrence for years for them to be present on missions."

"Earlier there had been some speculation over whether the number of five US citizens was accurate; has this been confirmed?"

"Not officially, DefenCorp AeroSpace, for whom it's believed the dead contractors worked, refuse to talk to any reporters but as far as we know the figure is accurate."

"Okay, Caroline, no doubt we'll be hearing a lot more from you in the coming days but for the moment, thank you."

six

The database query Diane Mesi had kicked off was likely to take at least half an hour. It was only when she started looking for something to do while she was waiting that she realised how hungry she was. She had arrived at the office before seven after skipping breakfast, over six hours earlier. She walked down the hall to the vending machine and on the way back picked up a newspaper that had been lying on a desk. Campas had said that he would drop by around two o'clock, after his meeting.

She scanned the paper while she ate. Her eyes were immediately drawn to an article on the front page, a report from a news conference in Detroit chaired by the police commissioner. He had been commenting on a fire-fight which had occurred the day before in one of the city's most notorious areas. A cab company had come under attack by a group of gunmen. The company was subsequently discovered to have been used as a distribution point for a notorious drug gang. Four Jamaicans were found dead on the premises while two other men, believed to be Russians, were in hospital receiving treatment for their wounds. The commissioner had conceded that the attack marked the latest in a spate of similar incidents in Detroit in recent weeks. He defended the police department's record, saying that the attacks were virtually impossible to predict and, by extension, prevent. The article ended with speculation as to whether the department was as committed as it might be, given how many of its members were privately expressing satisfaction at seeing these elements wipe out one another. Mesi knew it was a popular sentiment.

She opened the paper to read the editorial comment referenced at the end of the article. The commentary dealt more with the ongoing political battle raging on Capitol Hill than the specific Detroit incident. It bemoaned the opportunistic sniping that was being directed at the administration and argued that too much was being made of the escalating violence in the inner cities. An analogy was drawn with a painful purge which would benefit the patient in the long term. The writer pointed out that as Plan Coca squeezed the drug supply, people who traded illicitly would become more and more agitated in their struggle to control the remaining scraps. If the public could just harden themselves and see this difficult period through, it would all come right eventually. He went on to condemn the theorists who tried to promote the idea that something other than Plan Coca was in motion. If there was an international battle for supremacy between the drug powers, he argued, it was a by-product of Plan Coca's successes and was nothing to be overly concerned about.

She envied the author his certitude.

"Diane?"

Mesi turned around, greeted Campas delightedly and then brought a chair over for him from the empty desk next to her.

"How are you doing?" he asked.

"Fine. So how does it feel being on a diplomatic junket? Big time now, huh?"

"Yes, this is what I've always wanted, to be a security blanket for a minister who's afraid of embarrassing himself," he replied. "I tried to insist I could brief him adequately before he left but no, I had to drop everything and accompany him on his visit here. An entire three days between the State Department and the DEA."

"Don't knock it; at least you're valued!"

Mesi knew she must appear very subdued to Campas, different from the enthusiastic person he had worked with in Mexico. They made small talk briefly, exchanging pleasantries, before the discussion turned to work and issues related to the cartel war.

"I received a report this morning regarding Francisco Zaragosa. You remember we talked a couple of weeks ago?" he asked.

"Yes, any word on when he plans to return to California?"

"Try never. At first, we thought he might have fucked up and was being called back for some kind of reprimand. We couldn't have been more wrong. From what we've learnt, playboy Francisco is now a vegetable. Result of some kind of poisoning and the prognosis is that it's permanent."

"Christ, there's going to be major repercussions, isn't there?"

He nodded.

"Up to now, Esteban Zaragosa could usually be counted on as a voice of reason. His attitude was: as long as Madrigal made money, he was content to be number two. He provided a stabilising influence on Caesar Rodriguez."

"And that's all changed now?"

"I think so. Word is he blames Madrigal for what happened to his nephew. I think he'll make a move."

"And Rodriguez will back him?"

"I can't see why not, he's been yearning for this. He's never been strong enough to challenge Madrigal himself but with Zaragosa on side, there's no reason to hesitate. I think Madrigal, for the first time in a long time, is in real danger. It seems like the Kosovars have succeeded in creating the dissension you talked about."

"It's a continuation of the pattern, more in-fighting, more instability. It makes you wonder who gains," Mesi remarked.

"What do you mean? Rodriguez and Zaragosa obviously, if they succeed."

"Do they? Can they sustain what Madrigal has built? Maybe briefly but in the long run, I think they'll suffer financially. Who really wins?"

"The Kosovars? A fractured alliance with new leadership will be easier to supplant?"

"I know that's been the assumption, but if I look at the individual attacks … I don't know, they just seem *wrong* somehow."

"Well there have certainly been some puzzling inconsistencies," he agreed.

"Exactly. Take Conchillo, a perfectly executed operation followed by sloppy covering of their tracks, almost as if they went out of their way to ensure they were found."

"Maybe they didn't care. We know now it wasn't the first attack, maybe they figured Madrigal and Zaragosa already knew who was responsible?" he suggested. Mesi knew Campas did not really believe his answer but wanted to see where she was going with this by playing devil's advocate.

"Go back two years," she said. "Everyone's doing well. Why would the Kosovars or anyone else instigate a war? Even if they could seize a greater share of the global heroin market, the risks were astronomical. I know one of the suggestions was they'd saturated their current markets and needed to expand because of their commitments to various militias but …"

"I thought we agreed that Plan Coca could have convinced them to act. Seeing the Alliance engaged on one front already?" he offered. Again, she could see him resisting the urge to leap ahead, wanting her to step through her thought process.

"Did you have great hopes for Plan Coca when it was launched?" she asked.

He shook his head.

"Neither did I and we were in the majority. I'm convinced, despite what's coming from certain quarters, that we were right. I think the Kosovars would have held exactly the same opinion as we did."

"Okay, let's say they did; where does that leave us?"

"Well, if neither party stood to gain, maybe," she hesitated, then, after a deep breath, continued, "maybe someone else instigated the war. Maybe someone else benefits if the two tear each other apart."

"Someone else?"

"If it's true, there are two candidates – another crime syndicate or a government-backed agency." Mesi shook her head. "This sounds crazy, doesn't it?"

"Maybe not. No harm in talking it through! It's just the two of us throwing ideas around."

"Maybe you should tell Samuels that!" The weariness in her tone was evident.

"You're saying he wouldn't be willing to look into it?"

"Not if it came from me. I doubt he'd even give me enough time to present an argument."

"Why? Now that we're on the subject, I was surprised to see you weren't asked to attend any of the meetings over the last few days."

"I'm barely on the periphery of the investigation. I only get to attend internal strategy meetings."

"You're still on the investigation, though; he hasn't re-assigned you?"

"More because of historical involvement rather than any contribution he thinks I can make. It would be a bit obvious to remove me but I'm convinced Samuels is assigning me to tasks he believes are irrelevant to the main threads of the investigation." She held up an air ticket. "Case in point, he gets me out of his hair for three days while I head to France. I have to interview someone trying to bargain their way out of an assault charge by claiming he has information regarding the Kosovars' past operations."

"But that's crazy. Why is he doing this?"

If it had been anyone else she would not have been so frank but with Campas she felt secure enough to answer honestly. "Well, I've had some disagreements with the way he's tackling this operation, which hasn't helped our relationship."

"What kind of disagreements?"

"I've pointed out that all he's effectively done is use our manpower to supplement regional and border law enforcement. They're trying to predict where trouble is likely and take whatever action they can to avert it. We're not really doing anything to address the underlying cause."

"That's it? A difference of opinion and he's sidelining you?"

"There's more. Do you remember when I first visited you in Mexico? The plans I had as head of the new department, TAIT?"

He nodded.

"From what I'd been led to believe, we were going to have a significant role to play in DEA operations. I couldn't believe my luck in securing the post, especially considering the other candidates but …"

"When we last talked you said there had been some delay in finalising the funding?" Campas pressed.

"I don't believe TAIT was ever meant to be anything more than an expedient way of convincing external critics that the DEA was taking them seriously."

"What do you mean?"

"'The criticism was we're not proactive enough. So, the DEA's response was 'Look, here's a newly formed strategic analysis team to prove we're listening.' But being realistic, if they were truly committed, would they have appointed someone so unproven?"

"And that's why you think Samuels doesn't take you seriously?"

"Exactly. Even if he did rate me, which is debatable, he can't be seen to let a token appointee take a prominent role in the investigation."

Mesi knew he could see how demoralised she was but he respected her too much to try to offer meaningless consolations. She was certain there was a basis for her suspicions around her appointment.

"I don't know whether there's anything to your theory about third-party involvement, I'll do my best to look into it and see if I can convince Samuels that it's worth some time." He looked at his watch. "I'd better get back to Mayorga or he'll start sending out search parties. I'll call you when I get back."

She forced a smile and wished him a good flight home.

———

The cold sea wind whipped across the low fields adding to an inhospitable environment. There were signs across the landscape of the late spring bloom but these were muted by a sky full of ominous grey clouds. While the ancient stone walls bordering the patchwork of fields could be picturesque during the summer, at that moment, they only added to the oppressiveness. Two of the men in the open field had their hands dug deep into the pockets of their overcoats and stomped around in circles trying to combat the cold. The third man leaned against a wall, smoking a cigarette, lost in his thoughts and apparently inured to the weather. They had just returned from his daily exercise – a brisk ten-kilometre walk – and he was reluctant to go indoors just yet. He had been there for ten days and was beginning to feel claustrophobic. Not that he would complain too strongly, given the alternatives. Girard had told him there would be another visitor this afternoon. He wished he didn't have to go over it all again; each time was a stark reminder of what he had committed himself to.

One of the other men approached, interrupting his reverie.

"Come on Tuur, we're freezing our balls off here while we could just as easily be inside where it's warm."

He pushed himself off the wall and led them down the gentle incline to the stone cottage. Once inside the back door he removed his coat and pulled out a chair to sit at the kitchen table. His companions rushed through to the living room, where a warm fire was waiting.

A slightly overweight, middle-aged man, who had been standing by the sink washing some dishes, turned around to talk to him. "Well, Richard, our latest guest should be here any minute. I'd say after this we'll be almost done."

Richard Tuur didn't make much of an effort to disguise his irritation in the gaze he directed at Girard. "Honestly, Julian, it's that simple?"

"I don't see why not. You've met your side of the bargain so far. Keep it up and we'll reciprocate."

Julian Girard reached for an open bottle of wine, poured two glasses and gave one to Tuur. "I don't know why you insist on being so downbeat. A fortnight in a farmhouse in Brittany, enjoying the countryside, and then a helping hand to build your new life. It seems like a good deal to me."

Sometimes he appreciated the fact that Girard had such an easygoing nature; the confinement might have been much harder to deal with otherwise, but in this instance it was grating. The sub-directorate inspector should have known that when this was over, Tuur would have some real concerns about his safety, and by dismissing these so casually, he was being deliberately provocative.

Girard looked down at Tuur's balled fists. More than a few people had been unfortunate enough to experience the strength of those hands. Luckily the Dutchman knew better than to give in to his impulses at the moment.

"They've just pulled into the drive," one of the others called from the living room.

"Well I suppose that glass will have to wait until later. Do you want to go into the living room while I greet our guest?"

Girard opened the front door and saw one of his men who was stationed at the front of the house opening the door of the car that had just pulled in. A tall red-haired woman climbed out.

"Good afternoon. I'm Inspector Girard – Julian. Agent Mesi, isn't it? I hope you had a good journey?"

"Great flight. The short notice meant business class," she replied smiling, going over to shake his hand. "Diane."

Girard took a moment before entering the house. "You're aware of the circumstances surrounding Tuur being in our custody?" he asked.

"Arrested after a nightclub altercation and a background check revealed he'd deserted the Legion eight years ago, pending an investigation into some stolen ordinance. He managed to convince the authorities that he had information that was germane to the violence sweeping the drug community. That's when the sub-directorate entered the picture."

"Yes, we agreed to listen to him and, if we were interested, look at the possibilities. Initially, his story seemed not only far-fetched but unrelated to our investigations. When he expounded on his theory, however, we decided he might have something. My superiors authorised this," Girard gestured at the house. "He's required to put himself at our disposal for as long as necessary, and in return we'll help him to start over. Anything you hear, though, has to have the proviso added that we're dealing with a man who was facing serious charges that he would probably go some way to avoid."

"You mean he's making it up?"

"No, but I wonder if he hasn't embellished it a little. I've no doubt there's a kernel of truth to his story but, at the same time, he knew the situation he found himself in required something special. We can discuss what you think afterwards."

Tuur was standing with his back to the fire and his physical presence dominated the room to such a degree that Girard's men had unconsciously positioned themselves around its edges. Mesi resisted the urge to remain just inside the doorway and, following Girard's lead, sat on the couch facing the Dutchman.

"Richard, this lady is from the US Drugs Enforcement Administration. She's here to discuss what you've told us," said Girard.

Mesi reflexively smiled in greeting at Tuur, whose stare did nothing to disguise his hostility. Everything about him, from the hostile look to the tension in his heavily muscled frame, reminded her of a guard dog, bred for violence, its training barely keeping it in check. Details of the altercation which had led to Tuur's arrest came to mind and she pitied the unfortunates who had encountered him during the nightclub fracas. Breaking their stare, she looked down to consult her notes.

"Now, Mr Tuur, you've given an account of how you were recruited for an operation in July of last year, could you run through it again?" she asked.

"I've gone over it more than once already. You have the notes; why don't you just ask what it is you want to know?"

"Richard, I've explained to you that in order for our various associates to feel secure in your story, they need to hear it first-hand." Girard spoke as one might with an uncooperative child. "There's a chance that a fresh perspective may yield something new. We're all here to help one another. I know you want to make us happy and that can't happen until we know our colleagues are satisfied."

Mesi sensed that the inspector was annoying the mercenary and she wasn't sure it was unintentional. She was not convinced of the wisdom of such a tack but it was Girard's show.

"Let's start with how you were recruited," said Mesi.

Tuur gazed at her sullenly for what seemed a long time before beginning. "Since leaving the Legion, I've worked privately. Security sometimes but mostly ... other work. Africa, the Balkans, wherever. I was recommended for a place on a four-man assignment when someone dropped out last minute. There was a month's prep beforehand."

"Who hired you?"

"A man called Lorcy. He was the fourth member of the team. He organised a down payment of €60,000 and travel to Morocco to begin preparation."

"The payment, how was it made?" asked Mesi.

"An off-shore bank account was set up for me in Jersey and the money lodged." He glanced over at Girard.

"We've recently verified this," said the Inspector. "We were able to get help from the British authorities. After some pressure, the off-shore affiliate of the mainland bank allowed access to their records. Richard received that transfer and another one two days after the alleged incident, both from the same source. A company called Perseus Enterprises, located in the Bahamas."

"Anything on them yet?"

"The directors, rather predictably, turned out to be island residents agreeing to act as company officers for an annual fee. The lawyers who set up the company were being paid by the agent of another offshore company. We've started tracing it back but I'm doubtful it'll lead anywhere."

Mesi made a few quick notes and asked Tuur to continue.

"We stayed overnight in Dakhla and headed into the desert the next day. We crossed the Algerian border and arrived at a camp that was either a former barracks or training facility. Before you ask, I've already made it clear that I don't have a clue as to its exact location. We drilled for a raid on a factory, which was under armed guard. Lorcy had extensive intelligence regarding the security routines surrounding the factory and had drawn up a comprehensive plan of attack."

"What did Lorcy look like? Had you ever heard of or met him before?"

"No. He was not so tall, perhaps one-seventy to one-seventy-five."

"About five feet eight inches," Girard added.

"Dark complexion. I guess he might have been Greek or Turkish," Tuur said. "Look, I've helped one of Girard's men with a photo-fit; I can't add anymore, do you want to hear about the operation or not?"

"Of course, please carry on, Richard."

Mesi was surprised at Girard letting Tuur change the subject so easily but the inspector merely mouthed the word "later".

"We drilled repeatedly the next four weeks. Plan was simple, direct, mostly we concentrated on infiltration and clearing the building."

"Four weeks is a long time; you can't have been drilling all the time. What did you do for the remainder? Did you have any breaks when you went off site? You must have gotten to know one another?"

"We spent all four weeks at the camp. If we weren't drilling we sometimes practised long-range shooting. Otherwise, we listened to world-service radio, played cards and slept. It's standard fare for anyone who's served and we were being well paid for the tedium."

"Lorcy spoke about nothing other than the immediate mission all that time?"

"I already knew one of the men and we got along okay

with the other recruit, but Lorcy never socialised with us. He even slept in separate quarters. After four weeks, we were all eager to get the assignment over with. On the last day, we were told the location of the target, Conchillo, a small town in Mexico, not far from the US border."

When Tuur mentioned the Mexican town, Mesi's attitude to the interview was transformed. The initial invitation from the French authorities, which had arrived a few days before, must have been drafted shortly after Tuur's arrest. It had contained little detail, no mention of Conchillo and only a reference to the Kosovars. Deluged with countless vague reports from all corners of the globe, Samuels had happily palmed it off on her.

"Tell me how you travelled from Algeria to Mexico?"

"We were each given travel documents identifying us as Albanian nationals. We all had different routes from Casablanca to Mexico City and arrived at different times. We rendezvoused in a suburb of the city at a specific road junction where two all-terrain vehicles were waiting. Girard has all the details. Within four days of leaving Algeria, we had begun on-site reconnaissance."

She knew the documentation matched with what Campas and his team had found from examining passenger listings.

"How long did the reconnaissance last?"

"Three days."

"Why so long? Wasn't that dangerous?" asked Mesi.

"It was Lorcy's call, he said we had to wait. He was in contact with someone remotely and seemed to be waiting for a signal."

"Describe the attack."

"We split into two pairs. At Lorcy's signal, we took out

the two perimeter guards from about ninety-five metres. Then we breached the fence and eliminated the building guards."

"How?"

Tuur looked at her uncomprehendingly.

"Did you shoot them, bludgeon them, garrotte them? How did you kill the building guards?"

"My partner shot one with a handgun. Later, the other team member told us that Lorcy had used a knife on their guard." Tuur glazed over for a second. "We proceeded to the surveillance room, killed the only occupant and moved on to the processing area. We killed the three men working there. Lorcy and the other team member handled the guard room and joined us."

There was no more doubt in her mind. The confirmation that one of the guards had been stabbed convinced her that Tuur was genuine.

"What did the processing area contain?" she asked.

"Other than some basic equipment, the room was packed with heroin. I have no idea how much, only that it must have been worth a fortune. Lorcy ordered us to take up defensive positions outside while he planted the charges. Fifteen minutes later, the building had been destroyed and I was on my way home."

"You were never curious what it was all about?"

"We weren't paid to ask questions. If I thought about it at all, I assumed someone in Mexico had offended the wrong party and this was payback but I really didn't care."

"No one was tempted to take some of the drugs?"

"We had no way of getting it out of the country. Anyway, that wasn't the objective, and mission discipline was strong," Tuur replied with some pride.

"How did you get out of Mexico?"

"Lorcy left separately and the rest of us shared the other vehicle back to Mexico City, where we split up. I flew to Belgium and drove back to France."

"Any further contact with Lorcy or the others?"

"No. One of the conditions of the contract was that we were not to contact each other for at least a year."

Mesi nodded and looked down at her notes, lost in thought. "Why did you think this information would be important enough to the authorities for them to forget your outstanding charges?" she asked finally.

"I see what's been happening across Europe and the US," he shrugged. "I've seen coverage of the queues outside the methadone clinics in Paris, read the reports on the escalation of street crime."

"So, where's the connection to Mexico?"

"I think my operation was part of something larger. I know a little about the drug scene, here in France and other countries, so I'm guessing the travel documents we were given weren't accidental."

A satisfied grin spread across Tuur's blunt features. She could see he was quite pleased with his deduction.

"Personally, I think Richard's been extremely brave, whatever the motivation. He's run the risk of alienating some obviously dangerous people," said Girard, the remark banishing the smile from Tuur's face.

"Can we talk outside?" Mesi asked Girard.

They left the living room and walked back outside to the front of the house.

"Well, what do you think?" asked the Frenchman.

"I'll have to get more details but so far his account matches the findings of the investigation at the refinery

– 142 –

perfectly. It's interesting that he says they spent three days on site before attacking. I wonder if Lorcy was waiting for a time when they could do the most damage? Maybe a new consignment? Speaking of which, what's Lorcy's photo-fit like? I don't think I've seen a copy."

"I'll see you get one and a transcript from all the Q&A sessions we've had with Tuur," replied Girard. "Tuur's relatively okay discussing other aspects of the operation but whenever the conversation turns to Lorcy he becomes agitated. To get him to cooperate with the photo-fit, we had to threaten to rescind our agreement. I suspect the likeness may contain some deliberate inaccuracies."

"Why's he so reticent regarding Lorcy specifically? If he's telling the truth about the rest why stop when it comes to some hired gun? The details of the money transfer are far more incriminating. Potentially, they could lead us to whoever funded the operation, which you'd imagine would worry him more."

"I agree but I don't think Tuur's reaction to questions about Lorcy is because he's unintelligent or unaware of the implications of helping us. I've spent a lot of time with him, and listened to his story again and again, and my impression is that Lorcy said or did something that put the fear of God into him."

"Any progress on anything he's given you besides the bank transfers?" she asked.

"No. We haven't been able to locate the man who recommended Tuur to Lorcy. If we find him, we might learn more."

"For what it's worth, I'd advise you to send out an up-to-date account of what he's told us to all relevant agencies, asking for assistance and restating the invitation to question him. I don't think a lot of people you contacted would have realised how relevant he is, based on what was issued previously."

She made a mental note to call Campas later as she was sure he would want to question Tuur himself.

"Okay, we'll organise that. Shall we go back inside and see if we can wring any more out of Richard while he's in such an effusive mood?" Girard said with a smile.

The noise that drifted up to them from the streets into the second-floor apartment would normally be associated with fun and celebration. But their already-frayed nerves were not helped by the loud music and intermittent setting off of fireworks, each small explosion increasing the stress just a little bit more. Once a year, the little town of Quibdo came alive with La Fiesta de la Ascensión. It was a signal for people to forget their everyday troubles and to experience happiness, however briefly. The highlight of the evening was the judging of the floats everyone from small businesses to schools worked for weeks to prepare, in the hope that theirs would be judged best. The judging committee was comprised of the parish priest, the town mayor, some prominent local businessmen and one guest. It was this final member of the committee that kept the temporary occupants of the apartment from enjoying the festival. They meant to perform the dangerous task of killing him and then, just as importantly, escape with their lives. A few weeks earlier it had been arranged for the residents of the apartment to be absent for the week of the festival.

The two gunmen had arrived late the previous night and, once they had set up, their only task was to pass the remaining time without drawing attention. To achieve this necessitated crawling around on their hands and knees while in either of the two rooms whose windows looked down on the street. When the target reached the judging platform, the gunmen would open fire with Russian-made SVD Designated Marksman Rifles. These guns were more than accurate enough for the distance involved, and their capability to be fully automatic meant they could achieve a far higher rate of fire than pure sniper rifles. The intention was that the resulting confusion and panic would aid their escape.

Luis Madrigal had attended the festival for the last fifteen years without fail. His mother had been born here and this was his way of paying respect to her memory. She had died before her son attained any appreciable success. As soon as he could, he had established a festival fund for the town, enabling a much grander celebration. Anybody who wished to enter the float competition, but found themselves short of funds, could apply for a donation. The meal at the town square, which followed the competition, was now provided with as much free food and drink as could be consumed. The only price for all this had been for the Masses in the week before the festival to be offered to the memory of Laura Madrigal.

During the festival, more than at any other time, Madrigal's schedule taxed his security detail to their limit. He made it clear to them that he did not want to be surrounded by a phalanx of bodyguards every second he was there. He insisted on only two close protection bodyguards. He wanted to be able to take this unique opportunity to mix and share in the enjoyment of these people. The inhabitants of Quibdo lived a hard life but they refused to let their spirit be ground down and the festival was a joyous occasion. Occasionally one of them would approach him asking for help with a particular situation. He had never refused a case he felt was genuine and, over the years, word had spread of his generosity. Every year he received a warm reception. He spent months looking forward to the brief time he would spend here.

Looking out over the windowsill, one of the gunmen could see the people already assembled on the judging podium. They were all looking down the street. A small group was making its way through the throng from an intersection about a hundred paces away. He was certain that this must be their target approaching and turned to his companion, signalling they should get ready. The crowds made it difficult for him to single out the drug lord and he could only catch brief glimpses of the top of someone's head when the tall man at the head of the group momentarily moved to one side or another. He was reassured the obscured figure was Madrigal from the behaviour of people in the crowd as the group passed them. People would forget whatever had been occupying them and approach the concealed man for a quick word or greeting.

The gunman couldn't risk firing until Madrigal was in clear view on the podium and the hit was guaranteed. There would be only one chance and it had been made clear that failure would not be tolerated. Despite the gunman's years of experience, he found the pressure was getting to him. Was Madrigal going to stop and speak at length to every single person who greeted him? After what seemed an eternity, the tall bodyguard leading the group reached the stairs to the podium. The escort held back some people to allow room for two men to ascend the stairs. From his vantage point, the gunman could not see either man's face but it was obvious that the second man was too stout to be their target. He nodded to his companion and they took up their positions. This was their most vulnerable time and he could feel a trickle of sweat wind down his back under his soaked shirt. Leaning forward, he placed the gun barrel between the slit in the window and waited for Madrigal to turn so that he could see his face. Frustratingly the target was moving along the podium, shaking hands with each of the other judges, but at no point did he face the building. Sweat dripped into the gunman's eyes, stinging them, but he dared not wipe it away; he had to stay ready. The man on the podium was now engaged in a deep and animated conversation with the parish priest, the last dignitary to greet. Any second now. The conversation dragged on and he cursed them inwardly. What did they find to talk about? Why couldn't they just shut up? Out of the corner of his eye he saw his companion fidgeting in discomfort. You just better do your job properly, he thought. Again, the priest and the target shook hands. This must be it; their babbling was over. The man's face came into view at last. Was he looking directly up at the window? Clean shaven, bespectacled, pleasant features arranged in a smile. It was not Madrigal.

The door to the apartment suddenly crashed inward behind them. The other gunman spun round but before he could open fire he was cut down by a hail of bullets. The lead gunman was still trying to decide whether he should shoot at the podium when a burst of automatic fire ended his deliberations for good.

Three men quickly worked their way through the remainder of the apartment to confirm that there were no more assassins. A fourth man walked to the window and looked down on the podium to ensure no one had been alerted by the gunfire. Once they were satisfied everything was as it should be, he took out a cell phone and dialled a number to make his report. A few moments later, Luis Madrigal entered the apartment to examine the scene first-hand. After a cursory look around the main room he examined each of the assassins. Grabbing a handful of hair, he pulled their heads back to get a good look at them.

"Know them?" he asked one of the men.

"No but we've taken photos, it won't take long to identify them."

"Okay, clean this up and I'll see you back at the house tomorrow morning." He headed for the door. "I'd better get down there before the floats start arriving. And tell Marco he'll have to wait at least another year to judge the competition."

"Watch our later bulletins to hear more on that story. Now, during its initial stages, Plan Coca received unqualified praise, mostly due to what was perceived as its positive impact on drug consumption within the US," began Sandra Whittaker. "Recently, however, in addition to the difficulties the Plan faces in Colombia, negative aspects are beginning to surface at home. We're going to go to New York now, for a report on some disturbing developments there."

The piece began outside an unexceptional-looking, three-storey building and then moved through its main entrance.

As it passed down a dingy, leaky hallway covered in peeling paint, the reporter's voice explained that this was one of a number of community centres servicing the residents of the deprived Brownsville area of the city. Coming to a stop outside a door with a glass window, the camera peered through to show a room full of people listening to a thin Indian man. Every available seat had been taken and more people stood along the walls, with a few even sitting on the floor in front of the first row of chairs.

"This is Dilip Patel, a local shopkeeper," explained the reporter. "Five weeks ago he and a number of other local residents approached the centre's director and asked if they could hold these meetings."

The camera scanned the faces of the attendees. Most were middle-aged and elderly but there were some younger people, too.

"Dilip and the others," the report continued, "recognised the challenges facing the locality because of the extreme shortages in the drug supply. They felt it was imperative that there be some venue where members of the community could meet to speak about their concerns and suggest possible solutions."

The report switched to footage from an interview with the shopkeeper. First, he was asked who generally attended the meetings.

"All kinds of people; anyone worried about what we're living with. There are social workers, local businessmen, off-duty policemen. Mostly, though, it's just people who live here, who see what's happening to themselves, their families and friends."

He was asked which issues were of most importance to the local residents.

"The increase in violence. Brownsville's always been rough but over the last couple of months, it's gotten so much worse. Hold-ups, break-ins and muggings. No one goes outside unless it's absolutely necessary. We can't continue to live like this."

The reporter asked him if he had suffered directly himself.

"I run an electrical store and I've been held up four times and broken into five times in the last two months," came the anguished reply.

The footage changed briefly, showing various scenes from the area. Some images were mundane – people heading to work or walking their children to school – while others hinted at the economic reality of the area – homeless people pushing shopping carts, groups congregating on stoops sharing a bottle, abandoned buildings guarded by sullen-faced youths. While these were being shown, the reporter explained that besides the incidence of violent crime, the fragile social fabric of neighbourhoods like this was being torn asunder by the drug-related crisis.

The report switched to a black man in his early twenties who explained what had caused the social strife. The man, a local youth worker, spoke calmly, which only amplified the power of what he was saying.

"April, the price for half a gram of rock cocaine was ten dollars. A user could get that anywhere and if they tried hard enough they could probably get it cheaper. November, it's impossible to get the same amount for less than fifty."

The reporter asked him to explain how addicts had handled this increase.

"Well, they would have been totally unprepared. In order to cope they're being forced to resort to violence to *get the cash they need."*

He was asked whether the majority of these people have a history of violent crime and were simply having to increase their activity level.

"No, not at all. Of course some have always been violent but most would have survived without going beyond petty crime. Now the number of violent assaults and robberies grows on a daily basis."

The reporter asked whether this was an isolated problem, restricted solely to a small area of Brownsville.

"Isolated?" The young man smiled sardonically. "You think people here don't got the intelligence to jump on a train if they thought it could solve their problem? You can go to Bed-Stuy or the Bronx or any one of a number of places and you'll find exactly the same situation."

He was asked what the future held.

"It's only going to get worse."

Once again, there was a new interviewee. This time it was an older man with a kindly face framed in a greying beard and curly hair. The viewer was told that this was Marvin Wilson, the community centre director.

"We face an impossible situation," Wilson stated. "All the city's methadone programmes are oversubscribed, they can't take no more patients. Addicts gonna be forced into detox as their drugs disappear."

Wilson went on to explain that detox was difficult enough when people were mentally prepared and properly supported.

The reporter came in at this point and asked whether, regrettable as the short-term suffering was, it would not all be for the best in the long run.

"And in the meantime?" Wilson asked indignantly.

"*For every one person able to handle cold-turkey, how many can't? What happens to them, what happens to those around them; family, friends, their children?*"

Wilson had started calmly but his agitation was becoming more visible, his voice less controlled. "*And what happens to neighbourhoods like ours?*"

The reporter asked if Wilson thought the authorities had let them down.

"*I don't blame the police. They're swamped and they doing their best. But all these reports I see, editorials I read, politicians talking about how the problem is being contained within the drug community, how we've just got to ride it out. Well, the problem isn't contained. Most of the people attending these meetings have never taken drugs in their life.*"

What would it take for those in power to recognise the crisis, he was asked.

"*Do you think poor people the only users? Give it a little longer and you'll see more price rises and the problems we facing hit the middle class. Then, maybe the politicians will do a little more than tell us to tough it out.*"

The interview with Wilson ended and the reporter wrapped up the report. The newscast then returned to the studio and the immaculately groomed newscaster.

"*Plan Coca, it seems, is facing a difficult two-fronted battle, a battle we'll be following closely.*" Her tone went from grave to cheerful in an instant as she continued, "*When we return, Ken will have all the latest sport.*"

seven

"The operation Tuur described involved experienced people with access to serious finance," Mesi explained. "Convoluted fund movements, manpower, training facilities, documentation and first-class intelligence. So … "

"These characteristics, combined with the location involved, naturally brought you here," agreed Tom Hughes helpfully.

She had not been looking forward to approaching the Central Intelligence Agency. She had envisaged an uphill battle with a faceless bureaucrat who was not remotely interested in her investigation. Stories of Langley's uncooperativeness were legendary. And who could blame them? Between one scandal and another, it was understandable that they had developed a siege mentality. But Hughes had been a pleasant surprise.

She had been waiting for less than five minutes outside his office when he had come jogging down the corridor, apologising for the delay. His appearance – mid-forties, average height and reasonably good looking in a weather-beaten outdoors type of way – was totally at odds with her preconceptions. His tousled blond hair and open-necked shirt reminded her of some of the younger, hipper, lecturers who had taught her in college rather than a senior Agency specialist on Central and Southern American affairs. It had taken about an hour for her to take him from the first suspected engagement of the drug war through to her visit to France and Tuur's statement. Hughes had listened attentively, interrupting her narrative only occasionally, to clarify a particular point or make an observation.

"I've identified eighteen attacks on major Alliance resources throughout Latin America which are being treated as the work of the Kosovars."

"And you need to compile a list of people who conform to a very specific profile?"

"Exactly," she said. "I was thinking people who've served in Latin America in either military or intelligence roles. People who could now be working on a contract basis or may even have a vested interest in the final objective."

"I'm assuming you'll leave those copies with me?" he asked, indicating the heavy folder he had on his lap that she had occasionally referred to over the hour. "We'll compile a list of all known personnel who have worked in one or more of these countries; sort it so that those with most hits are at the top of the list," he said, flicking through the folder. "Once that's done, we can try to ascertain as many of their movements as possible from the past couple of years. Another thing we can do is get somebody to go back to all the relevant station reports for the regions for, say, a month before a particular attack to a month after it. See if anything which might be related was mentioned."

"That's great," she said and then felt compelled to add, "Look, I have to be honest. I'm pretty much on my own at the moment in thinking this idea of third-party orchestration is a real possibility. Everyone else still thinks it's a straight war between the Kosovars and Madrigal's Alliance. I appreciate what you're doing."

He shook his head dismissively.

"I think it's sensible to look at this." He patted the

file. "At the very least we need to be able to eliminate it as a possibility. Besides, even if the Kosovars are wholly responsible, they would still need someone with the kind of background you described."

She wished her superiors in the DEA were of a similar mind. When she had put forward her thoughts on the conflict having been orchestrated by another group, Samuels had been instantly dismissive. In the unlikely event Tuur was reliable, he argued, ignoring the corroboration of all the facts, then all it proved was that the Kosovars had hired him. The fake travel documents were meaningless. He had insisted that she drop it as a line of enquiry and dedicate herself to preparing dossiers on a number of suspected ex-KLA members living in Chicago and Detroit. That had been the final straw, which resulted in her doing what she had tried to avoid for so long.

She had stormed into Marshall's office, confronted him with her suspicions about TAIT being merely a tool for political appeasement and accused him of leading her on. She insisted, in light of the lack of support he had shown her and the wasteful way in which Samuels was utilising her, that she be let pursue the orchestration theory. The grandstand play had been a huge gamble, Marshall might very easily have been outraged. But, whether because of his chagrin at being presented with what was the obvious truth or some other reason, it had worked. He ordered Samuels to free her from all other assignments and provide her with any support she needed. She doubted she would get any real help from Samuels but was content with being freed to do something she believed in.

"Just out of interest, if there were a third party, who would you favour as the most obvious candidates?" Hughes asked. "Presumably another large player in the drugs market, one of the Russian or Chinese syndicates?"

"They're potentials but I have serious doubts that an established group would have taken the risks."

"Because?"

"Well, and this was why I first started having problems with the Kosovars as instigators of the conflict, all of the major players' cash-flows have taken a hammering. Surely they could have predicted the anarchy that's resulted?"

"Could it have been intended as a long-term strategy, something worth the damage for the ultimate gains?"

"Maybe," she said, "but what I think is more likely, is a smaller group who want to destabilise things, create an opportunity for themselves and exploit it."

"A possible variation on that is a subset within either the Alliance or the Fifteen Families who wants to grasp control and sees discrediting the current leadership, through creating this crisis, as their route."

"That's another of the less far-fetched options."

"How far-fetched do they get?" he asked.

"A terrorist initiative, possibly state-backed, designed to break down the social order of the consumer countries. One of the pharmaceutical giants stands to gain massively if drugs are decriminalised, so they associate insurmountable problems with policing it." She shrugged her shoulders. "Speculating on motivation is useless at this point, with so little to go on! To progress this, a lot more hard facts are necessary."

"Okay, I'll contact you as soon as we start turning stuff up." He stood up, signalling the meeting was over. "Come on, I'll walk you out."

As they were saying goodbye in reception, he stopped.

"Alan Hopkins?" he asked.

She was taken off guard by the question and hesitated a second before saying yes. She wondered how he knew her ex-husband.

"I've met Alan a bit in the course of my work. He's organised a few functions and attended several meeting on behalf of the Cuban-American lobby," he said, guessing her thoughts. Her expression was one of bemusement. "I'm sorry, I just made the connection and blurted it out before I realised. Foot-in-mouth syndrome! I hope –"

"No, no, don't worry about it. You just took me by surprise. Alan and I split eight years ago when he was only starting out as a lobbyist. We're still friends. I see him about once a month." She wondered why she had added that. "I'm surprised, though, that he mentioned me."

"I can't remember how it came up, but that's hardly surprising. Some of the receptions we go to can be so tedious, you'll happily discuss anything non-work related. I recalled him mentioning his ex-wife worked for the DEA. Again, I'm sorry."

"It's no problem, really. Well, thanks for your time today. I'll talk to you soon."

She heard someone approach and stopped what she was doing, swivelling around in her chair. Anderson, one of the junior agents, stood there holding a cardboard box that looked as if the bottom was about to give way.

"This just came for you. Shall I leave it here?" He indicated a clear space on her desk.

"Sure, thanks."

These were the files Hughes had promised her yesterday evening. They contained the listing and associated dossiers of operatives whose profiles made them the likeliest candidates for involvement in the attacks on the Alliance. The other item he had promised to look at, the re-examination of the station reports in and around specific incidents, had drawn a blank. Mesi had been disappointed and said it only proved how much care these people had taken, but Hughes had refused to leave it at that. He had initiated a series of interviews with the CIA's station personnel and their sources throughout the relevant countries. Between that substantial undertaking and the sheer volume of information contained in these files, Mesi was overwhelmed by his thoroughness and application.

After their first meeting, having learnt that Hughes knew Alan, she had called her ex-husband to get his opinion of the CIA man. Alan had told her that Hughes did not have the highest profile but seemed to be generally well liked. Popularity wasn't something normally associated with a man in his line of work but the times Alan had needed something from him, he had been totally engaging. She followed up her chat with Alan by calling one of her colleagues who had worked with Hughes on a number of inter-Agency initiatives involving Latin America. Apparently Hughes had been considered quite special in his formative years and destined for great things before his upward career trajectory levelled off fairly unspectacularly. The general impression of Hughes, her colleague added, was that he was a nice guy but he might lack the stomach for some of the harder, necessary, decisions Agency work entailed. Now, he did an adequate job co-ordinating the Central and South American station chiefs and was not called upon to leave his moral comfort zone.

Well, she thought, regardless of what others might

see as Hughes' shortcomings, he had been outstanding in coming through for her so far.

He had enclosed a covering note with the listing, suggesting they could work through it in parallel. While he was trying to get up-to-date information on the operatives he had identified, she could contact the various police agencies responsible for investigating the attacks. Perhaps one of operatives had crossed the authorities' radar. He knew it was a long shot but this kind of time-consuming, sequential work was the only avenue open to them.

Nothing else she had done since returning from France had resulted in any headway and she was thankful for something to apply herself to. Any feeling of progress would be welcome. Before contacting investigating officers like Campas, though, she thought it might be more useful to get in touch with Julian Girard. If Tuur recognised any of these operatives as the man called Lorcy then it would represent a huge step forward. She checked her watch and, after quickly calculating the time in France, placed the call.

"Agent Mesi," answered the voice.

The grave tone differed so much from her recollection of Girard that she immediately asked what was wrong.

"I assume you're calling in relation to Richard?" he replied.

"Yes, I'd like you to show him some photographs and ask him if he recognises anyone."

"That's impossible, I'm afraid. He was found dead early this morning."

She felt a tremor run through her. "How?"

"The preliminary report indicates suicide."

"Do you believe that?"

"Frankly, I'm not sure. I left Richard yesterday evening

in an apartment, under the watch of four police officers. He seemed happy, much happier than when you saw him. The hardest part was behind him; he had cooperated fully. Within a matter of days we would have had him established with a new identity, something he appeared to be looking forward to."

"How was he found?"

"He usually woke very early to go for a walk but his guards thought he was having a lie-in. When I arrived shortly after ten and he still hadn't surfaced, I went to his bedroom to wake him. His wrists had been slashed. There were no signs of a struggle."

"It's strange that if he was going to kill himself he would do it at this stage."

"That's what I thought," he agreed. "I got to know Richard quite well over the past month. Based on his service record and my own impression, I find this hard to believe. The only time I saw him express any doubt or fear was when we discussed this Lorcy and even then it was nothing I'd have thought would drive him to suicide. Still, who knows what was going through his mind?"

Girard promised to send her a copy of the final report as soon as it was ready and, sensing he wanted to get off the call, she wrapped it up. Afterwards, she tried to decide what the news meant. If Tuur really had killed himself, it had no significance and even if someone else was responsible, there was nothing there she could use to bolster her theory. Samuels' attitude would be that the Kosovars were merely tying up loose ends. Tuur's death had not changed anything other than to make things a little more difficult.

Reaching into the box, she retrieved the listing and the first handful of files.

———

Lawrence Wallace finished the call and switched off his cell phone. Once again he checked his watch then strode to within a few feet of the edge and felt himself being buffeted by the heavy winds. The building had been completed as far as the fifty-fifth storey and where he stood now, on the eightieth floor, there was only a bare structure. The views of the Chicago skyline, which the offices on this level would afford when the construction was completed, were breathtaking. The building would be wholly owned by Diversified Holdings, who would occupy the top fifteen floors and lease the rest. It would be a symbol of the pinnacle of corporate America, a physical manifestation of power and proof of influence. The impotence Wallace currently felt could hardly have rendered it less appropriate.

Earlier he had watched a news broadcast detailing the aftermath of a riot that had exploded in one of the city's deprived neighbourhoods. It had only lasted a few hours but the damage to property was substantial. The reporter had said that police felt the riot had been spontaneous and had sparked a few isolated incidents of looting in broad daylight. A local politician had warned of the growing number of addicts who had been priced out of the drug market. Due to scarcity of supply, prices had rocketed and people were being forced to go to desperate lengths. Some analysts were calling for government intervention to set up treatment programmes in the worst-hit cities.

The call he had just completed had been to authorise the release of more funds to the string of rehabilitation clinics he was financing. At the moment they were struggling to cope with the surge in demand. Staff morale had plummeted and some key personnel had resigned. Including this latest round of funding, the clinics had already accounted for twice the original budget and he doubted it would end there.

Despite his best efforts, he was anxious about this meeting.

He knew that the stance he intended to take would be difficult and he would come under pressure. He wasn't used to being in any position but total control. Normally when he entered a room, no matter how many others were present, he invariably became its focus, without ever having to try. It was just the natural order. A combination of more than forty years of calling the shots and a habit of not straying beyond his own select circles ensured others gravitated towards him. Despite his lack of celebrity, Wallace was recognised for what he was among his associates: a king. There were other names to describe individuals who wielded so much influence: movers and shakers, captains of industry, but the regal title fit best. After all, there was virtually no limit to what he and the small number of genuine peers could do if they wanted.

He wondered how much of where he found himself was due to hubris.

He had been born seventy years earlier, no more than a few miles from where he now stood. His father had been a baker desperate to continue the tradition of ensuring the next generation moved that little bit further up the ladder. He remembered the old man's pride when he had graduated from college. Pride and something else. Fulfilment. When his father had died a few months later, he knew the old man had been content.

He doubted he'd ever experience that sense of

contentment. The best he hoped for now was to make up some of the deficit.

After graduation he had initially worked as a manager in the automobile industry but quickly realised real success for him lay in another direction. His greatest talent was a remarkable ability for analysis. He could effortlessly break down the most complex of systems, processes and practices.

He also had a need to control his own future. The ideal application for this lay in strategic consultancy, advising businesses on how they could eliminate inherent weaknesses and optimise revenues. It had been slow going at first; it took time for the young Wallace to build up his credibility. But within four years he was employing more than thirty bright young business minds and had a host of blue-chip clients. Eventually, the mere announcement of their retention as advisors was enough to elevate an ailing firm's share price. Within the business circles in which he operated Wallace garnered a reputation bordering on mystical. His advocates boasted there was no situation or problem that was beyond him.

Much of his success had come down to picking his battles and recognising the right opportunity. A perfect example was Wallace Consulting being one of the first to recognise the potential for cross-pollination that consultancy offered. If his auditing division identified a shortcoming in a company, their professional services division could fill the gap. Similarly, though, Wallace had been the first to recognise the inherent conflict of interest and curb these questionable practices. This prescience guaranteed his was virtually the only company among the large consultancy houses to avoid lawsuits and a hugely devalued balance sheet. Wallace had displayed the same flair for judgement when he had taken defensive positions avoiding various technology and investment bubbles by divesting while others continued to rush in.

He worried now, though, that in his latest venture he had been too late in recognising the signs.

Despite his undoubted skill, luck had also played a part in building Wallace's eleven-figure personal fortune. In the late seventies, he had been approached by a consortium of white-collar executives who wanted to buy out the failing airline they worked for. Recognising the limitless potential for their intended low-fare, point-to-point strategy, he identified key weaknesses in their plan, amended it and took a major stake by funding the buyout. The airline was now one of the most successful carriers in the US, its share price having risen year on year for more than two decades.

After that, he had amended his own business strategy. More and more they entered into partnerships where they took equity in businesses he believed had potential but, either through liquidity issues or bad management, had faltered. A new entity, Diversified Holdings, was founded to oversee these investments and would eventually come to hold interests in over 300 fields of industry at last count – cosmetics, food production, alternative energy, pharmaceuticals and countless others. Yet, despite being one of the US economy's powerhouses, the multinational worked consciously to reduce its mainstream profile. Wallace's own name had been deliberately pushed to the background while the company's partners and subsidiaries were encouraged to develop their own brands and corporate identities. This strategy had ensured Wallace retained a large degree of anonymity despite the power he wielded.

And it had been this influence that had led him to

believe he could succeed in his latest venture. Just another problem in need of a solution, he had told himself.

Quite a few of the companies they held interests in were engaged in one of the most lucrative business of all: war. In addition to the forty or so arms manufacturers, there were some firms specialising in the provision of military personnel on a contract basis. Until a few years ago, they had held no special significance to him, nothing more than financial items on a consolidated profit and loss statement. That had changed, however, when he had conceived his strategy. He had realised that one of these firms would provide him with the "in" he needed and he had started to examine them more closely. One company soon emerged to stand out from the others.

Really, it was the company's CEO, Andrew Brewer, whose history and contacts marked him out. Wallace had orchestrated several supposedly chance meetings to sound out Brewer, and then, convinced as he could be of the man's expertise and discretion, he had gambled. It had been a huge risk, approaching Brewer and outlining his plan. At first it seemed as if he had made a mistake. Weeks went by with no response and Wallace had worried that he had fallen at the first hurdle. Then Brewer contacted him with his suggestions on how they should proceed.

Which had ultimately resulted in him waiting here.

He heard the lift groan to a halt behind him and the door being opened. When he turned around, Larsen stepped out of the lift and scanned the area.

"Impressive, isn't it?" Wallace said, trying to inject confidence into his voice.

Larsen walked past Wallace and for a second it looked as if he was going to step into mid-air. At the last moment he stopped at the very edge of the structure and sat down on his haunches, balancing on the balls of his feet hundreds of feet above the ground. The powerful gusts appeared to cause him no alarm. Just the sight of him balancing there was unsettling to Wallace.

"So, we're cleared for the next stage?" Larsen asked.

"We need to talk."

Larsen stood up and faced him.

Brewer was the normal conduit between the two of them but at the outset, as a way of ensuring too much control did not lie with the middleman, the two of them had agreed a protocol consisting of periodic face-to-face meetings. These occurred at significant junctures and up to now had consisted of Wallace simply rubber-stamping the major decisions to that point and giving the green-light to continue.

He waited for Wallace to explain this departure from the norm.

"I'm worried we're losing our way, that we're no longer controlling the situation."

"The different elements have engaged each other, exactly as we planned?"

"Yes."

"So, how are we 'losing our way'?"

"Don't you think it's a problem that we're still planning new operations, with no definite end in sight? I'd never envisaged it going on so long."

"We can't be sure yet that the conflict is self-sustaining. Madrigal's still showing signs of reluctance."

"We've already had more than twenty-five individual missions going back over two years. When will we be able to say 'enough'?"

Wallace could see the other man was reflecting on where he was going with this.

"We haven't deviated substantially from the revised projections," Larsen replied. "This isn't an exact science; we have to be flexible with the timescales."

"Look at how far things have escalated," Wallace said, abruptly changing tack. "You only have to pick up a newspaper or switch on a television to see the effects of what we've done. Does it really need to be fuelled further?"

"I don't think we can read too much into how things are being presented in the media," Larsen replied calmly. "I believe we need to focus on keeping the Alliance and the Kosovars motivated."

"And what they've done over the last few months isn't enough proof of commitment for you?"

There was an accusatory hint in the question.

"The objective is to ensure they damage one another irreparably, dragging as many of the other players as possible down with them. So far, despite the damage they've incurred, if the conflict ended now they could still recover."

Wallace noted that he did not bother to point out the obvious, that if this were to occur everything they had worked for and all the bloodshed would have been in vain.

The older man began pacing, annoyed that Larsen's arguments were preventing him from building any momentum in the conversation, momentum necessary to say what needed to be said. He had felt much surer before Larsen had arrived.

"I'm not sure the focus isn't too narrow," he said, trying another approach. "The reports Brewer and you have filed recently deal only with what's happening in the immediate environment. They're insufficient basis for a decision on further action."

"What is it you expect?" Larsen asked, his annoyance obvious now. "We have a long-term goal and a roadmap for achieving it. Nothing's changed. The reports have always focused on the one or two missions that are going on at the time. Why are you making this an issue?"

"We need to take stock. We need time to evaluate the broader picture."

"Are you saying we should stop?" Larsen asked incredulously.

One word now and it would all be over. Just say it, Wallace remonstrated to himself while trying to avoid Larsen's gaze. He started to form his answer a number of times but each time his nerve betrayed him.

"Proceed with Cartagena but that's it for now," he said at last. "Use the protocol to contact me when it's done. I'll have had time to perform a proper review by then."

"And the submissions for the subsequent two targets? We need to begin preparations, recruitment, training."

"Everything bar Cartagena is on hold. That's it, that's my decision!"

Knowing Larsen's history, if Wallace had been in the Dane's shoes he would have shouted in frustration at this retreat, but Larsen merely nodded and headed back to the lift.

Left alone, Wallace cursed himself for not having the courage to finish what he had started.

THREE YEARS EARLIER.

This is insane, he thought once again.

The middle of the night, sitting in a tiny rental car on the

West Side of Chicago. Waiting for someone he had never met before. The only streetlight in the vicinity flickered intermittently, struggling to illuminate the rain-drenched night. Occasionally, other sounds broke through the din of the rain hitting the car. Sometimes it would be an excited good-natured shout from those still out at this late hour and willing to brave the downpour, but most of the time there was no hint of good humour. This was the roughest of neighbourhoods and his uneasiness grew with each passing moment.

He considered leaving. Perhaps the person he was waiting for was not going to show. Maybe he had just been set on a wild-goose chase for most of the day and it was time to cut his losses. But he could not give up just yet. A small group of people, huddling up against each other to combat the rain, walked by his car and peered in. He was sure he had seen them pass by at least once before.

A tapping on the glass disturbed him and when he looked up he could see one of the men bent over, gesturing for him to roll the window down. After waiting so long, he didn't want to leave, so he complied with the request and immediately caught the strong odour of alcohol. The malicious grins did not bode well. To remain seated looking up seemed too vulnerable and seeing as how it was probably too late to drive away with them looming so close, he opened the door and got out. The atmosphere was tense but he hoped if he seized the initiative, he could avert any trouble. There were three of them, each physically intimidating, eyeing him hostilely.

"What do you want?" he asked.

"Why you sittin' there in the car?" one of them sneered. "You cruisin'? You some kinda faggot?"

The others laughed.

"Last time I checked, I wasn't breaking any laws," he replied. "So why don't you just mind your own business?"

Wallace had not been in a fight since high school and part of him felt as if he was outside himself, disconnected from events.

"Mind my …" said his inquisitor and, without warning, lashed out with a kick aimed at Wallace's groin. The blow grazed his hip, numbing his leg, and would have done much worse had he not stumbled back in time. Another step back and he felt himself crash into a chain-link fence. They fanned left and right of him and he braced himself for the onslaught.

"Leave him alone." The voice came from a man who had approached unnoticed while they were occupied. Two of them turned toward him and wavered momentarily, as if they were not quite sure what to do. A couple of exchanged glances seemed to bolster them and they resumed their advance on him.

Wallace could see, though, that despite their greater numbers, they were taking an altogether more careful approach than they had with him. With a clearer view now, he recognised the newcomer as Larsen and could see his total ease was unsettling them. One of them drew a knife and stepped up to him.

"Gonna' teach you a lesson!"

When Wallace replayed the scene later, it ran as if in slow motion. Larsen reached out, grabbed the man's wrist and twisted. An audible crack was followed by the blade being dropped. The man battled to remain standing while his knees buckled from the pain. A small smile played at the edges of Larsen's mouth and with his free hand he drew a handgun from under his jacket.

"Get going."

The two others couldn't move quickly enough and scrambled away, leaving their spokesman kneeling in pain while Larsen retained a hold of his injured limb. He released his attacker with a final twist and watched him set off in pursuit of the others. There were a few half-hearted threats shouted from distance, detailing what would happen when they returned. Larsen ignored them. He headed to a car across the street, and called over his shoulder for Wallace to follow.

Wallace found the setting Larsen chose for their meeting to be totally off-putting. A small, dingy, all-night restaurant, specialising in the greasy fare so many people loved. One look at the menu and his cardiologist's instructions from the last physical came to mind. He made do with a black coffee and took a seat by the window. The dirty late-night rain that continued to pelt against the pane only added to the gloom. At 3:00 a.m., the place was virtually empty, still too early for the first work shifts of the new day.

Larsen ordered an unappetising pile of food and proceeded to shovel it down his throat, oblivious to his companion. Wallace compared his first close-up look at the man to the photographs he had studied. If you looked for it, the slight cast his Mediterranean heritage gave him was just discernible. The face itself was not very engaging, spare features and intense auburn eyes creating a slightly feral aspect. Once he had worked his way through his food, he sat back slurping his coffee and gestured for Wallace to begin.

"You'd been watching, hadn't you? Why did you wait until the trouble started?" Wallace asked.

"I had to be sure you had no one else watching."

"You took quite a risk back there with such a nonchalant approach, didn't you?" Wallace asked, the recent scene still playing over in his mind. "What if they had a gun?"

"They didn't."

It was only then that Wallace realised what had actually occurred.

"You arranged that whole scene?" he said indignantly.

"It saved a much longer wait."

"What if it hadn't worked out? What if one of us had been hurt? Are you some kind of lunatic?" Then, more to himself, he added, "What am I doing?"

"Relax, they were low lives, not serious at all. They were simply trying to renegotiate. Stupid, all they had to do was follow some simple instructions."

Wallace shook his head.

"Obviously not simple enough; they assaulted me and pulled a knife on you. Was this meant to be a demonstration of the kind of judgement you normally show?" he asked.

"It wasn't meant to be a demonstration of anything," came the matter-of-fact reply. "I couldn't care less what you think. You asked for this meeting; remember that. As for back there, it was manageable. End of story."

Wallace could understand why Larsen had rubbed the occasionally pompous Brewer up the wrong way. The indifferent tone would not have sat well with him at all.

It had not been the original intention for either him or Brewer to meet directly with Larsen. They had needed someone who could translate their broad strategy into direct action, someone with a proven track record who would operate autonomously. To find such a person, Brewer had engaged an experienced team of researchers to compile a list of candidates with experience matching particular criteria. The researchers worked on a contract basis and were never given any hint of the final objective. The profile they looked to match included extensive experience in Central and South America and a knowledge of all aspects of covert operations from initial recruitment to final debriefing. Brewer and Wallace had scrutinised each person the researchers proposed and when they felt it was merited, the candidate had been approached for further evaluation via a series of cut-outs. They followed this procedure without a hitch three times but unfortunately on each occasion an obstacle came to light that ruled out the prospect.

Then Larsen's name was put forward. From first opening the dossier, Wallace had gotten a sense he had not with the others. He was intrigued.

Michael Larsen had been working as an independent contractor for almost ten years, displaying an equal aptitude in both urban and non-urban environments. The information they had about his formative years was sketchy. Born in Hirtshals, Denmark, his birth certificate stated only his mother's name. The researchers believed his father was probably a Portuguese man who had died before he was born. It was assumed he had a decent childhood in forward-thinking, liberal Denmark, although one of the profilers on the team had wondered to what degree his mixed heritage and lack of a father would have figured. Early school report cards showed a reasonable aptitude for languages but otherwise he had been a largely unexceptional student. Denmark was one of a number of European countries that maintained a system of conscription, but rather than wait to see if he would be called, Larsen had enlisted in the army directly after leaving school. Subsequently he qualified for the Jægerkorpset, an elite Danish unit that was well respected internationally. It was common practice for Jægers to train with the British SAS and the US Rangers. Individual Danes had finished top of the ranger class on more than one occasion and while Larsen had not achieved this distinction, he had comfortably completed the training.

It was difficult to find out much about his subsequent career with the Jægers given the Danish military's secrecy regarding the unit. Eventually, though, the researchers managed to locate some men who had served with him and were willing to talk. Apparently, Larsen had shown an affinity for individual missions involving long-range reconnaissance and other specialist skills. Although it was not explicitly stated, the interviewers were convinced Larsen had been used to remove individuals identified by the security forces as hostiles. His ex-comrades remembered him as friendly enough, willing to share an off-duty beer, but no one recalled him forming any especially close friendships. It had come as a surprise when he had quit the military after almost ten years and, despite the researchers' best efforts, it had proved impossible to find out what he had done for the next couple of years.

The first record of him working as a mercenary had been in Africa and then a short while later the Middle East. After this he had come to Latin America where, except for a few stand-alone missions, he spent all his time. He had seen action in Ecuador, Guatemala, Colombia, Peru and Venezuela. During one of the Ecuadorian-Peruvian border disputes he had come to the attention of US intelligence who had employed him to carry out a series of assassinations. It didn't take long for prospective clients, state and private, to realise his talents. Not only could he be counted on to eliminate difficult-to-reach targets, he also had the tact and imagination for more intricate, subtle tasks. Larsen's opinion was that money was money, regardless of the source. At some point the CIA had grown unhappy with this, particularly when he was engaged by parties whose interests ran counter to theirs. The subject of his elimination was tabled briefly and had it been okayed, the task would have fallen to the Colombian CIA station chief to arrange. The man in question, now retired, had worked with Larsen extensively and told one of Brewer's researchers that, for as long as the matter was under consideration, he had been a nervous wreck. For whatever reason, the order was never given and the relationship between the Dane and the Agency was subsequently patched up when he once again went to work for them.

Then, a crisis.

Atypically, he took a contract in Africa. An English mercenary there had launched a military campaign aimed at reinstating a President who had been forced into exile. His efforts were meeting with such success that powerful interests had begun to worry. The country was oil rich but, while the military dictatorship was happy to play ball with the foreign multinationals, the president-in-waiting had made it clear that investigations and reforms of the oil industry would be his first order of business. Plainly the mercenary had to be eliminated but his security was so good, his men so loyal, that no one had been able to get close. Larsen somehow managed to gain the soldier's trust and found a way into his inner circle. He spent many hours in the Englishman's company and even gained direct access to the deposed president. Larsen's paymasters couldn't believe their good fortune and as far as they were concerned he could name his fee if he took both of them out.

Instead, inexplicably, he had walked away and left disaster looming for his clients. It didn't matter that the mercenary's efforts ultimately failed, Larsen's reputation was left in shreds. That had been his last assignment; since then, even when people who were willing to overlook his transgression had approached, he had turned them away.

Brewer had real reservations about using Larsen in light of what had happened in Africa, but at Wallace's behest and because of the difficulty they had experienced locating a suitable operative, he agreed they could try. He set about the normal procedure of setting up an approach and this was where they ran into difficulties.

All attempts by Brewer's intermediaries to engage Larsen in contract discussions met with failure. At first no reason was given and then when the go-betweens persisted, he had said that he would only deal with the principal directly. Brewer wanted to walk away, but Wallace, worried at their lack of progress, convinced him to meet with the Dane. Brewer had been beside himself with rage on his return and said they had to forget Larsen and move on. When pressed by Wallace, all he would say was that Larsen had been deliberately disrespectful and confrontational, refusing to believe he was the principal. Brewer said he believed Larsen had lost the vital respect for the command structure and was consequently too much of a risk. Perhaps Africa had unhinged him after all.

Weeks passed but, despite their efforts, no other candidate strong enough in all of the necessary areas emerged. Wallace, frustrated at seeing the whole project grinding to a halt, had insisted Brewer set up a meeting between him and Larsen.

The instructions for the rendezvous had duly arrived two days ago. Wallace was booked on a commercial flight from Chicago to New York and instructed to listen for his name on arrival. The PA system had directed him to one of the airline ticket desks where he was given a ticket for a flight to Philadelphia, leaving in less than fifty minutes. After a mad dash, he made it to the flight and on to Philadelphia. The sequence had repeated itself twice more over the course of the day, until finally an exhausted and frustrated Wallace found himself back in Chicago. This time, rather than an airline desk, he had been directed to a car rental desk and was soon leaving the airport in a Toyota Yaris. He had followed instructions issued to him via a cell phone, which had been left in the door compartment, until he had arrived in the run-down section of the city where the altercation had occurred.

"I think we should get down to business?" Wallace suggested.

"Go ahead."

"What do you know about the international trade in illegal drugs?"

"Brewer got far enough along the proposal to specify your area of interest, before I sent him packing, so I did some homework. Fifty million regular users of one form or another worldwide, according to UN estimates. Cocaine and heroin are still the most prevalent but the synthetic market's growing quickly, particularly in Asia."

"And financially?"

"I've seen a global annual estimate for the trade of $400 billion plus. There's a huge interdependency with the illegal arms trade. Guns for drugs are the lifeline for a host of revolutionaries and militias."

"So, how much of a chance would you give a privately funded initiative of dealing a serious blow to the industry?"

Larsen idled with his mug for a few seconds while he considered his answer. "Diversified Holdings' balance sheet valuation is around $70 billion and that's excluding Wallace Consulting. Forbes recently calculated your private fortune at $20 billion but I'd say that's more the value you're comfortable being circulated. Doesn't matter, even if you could mobilise all your resources, it wouldn't make a difference. The US Government spend billions each year and all they do is marginally slow the market's growth rate. Financially, you're nothing to sneeze at but you've mentioned a private operation, which I'm inferring means unsanctioned. Unsanctioned means secrecy, which by necessity means more expense and less efficiency."

"I'm not talking about a scenario where my wealth is pitted directly against the various cartels," Wallace replied. "I'm not too conceited to see where my limits lie. But why is it, do you suppose, that most state-backed initiatives are doomed to fail?"

"I think part of it's down to how futile it is to try to stop people doing what they really want to, but I'm guessing you're referring to the limitations imposed on the various agencies by politicians?"

"Exactly," he said. "Between the inadequate level of funding, bureaucratic obstructions and political cowardice, their hands are tied."

"So, they're all doomed to fail. What's your point?"

"Look at the problem from a different angle. Some experts may have the know-how to combat the trade, some governments the funding and some extremists the will but they're not aligned. Agreed?"

Larsen nodded.

"So, tell me what's the only organisation with the resources, knowledge and lack of scruples required to cripple a major drug cartel?"

Larsen thought about the question and when he realised where they were heading he smiled.

"Another cartel."

"Exactly."

"How?"

"A third-party sows disharmony between two of the largest players. Manufactures a full-scale war, fuels it at every opportunity. If this were perpetuated long enough, I think the flow of drugs into the consumer countries would be compromised."

"You're going to use the Gorgon's head."

Wallace's puzzlement was obvious.

"To kill Poseidon's sea beast and save Andromeda, Perseus cut off Medusa's head and used it to turn Cetus to stone. One monster destroying another."

Wallace still looked lost.

"Forget it, how would you incite this war?"

"Attack strategic locations and shipments owned by a particular group. Destroy them, totally. Ensure the attacks are so extreme that they can't be mistaken for the handiwork of an established state agency. Do this repeatedly and then arrange for the evidence to point in a specific direction."

"And I'd coordinate these attacks?"

"Yes. With Brewer's help, you'd recruit and train a different team for each attack. They'd have only one objective to achieve and then they'd be disbanded. Intelligence for the attacks would all be supplied. You'd be required to participate directly in some specific attacks to ensure an appropriate forensic trail."

"You can't guarantee the correct response is elicited."

"No, we can't. All we can do is plan it to the best of our ability. There's also a limit to how many operations we can mount, the risks will grow with each subsequent attack. If it hasn't worked by a previously agreed point then we'll simply abandon it."

"You mentioned supplying the appropriate intelligence. Where would that come from?" asked Larsen, draining his mug.

"Brewer, through his own company and former employers, has access to a lot of sensitive information regarding production and storage locations as well as shipping routes etc. The information is out there, it's just no one's ever used it effectively."

"So what are you proposing, pit one Colombian cartel against another?"

"Bigger than that," Wallace answered, leaning across the table. "The largest player in the world is a group of affiliated cartels controlled out of Colombia. They're known as the Madrigal Alliance, named after the man who pulled them together. It incorporates virtually all of South America's producers. It also deals with the main Mexican cartels."

"As partners or subordinates?"

"That's a matter of conjecture. Anyway, if enough external pressure could be exerted, I believe the Alliance would crumble." Wallace scrutinised Larsen's face, trying to gauge his reaction to the proposal.

"And you have another group in mind to go up against them?"

"Yes. What's required is an adversary that won't be cowed by the Alliance's reputation, a group prepared to take the fight to them. We've identified the Kosovar Fifteen Families as the best option. They have enormous wealth and a global reach."

"Why would they choose to target the South Americans? For your plan to work, the reasons for the attacks have to be believable, what would they have to gain?"

"They each control a major stake in the global heroin business but elements in both organisations have pushed for expansion. Initially that would provide us with what we need to get the ball rolling."

"Have you considered that if it worked, and each started destroying the other, you might be providing the perfect opportunity for one of the other, smaller groups to move up?"

"That's exactly what I'm banking on," Wallace said enthusiastically. "One of the reasons for the amount of drugs currently being trafficked is the general stability. No one's motivated enough to challenge the status quo. But if the two main players were weakened then others would be encouraged to expand and the conflict would spread. It wouldn't just be two sides then, it'd be a free-for-all and the more energy they put into fighting one another, the more drug production and distribution will suffer."

"Okay but why? What's the point of it all?"

"If fewer drugs are available, society benefits. Too many lives are being lost to addiction. Ideally, we'll set the whole business back, two, three, maybe even five years."

"You want to save people you don't know, most of whom probably don't even want to be saved?" Larsen asked disbelievingly.

"A lot of drug addicts may be willing but only because they were initially exploited."

"And what about the dirt-poor growers who rely on the crops to survive?"

"I can sympathise but their situation doesn't justify –"

"Remember," the Dane cut him off, "once you initiate violence, you've no way of knowing how it might spill over. Have you thought about the dangers to innocents?"

"I'm not totally clueless. I've carried out detailed analysis, made projections, had Brewer scrutinise them. They all agree that if we do this properly the fall-out should be minimal. Of course, there may be some isolated incidents but I can't use that as an excuse to dodge my responsibility."

Larsen stared at him.

"Look, I know you're trying to measure my commitment but there's really no –"

"So, your daughter's murder requires violence on this scale? Have you considered therapy?"

Wallace was thrown by the remark. Not just its callous flippancy but surprise that Larsen would have known about Carol at all. The part of him that was not in shock, not revisiting the nightmare, reprimanded him for his naivety. It was only natural that Larsen would have looked into his personal life.

Eighteen months had passed and the wound was as fresh as ever. He remembered the phone call from his lawyer; the police had been unable to locate him and had to go through the old family friend. Strange how the sum of an entire lifetime could change beyond recognition with one phone call.

He managed to regain his composure, preventing himself from falling apart right there.

"I'm … I'm guessing this is your crude attempt to ascertain my state of mind but I'm warning you, don't try your mind games with me. I know why I'm doing this; the question is your participation, so let's stick to that."

"Tell me about it."

"What?"

"About how she died; the reports weren't very detailed."

Wallace was stunned; based on his off-hand manner, the other man might as well have been asking about the weather. Brewer had been correct; he must be unhinged.

All this time wasted, trying to convince a crazy man, he thought. There was nothing else to do, Wallace started to rise shakily from his seat but Larsen reached over and gripped his arm firmly.

"I need to know what's driving you, otherwise I can't consider it. You'll probably find others who don't care but I need to know."

Wallace returned reluctantly to his seat. "Why? Why is it necessary? You're a professional, you'll be well-paid."

"Do you know how many times people in the field have found out, when it was too late, that the reasons they thought they were fighting for were just a lie? Or how often important people have expediently reversed a position they've said was irreversible and left men stranded?" Larsen asked bitterly. Then his voice softened a little. "I don't resent risking my life. Like you say, I'm well paid, but I've reached the stage where I need to know why."

Wallace weighed it up for a few moments and, at last, by the slimmest of margins he agreed to revisit the nightmare and explain what had happened to Carol and Elizabeth.

After the event, he had been successful in exerting pressure on the city authorities to deploy a greater police presence in the relevant precinct but, despite the resultant success, his anger remained. He then turned his attention to the wider problems that drug addiction visited upon society. He had lobbied for tougher legislation, better funding for the relevant enforcement agencies and more stringent monitoring of their effectiveness. Before long, however, he recognised how little he was accomplishing. Like using a bucket to stop the incoming tide. He looked at other avenues. One option was to help those battling addiction. He researched the most successful treatments and had committed to starting a string of best-practice treatment centres. While it was gratifying to see progress there, it was still not enough. His thoughts finally started to move in a different direction. Once he was convinced this was the way to go, he had stood down as CEO of Diversified Holdings so that he could dedicate the time required.

When he was finished his account, he sat back, drained, and waited for Larsen to respond.

"Okay, regardless of how well we plan it, no matter what precautions we take, there's a chance that what you're planning could be discovered. Are you prepared for that? Is Brewer?"

"This means everything to me, I'm prepared for all eventualities. Brewer's a professional, like you."

"Other than you two, who else knows?"

"No one."

"Okay, we're done for now."

"What do you mean?" Wallace asked. "I need an answer."

"I'll be in touch."

"When?" he asked, exasperated.

"If you haven't heard within a month, start looking for someone else."

Aware of how vulnerable he had made himself, Wallace put a hand out to stop him.

"Why the insistence on meeting face-to-face?"

"If we do proceed, you need to be clear you're not insulated from me. Face-to-face reinforces that."

Larsen contacted Wallace two weeks later, agreeing to take the mission.

The incessant wind howling through the skeletal structure brought Wallace back to the present. In all of his years as the focal point for major decisions, he had never felt so much out of his depth. He had been determined to call it off and yet when he was presented with the opportunity, he couldn't follow through. He knew part of him had hesitated because of what Larsen had said regarding the targets being capable of full recovery. But that hadn't been the only thing that stopped him.

For some reason Larsen's opinion of him mattered to Wallace. Why the view of someone like the Dane should be so important was unclear to him but for some reason it was. He could see that Larsen had clearly given himself over totally to this crusade of his. When he had asked Wallace if the billionaire meant to abandon the mission, the mercenary had tried to appear dispassionate but not quite succeeded. Wallace did not look forward to breaking the news of his decision after the Cartagena operation but knew they had to stop.

Wallace remembered his early frustration at how long Larsen had spent researching the targets before launching a major operation. A year passed after him accepting before he saw concrete action. Major dealers in Chicago had been eliminated and drugs removed from circulation. It was only when Brewer produced copies of the police report of the nightclub killings that he understood the methods used.

He was surprised that he was not more revolted. Brewer mentioned that Larsen had insisted that if they were going to provoke the proper response, they could not afford to be any less savage than their quarry. None of the victims were innocent and as long as that continued Wallace had no qualms about the measures Larsen took.

Shortly after the Chicago incident, the operation really hit its stride and Madrigal's Alliance suffered more major setbacks. What was surprising was how few of the attacks merited significant media scrutiny, most escaping their attention altogether. Those that were reported made local, sometimes regional, headlines but that was the extent of it. Wallace had been concerned that the DEA or some other government agency might realise the orchestrated nature of the attacks too early, before the desired effect had been realised, but his fears proved groundless.

Something else that had confounded Wallace was how long it had taken to spur Madrigal into action. On select missions, clear indications were left of Kosovar involvement, but it had seemed that these were often missed, whether through virtue of being too obscure or through sloppy investigation.

The impact they had made on the flow of drugs into the US in their first eighteen months of operation was minimal – hardly surprising considering the total volumes involved. With the money he had ploughed into this, he would have been better off just buying the drugs directly and destroying them. It was not until the attack on the Mexican heroin refinery that anyone had started pointing the finger at the Balkans.

The escalation since then had been shocking. Starting with the attacks in Spain and Austria, it seemed some new atrocity was making headlines every other week. The latest estimates put the amount of cocaine and heroin crossing the border at fifty per cent less than the previous year. Areas of Europe, while not affected as dramatically, were also seeing major reductions. Prices were driven up as availability waned and the social stresses brought on by the shortages were deeply felt.

It all should have been profoundly satisfying. The task he'd decided to dedicate the remainder of his life to was starting to take shape, starting to succeed. And for the first few weeks it was. He didn't agonise over the plight of legions of addicts who were forced to endure a form of torture as their supply dwindled. Although he would have preferred that they be spared, these were the people he had assured Larsen he had thought about when the mercenary had mentioned overspill. But as the conflict escalated, more and more innocents were sucked in: people who had never touched drugs and had been merely getting on with their lives; passers-by who had been fatally caught up in pitched battles; law enforcement officers who had lost their lives trying to restore order; and countless other victims whose deaths were hastened by the further deterioration of conditions in society's most stricken areas.

One event had particularly impacted him.

Wallace had been coming back from a business trip and stopped in an airport lounge for a drink. While he was sipping his scotch, his eyes were drawn to a news report playing on the muted television above the bar. The images were from someone's phone and showed a little girl's body sprawled on the pavement. Emergency response personnel were at the scene. Wallace asked the barman to turn up the volume and he heard how four-year-old Marsha Corley had fallen from the fifth-storey fire escape to her death. She and two younger children had been left by their mother four days before when she had headed off to search for her next fix. After the food they had been left had run out, the report explained, they had become desperate. The little girl, unable to open the main door to the apartment, had resorted to the fire escape in an attempt to call for help. Since then images of Marsha, interspersed with memories of his granddaughter, had haunted him.

"To discuss the ailing Plan Coca, I'm joined by Dr Robert Holmes, author of a series of books on the international drugs trade, and Senator Charles Dalton, a passionate Plan Coca advocate."

Leonard Boswell, host of Behind the Headlines, paused a moment as if he was pondering the serious issue at hand. "Dr Holmes, let's start by looking at the recent revelations regarding the involvement of US companies in military operations on Colombian soil; what's the situation as we currently understand it?"

Holmes had a weather-beaten face topped with an untidy mop of grey hair and slouched so much that he looked in danger of slipping from his chair.

"There are five US companies which have contracts with the State Department as part of the Plan," the author responded. "The contracts account for more than fifty per cent of their revenue."

"Are these companies effectively providing state-approved mercenary services to the Colombian government?"

"Absolutely," replied Holmes. "That's the stock-in-trade of these companies, their stated business; a well-established business."

"*Rubbish,*" *countered Dalton.* "*These are professional companies engaged in the provision of expert training services under controlled conditions, nothing more.*"

"*Controlled enough to have had five of their employees killed a short time ago?*" *Holmes retorted.*

Before Dalton could come back, Boswell cut across him. "*Senator, there was strong reaction to the incident Dr Holmes is referring to. A fumigation run which went terribly wrong and resulted in the death of a number of US citizens working for the contract companies. Were we guilty of overreaction?*"

"*No, of course not. The deaths were tragic,*" *the Senator replied,* "*but it would only compound the tragedy if we were to allow them to be used by opportunists whose only interest is in undermining Plan Coca.*"

"*So, the issue of these companies conducting business in Colombia has been blown out of proportion?*" *Boswell asked Holmes.*

"*Well, I don't know about that but, certainly, if people want to examine aspects of Plan Coca there are other places they could start.*"

"*And where would that be?*"

Dalton fidgeted in his seat.

"*I think the biggest problem is the Plan's obvious failure to address the human rights violations which the Colombian paramilitaries continue to commit,*" *Holmes said.*

"*But isn't one of the Plan's main remits to eliminate FARC and the ELN?*"

"*It's not them I'm referring to. There's overwhelming proof that a number of other paramilitary organisations are operating under the direction of the Colombian Military. The well-intentioned policies of the US administration are* being used by elements in the Colombian power structure for their own ends."

"There's no 'overwhelming proof', simply a lot of unsubstantiated claims," Dalton shot back.

"Can you give any hard examples?" Boswell demanded of Holmes.

"Well, there've been numerous occasions where US equipment provided to the Colombian army has ended up in the hands of these organisations. Independent humanitarian organisations have verified these weapons were subsequently used to slaughter innocent people."

Before Dalton could question Holmes' claim, Boswell interrupted again.

"If the US government were to insist that all links between the Colombian military and these groups were severed, would this address your concerns?"

Holmes shook his head, "Unfortunately, there's strong circumstantial evidence that the majority, as much as seventy-five per cent of the Colombian command, have been directly implicated, by action or omission, in the campaigns of death squads."

"This is ridiculous," the furious Dalton exploded. "I can't believe the viewers out there are believing this nonsense for a second. What are you saying? That the United States of America is knowingly aiding paramilitary death squads?"

"I want to be clear that I'm not suggesting for a second that either US Forces or particular politicians who support the Plan are in any way involved," Holmes said, shaking his head. "But don't you think it's worrying that no one in the State Department would be aware of this collusion?"

"What's the precise nature of this circumstantial evidence you refer to?" Boswell asked him.

"*Consider how often the right-wing paramilitaries have moved in perfect sync with the Colombian army's Plan Coca manoeuvres. Time and again the army announces it's about to target an area that its unofficial allies have already established a presence in. The paramilitaries operate as an advance guard, quashing the organised civilian opposition to the crop eradication.*"

Boswell was facing Holmes by this stage, apparently absorbed by what the author had to say, with his back practically turned to the Senator. Dalton could see that it was quickly becoming a two-way exchange, an exchange which he realised would further damage Plan Coca's public perception. Unfortunately, there was no civil way in which he could re-assert his presence and the Plan would not benefit by its strongest champion appearing ill-mannered or aggressive. He resolved to sit tight in the hope that the normally even-handed Boswell would give him a chance to rebut Holmes' claims.

"*And what would you contend is behind the paramilitary's actions?*" the presenter asked.

"*Greed. There's the obvious greed involved in controlling areas which can produce such abundant quantities of coca and opium but there's also the fortunes which stand to be made from the planned infrastructural development.*"

"*How would that work?*"

"*Half a billion dollars has been earmarked as part of Plan Coca to develop the area specifically hit by the Plan. This is a laudable attempt by the US Government to ensure that the people hit most heavily by fumigation and crop eradication are helped.*"

"*So the areas which are supposed to benefit from the aid have suddenly become incredibly valuable?*" Boswell offered.

"*Exactly, the paramilitaries and those who back them want to move the people out of these areas so that they're the ones to benefit from this windfall.*"

"*Well, you've certainly raised some points which one hopes will be addressed by the pro-Plan contingent,*" Boswell said, turning to Dalton, leading the Senator to believe he was going to get his opportunity to point out the flaws in Holmes' assertions until the host continued, "*Now, onto another worrying aspect of the Plan, the link many of its critics have established between it and the ongoing violence in our major cities. Senator, Paul Forester writing today in the Washington Tribune quotes unnamed Capitol Hill sources who maintain that the DEA has been aware that the Colombian cartels have been engaged in a war with their European counterparts for some time. Your reaction?*"

One of Dalton's aides had mentioned the article briefly before they had gone on the air but there had been no warning that Boswell would raise it. Totally unprepared, nonetheless he had to attempt an answer.

"*Well, it may be that the European crime syndicates have seen how much Plan Coca has weakened the Colombian cartels and are seeking to exploit the situation but …*"

"*In fact, Mr Forester contends that the feud between these drug superpowers may be more to blame for the drug shortages of recent months and that the apparent successes of Plan Coca have been unfairly flattering.*"

"*That's preposterous. The success of Plan Coca has been well established and is a matter of record. All of this is pure conjecture coming from the anti-Plan camp.*"

"*I see … Well, thank you Senator, Doctor, I'm sure we'll be returning to Plan Coca quite soon.*" The camera closed in, blocking out the shot of the two guests to focus on a *head-and-shoulders shot of Boswell. "Now, when we return after the break, we'll have Andrew Pryor with us for our weekly look at the markets."*

———

eight

Andrew Brewer hurried through the park, oblivious to the happy scenes playing out around him. Kids threw frisbee, joggers and power walkers went about their circuits industriously, and all around small groups of people lay on the grass soaking up the sunshine. They may as well have been invisible. He hated these meetings. It would have been preferable if they could have conducted all communication remotely, but these personal contacts served a vital purpose of reassuring both parties of the other's continued commitment. It didn't help him that there was nothing obviously suspicious in them being seen together. There were countless plausible reasons why they might be meeting but he knew why they actually *were* meeting.

As usual his advance team had vouched for the security of the location, a location he had chosen himself. His appointment had arrived alone fifteen minutes earlier and multiple sweeps of the park had been performed. The other man reclined on a park bench, head back and eyes closed, enjoying the good weather. Sensing Brewer's approach, he stood to greet him and suggested a stroll along one of the park's paths.

"Well," Brewer's companion began, "favourable reports from Colombia. The pipelines have been free of attack for six weeks now. The pressure the Alliance is under has effectively crippled the rebels. I'd be surprised if they last out the year. I think it's time to start tying up loose ends."

"Sooner the better," agreed Brewer.

"A quick run-through on the other objectives. Madrigal first. He's very vulnerable. A leadership challenge is imminent. This time the challenge will succeed!"

"Serves the bastard right," smiled Brewer viciously. "All he had to do was play ball but he insisted on sticking his nose into areas that didn't concern him. Once he's out of the way, with the new territories we've gained, it should be no time at all before production's running at an all-time high."

"For there to be any point in revamping production, the hostilities will have to stop," the other stressed. "Steps are being taken to persuade the Kosovars to desist but they'll have to see that the Alliance is also stopping."

"With the Alliance in such disarray, I can't see why that wouldn't be forthcoming. They all desperately need a chance to get revenues flowing again."

"Yes," he agreed, "but we'll only get one shot at a ceasefire, so Larsen needs to be reined in. Can you take care of that?"

"Of course. I assume he'll need to be eliminated?" Brewer asked, failing to hide his enthusiasm.

"Leave that to me, all you need is to stall his next operation; give me some time."

"Are you sure? I've handled all of the field operations to date; I can set something up with one phone call."

"No, you're doing enough already. I'll deal with him."

Brewer would have preferred to plan Larsen's death himself. He suspected the other man did not trust his objectivity where the Dane was concerned.

"Okay, if you insist," Brewer said.

"I know Larsen's potential and we need to be sure

about this. If he were to learn ..." He drifted for a moment before he snapped himself out of it. "Anyway, returning to our objectives, between the negative press following the contractors' deaths, which you so ably organised, and the coverage of the drug feud, Plan Coca's in tatters."

"Still, there's been no indication yet that the plug will be pulled," Brewer reminded him.

"It's already been agreed at the highest levels," came the reassurance. "All that's required is to provide the administration with the appropriate opportunity. The ceasefire we've discussed will serve. They'll rush to issue an announcement of the Plan's suspension."

"Suspension implies temporary," Brewer pointed out.

"That's simply an exercise in face-saving, it won't be relaunched. I doubt a similar strategy will be contemplated again in our lifetime."

"Excellent. Alright, all other loose ends are well in hand. Excluding Larsen, the other participants who constitute possible threats can be handled within the week."

"With no danger of Larsen being alerted?"

"None whatsoever," Brewer answered confidently. "We deliberately structured the operations so that he was provided with a completely new team each time out. When the mission was over he never saw them again." Brewer's companion did not appear to be quite convinced by his certainty, so he added, "Tuur was a perfect example. Once you alerted me of his indiscretions, he'd been taken care of within seventy-two hours, and Larsen's still none the wiser."

"How do you think Wallace is going to react when it starts grinding to a halt?"

"He'll be relieved to get as far away from the whole mess as he can. He's lost the stomach for his vendetta and, once you arrange for Larsen to be dealt with, he'll have the perfect excuse to drop it. I'm still not convinced we shouldn't just get rid of him too."

"All in good time, if he doesn't pose an immediate danger, I'd rather wait. We're already making a lot of moves and he's still got some very powerful connections, why take an unnecessary risk by alerting them?"

"That about wraps everything up then!" said Brewer, preparing to say goodbye.

"Not quite. There may be one more person we need to consider."

"Who?"

"A DEA agent, Diane Mesi, who's approached the Agency for help. She's looking at the possibility that the conflict is being orchestrated by a third party."

"I thought you said the investigations were being managed. How did this happen? Jesus, how much does she know? Who has she been talking to?"

"Take it easy. She's in a minority of one, isolated and a long way from figuring out what's going on. If I'm correct, she's heading in entirely the wrong direction."

"How can we be sure? Shouldn't she be dealt with as a precaution?"

"The situation's being watched closely. If at any stage it seems more prudent to handle her, we'll know."

After Brewer had been pacified a little more, they finished up the meeting and he headed back to his waiting limousine. By contrast, his companion, deciding it would be a sin to waste the glorious weather by returning to the office immediately, started another leisurely circuit of the park.

She pushed herself back from the desk, stood up and tried

to stretch the day's tension from her shoulders. Another long frustrating day was coming to an end. Any sense of momentum generated after her visit to Tom Hughes at the CIA had almost totally dissipated. Mesi had spent countless hours talking to the various police officers responsible for the investigations of the attacks on Alliance resources but had gotten nowhere. There had been no evidence of involvement by any of the first group of operatives whom Tom had identified and she was now working her way through a second batch. Meanwhile Tom had been equally unsuccessful in turning anything up from a series of interviews with personnel from the various stations under his control. She knew that a lot of investigations succeeded through this kind of tedious, repetitive investigative work but it was becoming difficult to keep her hopes alive. Tuur's death had been a real body blow. Had he been alive perhaps he could have worked with Tom to learn Lorcy's real identity. That one breakthrough might have been all they needed. Wearily, she walked over to the water fountain and splashed some cold water on her face.

Her lack of progress had only encouraged Samuels in believing he had been right all along. She still found it hard to understand why he had such a preference for believing that it was a straightforward war between the Kosovars and the Alliance. Yes, her theory meant they still had work to do to discover what had kicked off the conflict, but look at the alternative. If this was just a bloody transatlantic crime war then how did you even begin to go about stopping it? At least a third party provocateur, if identified, might be neutralised.

She looked at her watch and saw it was after eleven o'clock. More than sixteen hours in the office. She should really head home: some sleep and time away might help. She mulled it over and decided to give it another half hour before calling it a day. She decided to put Tom's folders to one side and try a change of approach; she couldn't bear to trawl through another file for the time being. She took out a sheet of blank paper, turned her back on the computer and started randomly writing facts about the investigation, possible theories, ways to progress, whatever came to mind. At first, all it accomplished was to relax her a little, limber up mental muscles fatigued from hours of poring over documentation. But then something gradually started to emerge.

None of the crime scenes had supplied anything other than the indications of Kosovar involvement. She was convinced this had been left deliberately, meaning the perpetrators had successfully avoided leaving any real indication of their identity. If this kind of professionalism was a constant throughout all of their activities, the investigation was doomed to fail. However, what had been obvious, especially after speaking to Tuur, was that the Mexican operation had required good advance intelligence. Tom and she had dedicated a lot of time to finding people who might have contributed to it. But due to the fact that she was the only full-time person on the investigation, they had pursued the intelligence angle solely by looking for likely candidates in Tom's files. At the edge of her consciousness, she began to realise there was another route to explore. It was a long shot but worth a try. Was there a chance that even one of the reconnaissance phases of any operation had not been performed to the same standard of professionalism as the subsequent attacks? If so, a trail may have been left. A trail she could follow.

She spent some time trying to figure out a way to test this before deciding that what was required was a query that linked several distinct databases, something far beyond her own modest SQL skills. Luckily she got on well with one of the senior data operators and he agreed to return to the office after she had apologised for disturbing him at home but stressed the how important it was. When he arrived she explained what was required. She wanted to compile a list of people who had entered more than one of a list of specified countries up to ninety days before a number of associated dates. The countries had all been the sites of possible operations and the dates those of the attacks. Ninety minutes later, after the query had been built and started, she headed home.

The scope of the search meant it took the query over thirty-six hours to run. One hundred and fifteen people were found to have visited more than one country within the specified timeframes with thirty-four visiting more than two. Mesi set about the task of running background checks on these thirty-four, which took the remainder of the working week and right through to Saturday evening. Nineteen people worked for multinationals involved in either telecommunications or manufacturing. She put these to one side. Eleven more were students who had been travelling during their vacation and were now back at college. These too could be disregarded for the moment. The last four were more difficult. All appeared to provide a consultancy service which was vaguely defined. It took almost a full day to nail down what the first two did before being able to dismiss them. It was only on the third of the four that she hit pay dirt.

Richard Kates worked as a contractor for a venture

capital company ostensibly looking for viable investment opportunities in emerging markets. The first thing that drew her attention was his extended tenure in the Marines, hardly the typical background for an investment advisor. A closer look at the company he was contracted by revealed a significant proportion of its ventures were related to either security consultancy or arms manufacture and she started to feel a stir of excitement. The company's funding was particularly interesting. Eighty per cent of it came from a trust, set up and run by a Washington law firm, with the remainder coming from a variety of sources. Piercing the trust would be difficult and time-consuming. Looking into the management of the company was more easily arranged. It was at this point that the name of Andrew Brewer emerged.

She kept reminding herself not to jump to conclusions, yet the longer she looked into Brewer's background, the more difficult it became. He had formerly worked for the CIA, spending more than twenty years with the Agency before entering the private sector. The company he had subsequently founded, Spartan Personnel, had enjoyed a spectacular rise as a provider of lucrative defence contracts, making a practice of beating more established competitors during the tendering phase. In addition to his role as CEO of Spartan, Brewer served on the board of a number of smaller concerns, one of which was the venture capital company who had employed Kates. Her instinct told her that Brewer was the key she had been looking for, he had all the necessary contacts and means to put together operations like these, but caution forced to her to consider whether she was making too much of a tenuous chain of coincidences. After all, there was so much legitimate international business travel these days that almost any pattern might be present if you analysed flight records for long enough. Even if Kates was connected to the attacks, where was the solid basis for saying Brewer was involved? Was she so desperate that she was resorting to leaps of pure fantasy? Maybe so, but it was not as if she had a lot of alternatives. She couldn't leave it here; she needed to pursue this to its conclusion.

If her hunch was correct, she needed to determine what it might mean. Andrew Brewer, affluent businessman and respected former government employee, had set the major drug powers of the world at one another's throats. What motive might he have? Was it to add such instability to the South American continent, where Spartan did most of its work, as to lead to a greater need for his services? That didn't seem plausible but she was at a loss to think of another obvious motive. She knew she would need a compelling one if she was to convince Samuels or even Marshall that they needed to look at someone of Brewer's reputation.

She debated whether or not to call Tom. He was sure to have known Brewer considering their similar backgrounds and he was far better placed to comment on whether her suspicions were remotely credible. She reached for the phone and then stopped herself. It might be unfair, she thought, to put him in a position where he risked incurring the enmity of Brewer based on nothing more than her hunch. From the little she knew of Tom and based on how hard he had worked to help so far, he might feel obliged to take the risk. No, she would wait until she had something more solid to go on. She realised the danger that investigating Brewer posed to her own career but she couldn't let this go. A check of the map revealed that Kates' residence in

Charles City, Virginia was within driving distance of DC. If she drove up there the next day, she could conceivably be a step closer to Brewer before the weekend was over. After so little progress for so long the prospect was impossible to resist.

Early Sunday morning Mesi left the city, trying not to let her excitement get the better of her. The scenery changed gradually from urban sprawl to unspoiled countryside. It was a pity, she thought, that it took something like this to get her out of the city. Kates' tax returns since the Marines had specified his main source of income as consultancy and a small recreational facility he owned. The facility hosted survival days for businessmen who wanted something more than the standard paintball experience, and he lived only a few miles away from it. She had no idea whether he would be home; for all she knew he could be travelling, but she could not call ahead. If she was to have any chance of learning something, she needed every edge she could get. Pre-warned, he could either have time to fabricate a plausible story for his trips or simply disappear. She passed a sign indicating only five miles to Charles City and felt butterflies start to flutter in her stomach.

Roger Abeylan looked through his field glasses at the small window, satisfied with what he saw. For three days they had shadowed Kates, waiting for the right time. The instructions were clear: avoiding detection was paramount, the body must be disposed of so that it would never be found. Abeylan didn't know what his target had done or who wanted him dead. He was happy to work through a broker – ignorance provided protection. Forewarned of

Kates' military service, he was careful not to rush. The opportunity had finally presented itself when Kates had headed out to the deserted survival centre on the Sunday.

The facility was situated about a mile from the road and accessed by a dirt trail. Kates sat in the small hut which, along with living quarters for clients staying overnight and a storehouse, formed three sides of a square. Abeylan and his partner lay concealed in the high grass on the perimeter of the square. Even though they were confident the target was alone, they had decided to wait for him to exit rather than try to take him in the building. They would shoot him as he came down the front steps, bring their car up and load the body in the trunk. There was less chance of the unknown that way and less clean-up after the fact. Once they had ditched Kates' car in the parking lot of the nearest train station, they would dispose of the body. Simple. Moving the car was a slight risk, but worthwhile, as it would delay questions being asked, an important consideration to the client.

At last Kates stood up and put on his jacket. Abeylan signalled to his companion to get ready. They fired when he reached the second step. The body jerked, pitched down the steps and lay still. They moved in cautiously, only relaxing when there was no doubt of the kill. While his companion fetched their vehicle, Abeylan waited with the corpse.

Perfect, he thought, almost done.

There had been nobody at Kates' house and his neighbours had been unable to say whether he was away. Mesi decided she would try the survival centre, and if he wasn't there, she would write the trip off as a waste of time and head back home.

What would she do if she did not get to talk to Kates? She felt she had definitely stumbled onto something with him and his connection to Brewer but, other than the time Thomas Hughes could spare her, she was working on her own. Given the number of ventures Brewer was connected to, a thorough background check on his corporate involvement could take months, even leaving aside his time at the Agency.

Driving into the compound, she saw two vehicles in front of the main office and, momentarily, felt a rush of satisfaction. She had tracked down Kates; things might just be starting to look up, she thought. A man opened the trunk of one of the vehicles and started back around to the far side of the vehicle. His back was to her so he didn't see her approach or hear her car and by the time she had closed the distance, he was already obscured. She slowed the car and was just about to cut the engine when he re-emerged accompanied by another man. Then she processed what was unfolding in front of her. The two men were labouring to carry what she recognised as a body bag.

She started doing a U-turn. One of the men released his burden and levelled an automatic machine gun at her. Making a snap decision, Mesi gunned the car straight at him rather than continuing the turn, which would only offer an easier target.

Her car smacked into the back of the parked vehicle, pinning the gunman's legs between them and hurling the machine gun from his hands. Her body whipped forward on impact and hit the activated airbag with a hard jolt. Struggling to extricate herself from the airbag, she pawed at her door handle, aware of how vulnerable she was. She feebly pushed herself out onto the ground and drew her automatic as a hail of bullets ripped through her car, shattering the windows in a crescendo of flying glass. Her left shoulder ignited with a stabbing pain but, ignoring it, she scrambled on her haunches, up along the side of the car, hoping to position its engine block between herself and the remaining gunman. The man she had hit was lying across her bonnet, thrashing in pain, his legs crumpled terribly between the vehicles. Their eyes locked, both frozen for a second, before he gathered himself to alert his companion to her movement. If the gunman learned her exact position, his firepower was so superior that it would be over immediately. Left with no other choice, she fired three shots into the pinned man's chest. There was an instant burst of fire and she could almost feel the bullets punching through the air above her. She was fairly sure he was on the far side of the two vehicles but did not know what direction he was moving in. Dropping to the ground, she caught a glimpse of his feet and saw him edging slowly back along the vehicles in the same direction as her but further toward the back of her car. Some way of initiating action was required; waiting and trying to respond was sure to get her killed. Calculating how quickly he was moving, she gambled, scuttling quickly on her hands and knees around the vehicles behind him towards the driver's door of their car. She tried the handle gently. It opened with a sound she was sure he must have heard. It was too late, though, to go back. Crawling as quietly as she could, face down, across the seats, she lay there with her eyes trained on the passenger door window and prayed he did not see her first.

The vulnerability of her situation struck her. If he changed direction or simply started spraying both cars indiscriminately, she would be dead. Her nerve wavered and she fought to resist the temptation to retreat from her position and make a run for it. The knowledge of how easy a target she would be over open ground was all that stopped her.

The pain in her shoulder reared. For a moment she felt light-headed and lost touch with where she was before snapping back with an effort. Unsure how many seconds she had drifted, her heart was pounding, waiting for him to appear. Beyond her ragged breathing, she could hear nothing else.

Hold the gun steady; focus just beyond the scope.

She repeated this mantra over and over, trying to ignore the mounting discomfort. She glanced around and started to doubt whether she could see far enough beyond the window from where she was lying. If he was even a few paces away from the vehicle she might not be able to see him pass. She needed to adjust her position. Was it too late? Would she give herself away?

Just do it quickly!

She lost sight of the window for the briefest moment while she shifted her elbows on the seat, and when she looked back along the gun-sight, her vision was filled with the surprised face of the gunman. The barrel of his gun appeared.

Oh God.

Her whole left arm was numb, the hand unfeelingly supporting the other which was gripping the gun. It should have been such a simple thing to get her finger to squeeze the trigger, but despite the frantic instructions from her brain, nothing was happening. She looked directly into the muzzle pointed at her. The next second the world simply became a cacophony of noise.

It took some time for her to register what had happened, that, somehow, she had survived. A quick mental inventory of her physical state revealed that other than her shoulder, there was nothing else seriously wrong. She clambered across the seats to look out the shattered window. His torso had been hit at least twice and he lay there motionless. Collapsing down into the car, she sank into unconsciousness. More than an hour passed before she could rouse herself to call for assistance.

Samuels and Marshall had to wait more than a day before they were allowed to see her. She had been hit in the upper left side of her body. There was one clean exit wound while another bullet had shattered her collarbone and dispersed bone fragments through her trapezius. The doctors had removed the bullet, strapped her up and treated her for blood loss. Once she was out of surgery, she had been heavily sedated and left to sleep.

When they entered her room, she sat upright in the bed, TV on with the sound turned down. The heavy strapping, IV drip and her pale complexion combined to paint a pathetic figure.

"Diane, you sure know how to frighten us! I don't know what to say, you shouldn't have felt the need to go out there alone," Marshall said awkwardly.

She nodded slightly, trying to stay as still as possible but even that small movement brought on a wave of nausea.

"We have some news on one of the assailants," Samuels said, adopting a business-like air. "His prints identify him as a Cuban immigrant, Roger Abeylan."

"He had a record?" she asked.

"In Miami. The police there say he was very bad news – a suspected contract killer. He served time but they never had enough to put him away for good."

"One of the officers we talked to said he suspected Abeylan had connections, friends, the type that could walk through walls," Marshall added.

"Spooks?" she asked, receiving a confirming nod.

She told them about the link between Kates and Brewer. She could see the possible implications register with both men despite any doubts they might have.

"Someone, let's put the issue of whether it was Brewer to one side for the moment, was obviously looking to sever the ties to Kates," Marshall said. "Problem is they succeeded. We don't have anywhere near enough to approach Brewer. If there was someone else like Kates out there we could talk to … "

She shook her head, the air of defeat evident.

"Kates was our one chance. The only reason he showed up was someone's sloppiness. Even if they've made other mistakes, it's clear they're cleaning them up."

"There's no chance of finding this Lorcy you've spoken about?"

"What do we have? A questionable physical description and a fictitious identity. I've been trying to track him down since I returned from France. For all we know, he's been handled the same way as Kates."

"What about putting Brewer under surveillance?" Samuels proposed.

Mesi didn't think Samuels had quite come around to agreeing with her suspicions of Brewer's involvement, but he clearly wasn't blind to the scene before him or to the consequences if she were subsequently proved to be correct while he had simply ignored her.

"We can talk about it," Marshall answered and then added a warning. "But considering who Brewer is and the circles he moves in, I don't know how feasible it is." He quickly changed the subject, turning to Mesi, "Diane, we've been told we can't stay too long but one of us will come back tomorrow. The doctors have said it's going to take time for you to recover and I want you to listen to them. I'll make sure you're kept up to date on developments."

After they had left, she looked at the mute screen and desperately tried to ignore the wave of depression threatening to engulf her.

The place he had picked for the meeting could not have contrasted more with their previous rendezvous. This was a part of Washington where green areas and recreational spaces were very low on the list of priorities. Down here, there were just two imperatives: get as much as you could and do all you could to hold onto it. Drugs flourished here, the inhabitants needing the temporary escape they afforded more than most. Children learnt lessons not found on any school curriculum, and their parents, already ground down by the bleakness, could do little to help them. Generations ago people here had left their doors unlocked and kids had played on street corners. Now flak jackets and armour-piercing bullets were the order of the day.

He had chosen the lobby of an abandoned tenement right in the centre of the projects. The setting matched his mood perfectly. Poor judgement had jeopardised everything. He watched from a darkened recess as Brewer came through the main doorway and looked around searchingly. Brewer's unease was palpable and the other man remained where he was, unannounced, watching, letting it build. As the contractor's agitation became more and more pronounced it manifested in frequent glances at his watch and lots of pacing back and forth. At all previous meetings, he had let Brewer set the time and place, happy to indulge him and accommodate his preference for having a small protection team. This time, he had issued a summons, which did not allow for any such luxuries. Deciding there was no more pleasure to be gotten from watching the contractor squirm, he emerged from the alcove. Brewer saw him approaching and, realising he had been spied upon, became visibly annoyed.

"What the hell kind of game is this? I don't think spur of the moment meetings are very wise. When we deviate from procedure we run the greatest risk."

He almost laughed at Brewer's transparent attempt to seize the initiative.

"Isn't there something we need to discuss?" he asked.

Brewer stared uncomprehendingly at him.

"Roger Abeylan?"

"Abeylan?"

"You do know him, don't you?"

Brewer realised something must have gone wrong and the angry façade disappeared.

"Yes, I've used him in the past. He's always proven first class, as a matter of fact, I've decided to use him on the current clean-up phase. Is that a problem? We did agree to leave the details to me?"

Again the obvious attempt to exert authority. He said nothing, letting Brewer work himself up even more. "His assignment has been given. It's multi-stage but there are protocols. We can abort if you're unhappy."

"Tell me, one of these stages, does it involve Richie Kates?"

Brewer was surprised to hear him mention Kates by name; he had not thought his companion knew any of the individual operatives.

"Yes, he's someone I've evaluated as a potential security risk. Given time, he might be able to piece some of the operation together. We used him on some of the reconnaissance missions."

The other man shook his head, not believing what he was hearing.

"At approximately four o'clock yesterday afternoon, a tactical response team and medical unit were alerted and told to make their way to Kates' workplace where a DEA agent had come under fire."

The short pause that followed lasted only a second or two but to Brewer it seemed interminable as he struggled to digest the news before coming to the only feasible conclusion.

"Mesi?" came the worried guess.

"She'd gone out there to speak to Kates. When she arrived, Abeylan and another man were loading Kates' body into the trunk of a car."

The fact that the DEA had Abeylan's name meant that the Cuban had been either apprehended or killed.

"Is he in custody?"

"No, luckily," Brewer's companion said, making no attempt to hide his scorn. "Mesi somehow managed to kill Abeylan and his accomplice. Before you ask, she survived reasonably unscathed."

Brewer rubbed his face, trying to calculate how much damage had been done. He knew there might be a link from

Kates to him but it was so insubstantial. "Okay, we've had a setback but it's recoverable. Kates was dead before anyone could talk to him, and even if Abeylan was questioned before he died, he was working through a cut-out. There are no direct ties to us." With no response forthcoming, Brewer felt the pressure build. "I can arrange another team to follow up on Abeylan's remaining work," he continued. "It won't take more than a day or two. The top people in the DEA may be forced to throw a few more resources at Mesi's investigation but all the loose ends will have been dealt with before it goes anywhere." Brewer was being carried along by the momentum of his rationalisation by this stage. "The conflict will start to subside and they'll lose interest. It's not as if the DEA are eager to dig too deep in Colombia, not with their skeletons. We'll be exactly where projected, in control and –"

He was cut short by the other man's cell phone ringing.

"It's done? ... Only the driver? ... You're sure? Good. I'm just finished, you can send in the clean-up team." He finished the call and, reaching into his overcoat pocket, removed a gun fitted with a suppressor. "When I stop to think, it's probably better this way," he said coldly. "You're a liability and at some stage you're bound to screw up again. Who knows who you'll pull down with you? I mapped everything out; all you had to do was arrange a little subcontracting and you couldn't even handle that." He pointed the gun at Brewer. "You would have been Mesi's next call and all because you were too sloppy to put the sufficient layers between you and Kates. Jesus, it's a miracle you've lasted this long."

"Please, it's not that bad. Don't do this, we're so close."

"You're not close to anything."

Brewer dropped to his knees, pleading unintelligibly before the single shot cut him short.

The killer stooped over the body, checking it quickly, then stepped over it to exit the building. By the time he reached his car he was fully focused on the next step.

The first sight that greeted her when the nurse pushed her into the room was Tom Hughes standing by her bed, smiling awkwardly, flowers in one hand and a bunch of magazines under the other arm.

"Tom, it's great to see you."

"I would have come sooner but I only just heard. Here, it's a fairly eclectic mix, I wasn't sure where your interests lay," he said, handing her the magazines.

Mesi sensed the nurse taking an interest in their conversation and asked her if she could find a vase for the flowers.

"So, how are you?" he asked, pointing at the strapping. "It looks pretty horrendous."

"I've just had a meeting with the surgeon, who said that once this is off and providing I stick to a regime they've mapped out, there's no reason why I won't recover full mobility."

He asked her what had happened, saying that what he had managed to glean from Samuels was very sketchy. She explained the process she had gone through to find Kates and the link to Brewer. She could see that he had grown more visibly upset during her account of the link to Kates.

"So, why didn't you call me when you found out Brewer might be connected, I thought we were working on this together?"

"I didn't want to put you in an awkward position," she

said, uncomfortable under his reproachful look. "When I saw Brewer's background, I figured he might still have pull within the Agency. I felt it'd be unfair to subject you to that. I'm sorry."

"Look, from now on we work this as a team. I bought in to your theory about a third-party instigator when you first came to me. Why do you think I've spent so much time getting material together for you?"

"That's true but –"

"No 'buts', fair's fair; there has to be give and take. If you think you've made a significant breakthrough, I should be kept in the loop, at least as much as Marshall or Samuels permit. Agreed?"

"Absolutely," she responded with a smile, "you'll hear about everything from here on in. At least I'll have a sounding board. So, what do you know about Brewer? Have you ever had any dealings with him?"

"No, no. I know him by reputation but we never had occasion to work together, which might seem odd seeing as how he did a lot of work related to Latin America, but the Agency is pretty big and he was a few years ahead of me."

"And nothing since he left?"

"Unfortunately, he's operated at a far more rarefied level than yours truly. If he is connected, it shows that, despite the number of people we've checked, we haven't been casting the net wide enough."

"Why do you say that?"

"Well, if we'd continued the way I'd suggested, we'd never have come across Brewer because strictly speaking he was never a field agent, more of a co-ordinator."

"One thing that struck me when I was researching him was how well he's done with Spartan in such a relatively short time-span. Do you think he's been unduly helped because of his former position?"

"I'm sure he's funded a few nice junkets for the odd congressman but that's par for the course. If his background is any benefit it would only be if everything else were equal between tenders. Then the cachet of being ex-Agency might tip the scales. There's far too much scrutiny of arms expenditure these days for anything untoward in the awarding of contracts."

"Yeah, I guess."

"You must be happy, though, in one respect. Samuels can't ignore your suspicions now, he's sure to get behind your investigation 100 per cent."

"Don't be so sure," Mesi said ruefully.

"What do you mean? He's not still refusing to consider the possibility of orchestration?"

"Quite honestly, I'm not sure. We're going to establish surveillance on Brewer but I know he's still reluctant. Even if we did prove Brewer's involvement, I think he might argue that the Kosovars commissioned him."

"Which is possible," Hughes replied apologetically, clearly hating to point out the unpalatable truth.

"I suppose," she agreed.

"Look, one step at a time – first we get enough to question Brewer. I'll start pulling files on the missions he worked and personnel he used. I may not be able to show you original material due to classifications but I'll see you get all the salient information."

He started to say goodbye, promising to call back later that evening and then, after hesitating briefly, leaned over and kissed her lightly on the cheek.

Mesi was surprised by the move but not altogether

unpleasantly. She was not sure what to say and an awkward moment ensued.

"Sorry about that; impulse," he said. "If I was out of line …" He held his hands up.

She sensed his tentativeness while he waited for her to say something.

"No, don't worry," she smiled.

"How about I come back later this evening after I leave the office?"

"I'd like that."

———

nine

Larsen had waited more than four days in Cartagena before the information had arrived.

Rather than flying into the country, he had chartered a small sailing boat in Panama and sailed from there to Cartagena. It was easy enough to organise a slip at one of the marinas and then follow the usual custom of having an agent check him into the country. A day later, he had a stamped passport and visa in his possession, just another tourist in what was regarded by many as South America's most beautiful city.

Before his recent meeting with Wallace, Larsen and Brewer had reviewed how the initiative was progressing. While they had been satisfied they had managed to spur Madrigal into retaliation, they were somewhat disappointed. It appeared to them as if both sides, after a period of activity, were easing back on the hostilities. By this stage the projections had called for both sides to be funnelling most of their energies into destroying the other. Despite the impact that had been made on drug trafficking and consumption, the results were still some way short of what they had originally envisioned. If anything was going to force Madrigal to redouble his efforts, surely an attack on home soil would be it. Now, with Wallace's waning enthusiasm, this operation had taken on even greater significance, as it might represent the final opportunity to escalate the conflict.

The key issue had been identifying a target significant enough. There had been two ways they could go: assassinate a senior figure or destroy a valuable asset. The problem with the first option was that most of the authority lay with Madrigal himself, so he was the logical choice for an attempt. However, besides the difficulty involved, killing the drug czar might not actually help their cause. The vacuum created by his death would spark an internal feud between various candidates who fancied themselves as his successor. Such a development would divert even more energy from the external struggle with the Kosovars, precisely what they did not want. So they decided to go with the option of destroying something that the Colombians would value. They knew there were major shipments of cocaine regularly leaving Cartagena from the port of Santa Marta and, given the Alliance's weakened state, an attack on one of these would fit the bill perfectly. The fact that large numbers of tourists regularly travelled to Cartagena strengthened the argument for choosing this location.

Brewer had suggested they follow the usual procedure in which he organised reconnaissance and Larsen went in later with the operational team. The suggestion was for them to take their time and monitor at least two or three of the previous shipments. Based on this intelligence, Larsen would draw up a plan of attack and recruit a team. After the standard period of drilling they would head in. On the heels of his discussion with Wallace, however, Larsen was afraid the plug could be pulled any day and insisted on an accelerated schedule. He would perform the reconnaissance himself, taking only enough time to see one shipment leave harbour. In parallel, Brewer would arrange for a small team of experienced men whose details they had on file to arrive in Cartagena shortly after Larsen's arrival. Given the frequency of the shipments, the attack could follow fairly swiftly on the heels of their arrival. With luck, they would be in and out in a couple of days, lessening the chances of detection.

To complete the first phase of the reconnaissance properly, Larsen would need to talk to someone familiar with the cartel's shipping operation. Brewer had said he was confident he could get the name of a contact in the harbour master's office who could give them the specifics they required. Due to the time pressure he felt they were under, Larsen had set sail for Cartagena expecting the name and meeting arrangements to be ready for him on arrival. In the event, it had not arrived and, after a day of waiting with nothing materialising, he decided to spend some time seeing what the city had to offer. If he stuck exclusively to the boat it might start to attract unwanted attention.

Cartagena had two main attractions, the historic El Centro and the beach nightlife of Bocagrande. He had spent only a couple of hours on the first night walking along the beachfront of the latter. Between the constant stream of noise coming from the bars and the hordes of drunken revellers stumbling from one classless venue to another, he failed to see the attraction. El Centro was a definite improvement. It was centuries old and the ancient forts and original wall which had been built to protect the city against sackings and raids gave the place a real sense of history. Drake had laid siege to the city in one of the most famous episodes. The sailor had been eager to plunder the city for Queen and country. Larsen found that the winding narrow streets with their ancient buildings were like night and day compared to the trashy Bocagrande. If he had not been so anxious about the upcoming mission, he would have enjoyed his evenings moving through the cobble-stoned avenues, occasionally stopping at one of the plazas for dinner or a glass of wine.

A child who looked around seven or eight approached him smiling and held up a soda, his other hand outstretched, palm open. Larsen wasn't particularly thirsty but he gave the child a few coins for the can anyway.

He'd noticed the large number of street children. During his research, an article he'd read mentioned how Clinton had chosen Cartagena for a state visit in 2000 when he was launching Plan Colombia, the forerunner to Plan Coca. The authorities had decided the children's presence would ruin the city's photo-op before the world's media and their solution had been straightforward: they'd rounded them up, herded them onto buses and transported them to other cities where they were simply dumped.

Larsen wondered how much longer he'd have to wait for Brewer.

"Why are we so concerned with distribution in the US? Why not just pull back and limit ourselves to production and wholesale? If we terminated any special relationships we have and offered equal terms to everyone, we'd be insulated from the trouble."

Madrigal knew that Rodolfo voiced an opinion that had growing support among his compatriots. The only reason they were currently so vulnerable, the argument went, was that they had linked themselves too closely to the consumer end of their markets. Madrigal's strategy over the years, in forming so many alliances, had been specifically to ensure that the Colombians were involved in the process end-to-end, from harvest to street corner. This approach had ensured that their profits had soared during the good times, but it also made them more vulnerable when any part of the chain was threatened. Their cash flow was closely tied to how well the retail market performed and, currently, it was struggling. The combination of the stiff new competition that was emerging and the heightened danger to their retail partners meant revenues had plummeted.

"Giving up what we've fought hard to build won't accomplish anything at this stage other than to aid the Kosovars," he explained. "If we move back along the distribution channels, it's an effective retreat. They'll step into the gap. They'll send more heroin to the US and pursue partnerships with those groups we abandon. They'll cut us out of that sector entirely." He surveyed the room, aware some of them remained unconvinced. "They can't compete with us on coca production but, if we hand them control of the markets, we'll eventually be forced to deal with them. In effect, we'll be giving them what they want most – power over us. We have to persevere."

The group discussion broke off into a number of smaller, self-contained conversations, a common theme of disgruntlement running through each. He had intended to ignore them when something one of them said caught his attention. "What was that, Antonio?"

The man to whom he directed the question looked up quizzically.

"That last comment you made?"

"I only said, with everything else that's going on, how annoying it was that the foreign contractors continue to behave as if they're on vacation. They should have the decency to limit themselves to Putumayo." The man shifted uncomfortably under Madrigal's gaze. "I know you've given orders that we are not to cause trouble around Cartagena but it would be nice to teach them a lesson."

"What contractors, what are you talking about?" he asked, growing more annoyed with Antonio's vagueness.

"Rodriguez's man, Saldivar, he was with me yesterday. He mentioned he had seen someone he used to know walking through El Centro a couple of nights ago. Someone he had worked with in Venezuela."

Madrigal's instincts told him this was something he should pursue. "Did you look into it?"

"No, I didn't see any reason. I assumed he was one of the US contractors from Putumayo, taking some time off."

"Did Saldivar say anything else?"

"No, nothing."

After the meeting had broken up, Madrigal contacted Rodriguez on a secure line. He asked a little about Saldivar's background and was told about his extensive intelligence work before Rodriguez had recruited him. He arranged to speak with Saldivar directly and, when he finished, he reviewed the little he had learnt.

During Saldivar's eighteen months in Venezuela, twelve had overlapped with a man named Alvarez whom he had seen in Cartagena a few nights earlier. According to Saldivar, the Americans had used Alvarez as a last resort, to eliminate specific individuals who were proving troublesome. Contrary to what Antonio had said, Saldivar thought Alvarez was either Spanish or Portuguese. Alvarez had been close-lipped about his past, but Saldivar did recall some rumours that he had formerly served with the French Foreign Legion. From what Saldivar had said about his area of expertise, Madrigal didn't think him the type who would be used in a campaign like Plan Coca. So what else might he be here for? Of the likely possibilities, there were a few which did not augur well for the cartel. The only other useful facts Saldivar had been able to provide were the time period during which Alvarez had been in Venezuela and the name of his CIA control. Hopefully, it would be enough.

Madrigal received the completed dossier within two days. There had been a lot of false starts and deliberate misdirection to contend with but his sources were the best and had managed to produce a detailed picture of the man Saldivar had seen. His name was not Alvarez but Larsen. His father had been Portuguese, his mother Danish. He was not a product of the romanticised Foreign Legion but of the lesser known Jægerkorpset or Hunters, an elite Danish special force. A detailed history of his service record and reports on some of his subsequent labour confirmed his areas of specialisation. Larsen was used for one of two purposes, to spread terror or to kill. Whatever his mission in Colombia, Madrigal was certain it had to be connected to the Kosovars. The photographs he had obtained were all a few years old but would have to suffice. With the manpower at their disposal, he was confident they could locate Larsen if he was still in Cartagena. He called Antonio to tell him to prepare for the search.

During the days while he waited for Brewer to secure the contact in the harbour master's office, Larsen revisited his original reasons for agreeing to participate in Wallace's crusade. Even before Africa disillusionment with where his life had brought him had set in, but that assignment had proved a revelation. He had met people there, some of whom he had formerly worked with, who had travelled much the same road as him and should have been just as burnt-out and disillusioned. But there they were, in large numbers, fighting for a seemingly lost cause. And the strange thing was how happy they were. They must have known how steep the odds were stacked against them but it had not mattered. They had found something they believed in and perhaps just as importantly for many of them, someone they wanted to follow. Not the exiled president, as impressive as he had been, but the charismatic English mercenary who had decided to take up that fight. The more time Larsen had spent in his company, the more the idealism had worked on him. The Dane had hated what he had become but believed it was too late to do anything about it, resigning himself to simply waiting until events inevitably caught up with him. But during that time he had started to believe there might be another way. It had of course been impossible for him to reveal why he had really gone to Africa; even if the mercenary had forgiven him, his men would not. He had chosen instead to quit the country, leaving behind him a warning regarding the forces that were marshalling against the exiled president.

The episode had left him convinced that he too needed to find something he could give himself over to. Time had passed and it had begun to look less and less likely that an opportunity would present itself. When Wallace's approach came, he had convinced himself that the billionaire's proposal could be his personal grail.

It turned out he had been wrong. About the crusade and about Wallace. His patron did not have the resolve necessary, and if the main architect had lost faith what did that say about the overall strategy? Really, Larsen had only himself to blame. He had been too desperate. Yes, he may have taken a couple of weeks to accept Wallace's offer but inside he knew that he had committed the moment he sat across the table from Wallace in Chicago. The only choice left for him now was to try to keep everything going until their prime targets were at least consumed by the conflict.

The days passed with no word from Brewer and no response to his attempted communication. He was worried, wondering what was going on, and had resolved to leave Cartagena when, on the fifth day, Brewer's encrypted communiqué finally arrived. It stated that while he had still not secured a contact in the harbour master's it was no longer necessary. Through alternative sources, he had managed to learn the exact location from which the cartel would be making a major shipment in six days' time. If Larsen could perform a proper reconnaissance of the area in the interim, he and the team would have the perfect opportunity to strike. Unhappy with the sloppiness which had crept into Brewer's work, he was tempted to abandon the mission. The problem was that he was here now and if he didn't go through with it, Wallace might not give him another opportunity.

He contrasted Wallace's change of heart with the billionaire's impatience for him to initiate their first major operation and his satisfaction when they finally did.

Two years earlier.

The Guttierez family controlled more than twenty per cent of Chicago's drug supply. Working as distributors and retailers for the Madrigal cartel, they provided the perfect conduit from large shipments to more manageable lots that local drug figures could handle. They hailed from the Dominican Republic and dealt with groups from every ethnic background, Jamaican Yardies to homegrown gangstas. Within three short years they had established their position in the city and demanded everyone's respect. Early run-ins with the established powers had convinced people that it was easier to live with the Guttierezes than to try to push them out.

Leti Guttierez, the youngest member of the family, had carved out a reputation for herself beyond the illicit world the family laid claim to. She had bought the run-down Silver Salsa nightclub and transformed it into one of the city's most exclusive nightspots. The venue was a beacon for the Latin community. It grew in popularity and soon became the in-place to be seen. One of her coups involved convincing a multi-platinum-selling diva from their home country to give an impromptu performance at the club. She had then purchased one of the major local radio stations and changed its programming to cater to the increasingly important Latin American demographic. Leti's good looks and connections in the record industry ensured that her regular public appearances garnered a great deal of positive attention.

Manuel, the head of the family, was not as outgoing but vicariously enjoyed the celebrity his younger sibling attracted. He had ambitious plans for all of them over the next few years. Payments to the right quarters ensured that they were never exposed to serious scrutiny. The local authorities were firmly in the family's pocket and federal agencies' investigations were continually hampered by breaches in security. Occasionally, they would deliberately sacrifice a lower level figure or a relatively small shipment just to ensure no undue pressure was exerted on their co-opted police contacts.

One Thursday night, all three family members were partying at the club. Leti and the middle brother Ricardo were holding court in different areas of the nightclub, while Manuel stood by the bar enjoying the music. Later, the finals of the salsa dancing competition, which the club had been running for three months and which had received citywide coverage, were due to be staged. Despite the fact that it was a Thursday, more high-profile guests than usual were attending. The irony of a number of city councilmen and senior detectives getting sweaty on the dancefloor while over $20 million of various kinds of drugs sat upstairs in a secure vault amused Manuel. The barman tapped him on the shoulder and handed him a phone. One of his senior men, Freddie, was upstairs, having returned that evening on a flight from Mexico. He was ready to make his report. Manuel had been eager to hear from Freddie about proposals they had put to Esteban Zaragosa regarding the possibility of a substantial increase in the amount of throughput they could handle. He went to the two groups and extracted his siblings, pleading with their disappointed hangers-on that he would be stealing them for only a few minutes. He told them that Freddie had returned and that the confirmation of a new phase in their endeavours was imminent. The three made their way up the stairs, but when Manuel entered the large office area behind his brother and sister, he thought it strange that Freddie was seated behind his desk. Two more of their men were seated on the leather couch and no one stood to greet them. Aware that something was amiss, Manuel tried to step back out but was pushed roughly from behind into the office and heard the door slammed shut behind him. Looking around, he saw a man standing there levelling a silencer-equipped pistol at his head. Two other men emerged, one from behind a filing cabinet and the other from behind the desk. Like the first, they were dressed in black trousers and bomber jackets. Each trained a pistol on one family member. His brother and sister were forced to the ground and the first gunman tripped Manuel so that he fell and landed beside them.

Larsen nodded and his two companions shot the men seated on the couch, the impact of the bullets causing bloody stains on the wall behind them. He drew a large knife from under his jacket and walked around the desk to stand behind the trembling Freddie.

"We want you to open your vault. If you do, we'll walk out of here with no more fuss; if you don't, we'll kill you. Decide quickly before someone comes looking for you."

"You don't know who you're fucking with … " began Ricardo.

He stopped in mid-sentence as Larsen grabbed Freddie's hair and, pulling his head back, dragged the blade slowly across his neck. Blood sprayed out across the desk, some of it hitting Leti, prompting her to launch into hysterics. The loud thumping beat from the music downstairs dismissed from Manuel's mind any hopes that his sister's anguished cries might summon help.

"No more delays, Manuel, either open the vault or lose a family member."

Manuel looked from Larsen to his family members who were seated on the floor, a gunman standing over each. He thought about the contents of the vault. Could they absorb the loss? Yes. How long for them to recoup the lost revenue? No more than six months. Would the gunmen spare them? Perhaps not but what choice did he have?

Maybe their position and the implications of their murder might dissuade the gunmen.

Larsen's voice interrupted his considerations.

"Too slow."

A nod to one of the gunmen and a pistol was placed to the back of Ricardo's head. Manuel watched in horror as the bullet exploded through Ricardo's face and his lifeless body fell across the prone figure of the sobbing Leti.

"Your sister's next. Three seconds. One, two …"

"Okay, okay," he shouted. "I'll open it! Let me up!"

Larsen indicated for Manuel to move to the door of the specially constructed vault at the back of the office. Manuel entered the manual combination, punched in the six-digit pin code and pulled the heavy door open. Taking a quick inventory of the room, Larsen confirmed the intelligence had been correct and that the anticipated hoard of traditional and synthetic drugs were present. Walking Manuel back to the middle of the office, he signalled for the other two men to begin packing the drugs into a number of holdalls. Ten minutes later, after a series of trips down the fire escape, they had removed the entire contents of the vault. After the last trip Larsen told them to wait downstairs for him.

Manuel watched in horror as Larsen walked over to the weeping figure of Leti and yanked her off the ground. The knife-stroke was mercifully quicker than the one that had killed Freddie but gruesome nonetheless. He screamed in rage and launched himself across the room at this monster. Reaching out savagely for Larsen's neck, he was easily fended off. Larsen stepped in close to him and Manuel caught the scent of mint on the killer's breath. Everything slowed as the smile spread across Larsen's face. Manuel's head was yanked back and an indescribable pain exploded in his lower abdomen when the knife was thrust in. Before he lost consciousness, he felt the blade being dragged upwards.

The modern port, with its rows and rows of stacked cargo containers waiting to be loaded or transported inland, was nothing more than an enormous metal warren, betraying no trace of its rich history. A light rain had begun to fall, which obstructed visibility and helped him to evade the security personnel patrolling the port. Once he had gotten inside the perimeter, he took some time to get his bearings. Although he had a map, he knew it would still be easy to become lost. He was making a mental log of specific structures when he thought he saw a flicker in the darkness. He waited, motionless, for ten minutes, before deciding he must have imagined it. The next thirty minutes were spent making his way circuitously towards his destination. As he moved in and out from the portside, he tried to get a sense of the place. If something was to go wrong during the actual mission, they would need to know as much as possible. Unlike previous operations, they would be going in relatively blind. Given the calibre of the men they had lined up, that would not be too great a problem provided he did his job properly tonight.

He was about five minutes from his destination when something caused him to look back.

There.

This time there was no doubt. Movement, something too big for a four-legged inhabitant. Someone was following him. He quickly discounted the notion that it was security; why waste time stalking him when they could just approach openly? That left only one obvious candidate. In the millisecond he spent deciding what he should do, he understood what had happened. Too late, things fell into place: his nagging feelings over minor incidents throughout the course of their campaign, Brewer's uncharacteristic delay in identifying the contact, the inexplicable difficulties in getting events to conform to their projections. The Washington contractor had set him up. When the betrayal had begun was impossible to know, as was the motive behind it. Was Brewer engaged in some gambit of his own? Or perhaps he had acted at Wallace's behest, after the billionaire's appetite for his crusade had waned.

On enemy territory, totally vulnerable, he cursed his stupidity.

Picking up the pace quickly, he ran along one of the docks. With no further need for concealment, he concentrated on speed. Depending on how many there were, he hoped he might be able to get far enough ahead to circle around and escape the port somehow. From the corner of his eye he saw, between the gaps in the rows of containers, figures racing along parallel to him, trying to cut him off. He was not distancing himself from them sufficiently and knew he would soon run out of quayside at this rate. He needed to change tactics. Drawing his Glock, he looked around frantically. His pursuers also stopped and he could see some of them making their way towards him down one of the passageways between the containers. The remaining pursuers were, no doubt, spreading out so that they could surround him. The only option he could see was to turn and run in the opposite direction towards some storage buildings at the other end of the quay. If he could reach them, it might make it difficult for his pursuers to track him. As he set off, arms and legs pumping trying to cover the expanse, the absurdity of the image struck him. Sprinting, first one way then the other, his lungs burning while they gave chase. It was like some demented version of a child's game but he knew there would be nothing childish about the consequences if they were to catch him. Ten metres ahead of him, one of them, who had obviously not tried to keep up with his initial dash, stepped out and raised a hand for him to stop. He dived head first through a large puddle and fired four shots as he slid at breakneck pace towards the man. Whether it was a desire to take him alive or disbelief at his crazy manoeuvre, his adversary had not been prepared to exchange fire and this gave Larsen enough of an edge. Three bullets had struck the man before he was able to retaliate. The returning burst went harmlessly over Larsen's head and, back on his feet, he resumed his dash, ignoring the large gashes in both elbows and one of his hips. Seeing their companion gunned down released the others from any restraint they had shown up to now. A fusillade of machine-gun fire was unleashed. Most of the heavy torrent flew harmlessly by him but there were so many that one grazed his shoulder and another lodged in his thigh. He was just metres from the open warehouse and hobbling along desperately when a shot rang out from between two rows of containers. The bullet entered him from the side, shattering his ribs on entry. The impact spun him from his feet and only the momentum from the sprint carried him forward. He was tantalisingly close now to refuge. He struggled to make it back to his feet, the pain threatening to overtake him, and limped toward the building. The air around him was lit up by gunfire and he realised he had no chance of making it. Left with no choice, he turned to face them and opened fire. He was hopelessly outgunned and knew that it would be over in seconds. He had to concentrate to keep the Glock from slipping from his fingers, rain and blood hampering his grip. His return fire was ineffectual as he failed to hit any of his pursuers. Another shot hit him in the chest and he staggered back, then one more before everything was enveloped in a blinding light.

"He couldn't be taken alive?" Madrigal asked, barely controlling his fury.

"No, I'm sorry. It was impossible."

"You knew where he was likely to be and had the opportunity to have as many men as you wanted waiting but still he was impossible to capture?"

"I'm sorry, sometimes these things are difficult to control. Dangerous situations –"

"Are you telling me about danger?"

"No, no. I'm just saying … he opened fire, despite the futility. I believe he would have done anything to avoid being taken, even suicide, which is what I think this was."

Madrigal rubbed his temples. "You say there's no sign of a body?" he queried into the speakerphone.

"No and I don't think there will be either. The explosion would have obliterated it."

"There's absolutely no chance he got out?"

"No. No way … he was hit repeatedly before the welding equipment exploded. There's no chance anyone could have survived."

Madrigal ended the call without a further word. One slight chance and now it was gone. There was no victory in killing Larsen despite the likely averting of a planned attack. A few days before, there had been a faint glimmer of hope …

It had seemed promising; they had caught sight of

Larsen after only a day of searching. The intention had been to pick him up the next time he ventured out, which turned out to be the botched episode at the port.

He had hoped that, by capturing the Dane, he might gain some insight into what lay behind all this. From the start nothing had made sense – the Kosovars never had any reason to declare war on them. He felt as if they were all being moved around the board for someone else's amusement and, now, an opportunity to get the answers he desperately needed had slipped away. Even if he managed to defeat the enemy or somehow fashion a truce, it was too late to matter for him. His leadership had been weakened irreparably and he knew the vultures were circling.

The broadcast switched from the financial report back to Sandra Whittaker, the main anchor.

"Today the State Department made the announcement a lot of people have been predicting for some time. Plan Coca has been suspended indefinitely, pending a detailed review. No date was given for when this review would begin. Long-time critics of the Plan have claimed today's announcement as an unqualified victory. To discuss this development and share their views on how history will record the Plan, we're joined by Caroline Williams and Professor Thomas Nelson. Caroline will be no stranger to our viewers having spent the past two years as our correspondent in Colombia. In that time she has received numerous awards for her coverage, most recently the prestigious Walter R. Randall award for best coverage of a foreign story. Professor Nelson is a lecturer at the Georgia Center for Economics and author of a number of books on the international drug phenomena, including the best seller, Harvest of Tears."

"*Professor Nelson, if I can come to you first, the Plan once drew rave reviews, with only a few dissenting voices but today it ends its life mired in criticism and acrimony. What went wrong?*"

Nelson, a balding chubby figure with a jovial demeanour, greeted the question enthusiastically. "*I don't know if anything went wrong as such. Plan Coca was a military operation funded by the United States. No protracted military operation can precisely follow a script or operate in a vacuum. I don't believe proponents of the Plan understood this.*"

"*Are you referring to the negative coverage given to the death of US personnel in Colombia or what was seen as the external effect of the Plan, the widespread armed conflict which ensued and social disturbance attributed to drug shortages?*"

"*Both. The death of the US contractors was a public relations nightmare, exacerbated by the State Department's bad handling. The external developments provided ammunition for critics of the Plan and, despite some questionable assumptions, no effective counter-arguments were ever aired.*"

"*What kind of assumptions?*"

"*The two most popular theories put forward painted the Plan in the most negative light. The first was that the Plan was so successful it prompted the other cartels to move in on the South Americans' markets. The other was that advocates of the Plan were cheap opportunists who tried to take credit for shortages the conflict had in fact caused.*"

"*Effectively a no-win situation?*"

"*Without a doubt. The Plan came to be viewed either as a cause of social strife or an expensive sham. The pro-*

Plan spin doctors failed miserably. Politics is all about perception, so today's announcement was inevitable."

"Do you think the criticism was justified?"

"To an extent but not to the degree we saw. Yes, the Plan probably caused some unforeseen problems in the consumer countries –"

"Such as the closures we've seen of numerous drug treatment centres. Staff quitting, complaining of unworkable conditions?" Whittaker cut across.

"Yes, problems like these," Nelson agreed. "Military solutions are blunt instruments, there's always going to be some unforeseen consequences. As to whether the Plan received undue credit for being the sole reason behind the fall-off in drug availability, that's a little like arguing which came first, the chicken or the egg."

"You do agree, though, with the consensus view that the war between the drug powers ultimately did more damage to the supply lines?"

"Yes but you have to ask whether the conflict would have occurred if not for the Plan?"

Whittaker turned her attention to her other guest.

"Caroline, from the outset humanitarian aid organisations maintained that unless the Plan placed more emphasis on social programmes rather than military initiatives it was doomed to fail. Do you think a different focus could have been successful?"

"Yes, I think a long-term approach which addressed underlying social issues would have had more chance. Certainly, there would have been less potential for criticism. That said, people wanted a quick fix and saw only a military effort providing it."

"From the perspective of someone who followed the Plan

on the ground as you did Caroline, do you think it's fair to attribute the trouble related to drug shortages in the US and Western Europe to Plan Coca's efforts in Colombia?"

"I'd have to say no. Initially, especially during the early fumigation missions, the official line was upbeat about what was being accomplished and reports from US cities seemed to agree."

"But that was subsequently proven to be a false impression?"

"Yes, over time we developed sources close to the crop growers and rebels. We found it wasn't the official manoeuvres that were causing them most problems."

"So, what was?"

"Well the right-wing paramilitaries for a start, they inflicted far more damage than any of the official troop movements or fumigation runs. Even when the Colombian army did achieve something notable, it was usually because the paramilitaries were helping them."

"And the lower prices their harvest commanded also caused them difficulties, didn't they?"

"That's true, their ability to obtain arms was compromised due to the fall in revenue, which in turn undermined their efforts to hold territory. The lower prices were, of course, because of the pressure the cartels came under from the conflict."

"Professor Nelson, regarding the feud between the dominant producers and traffickers of narcotics, is it over? It's been more than a month since the last major incident."

"I would guess that an uneasy truce has been reached, if for no other reason than the feud was hurting both parties equally."

"Finally a question for both of you. Is there any aspect

in which you think the Plan could be termed a success?"

"I think in absolute empirical terms the Plan was successful," Nelson responded. "The amount of drugs being trafficked into countries diminished severely, albeit perhaps temporarily. Whether the Plan was directly responsible or acted as a catalyst is immaterial."

"Even within that narrow definition of success, I think the Plan has been over-estimated," Williams said. "With the benefit of hindsight, I'd say the Plan failed in all the ways that mattered."

"Caroline, Professor Nelson, thank you."

ten

Wallace bent down, cleared the dead leaves from the gravestone and positioned the flowers carefully.

Following his usual routine, he walked the short distance down the path to sit on a bench under the branches of an aged oak tree. He could still see the grave from here and liked to think they could hear his thoughts. Recently, he had not been coming as often as he ought and he pledged to get back to regular visits.

He had felt as if a huge load had been lifted from him in the last few weeks. The violence appeared to have completely ceased after two to three months of steady decline. At the height of the troubles, he could not turn on the news without hearing of a new episode or being presented with a disturbing feature on the social meltdown. Who would have thought he would ever welcome the day when the news consisted solely of gloomy economic forecasts and mounting Middle-Eastern tension. Closing his eyes, he rested back on the bench and let the tension seep out.

A slight smile appeared when he thought of the latest status report from the rehabilitation clinics he had founded in Elizabeth's memory. He had talked to the head of administration three days earlier and the news could not have been better. The demand for new admissions to their treatment programmes had subsided and they were steadily working their way through the backlog. Circumstances were still tough but they could see the light at the end of the tunnel. Surprisingly, despite the gruelling ordeal they had gone through, they had not lost too many permanent staff from the six clinics.

But he could not control where his train of thought took him and yet again he began wishing the clinics could have represented the limit of his ambition. Instead he had been tempted to look for other ways to create a legacy. There had been no word from Brewer for three months; all attempts to contact him had failed. Regardless of how much he tried to convince himself that there could be any number of explanations, he knew the truth. Brewer had paid the price for becoming involved with his crusade. They had put a contingency plan in place if the normal channels of communication broke down. There was an e-mail address to which he could send an SOS and, within two or three days, the message should have been picked up by Brewer. He had lost count of the messages he had sent.

Worried by this development, he had tried to activate the protocol to arrange an impromptu meeting with Larsen. It had not taken long for it to sink in that he would not be hearing from the mercenary either and with this awareness came a number of unpleasant insights. Larsen had been planning one last operation, for which Wallace, against his better judgement, had given him the go-ahead. If Larsen had somehow perished in its execution then Wallace's culpability was all the greater. If he had possessed the necessary courage at their last meeting, the mercenary might still be alive. He had seen how driven Larsen was, how difficult it would be to pull the plug there and then, so he had convinced himself one more mission could not make a huge difference. Due to his cowardice, Larsen had died for a cause that no one believed in any longer.

The worst part of these discoveries was what they had taught him about himself. Rather than concern for the men he had placed in harm's way, his first reaction had been one of fear. What if the trail led the parties responsible for their disappearance to his door? Time passed and his fear receded. It looked like the professionals he had employed had shown a loyalty he was lacking. How else could he explain his failure to try to find more concrete evidence of what had happened to them and his willingness to leave events to run their course? His relief at being able to walk away disgusted him. If he was honest, he suspected that, had he been told he could choose this outcome a number of months before, he would have happily settled for it. His appetite, for what he had once felt had almost divine sanction, had waned to the point of extinction.

This is how it ends, he thought. He had sparked a wave of violence leading, one way or another, to the death of hundreds and the misery of countless more. He had caused men who had trusted him to go to their deaths while he had remained in the background, safe from harm. He had accomplished nothing of permanence. And he was grateful to have survived. He still had wealth, reputation and his involvement in the foundation. The latter would help him in the long run to ease whatever recriminations cropped up from time to time. On reflection, he had come out of it remarkably well.

A couple of visitors to the cemetery saw the silver-haired man sitting alone on the bench, cradling his head in his hands as he wept, and hurried along, not wishing to intrude on his grief.

—

First day back at the office. It had been twelve weeks since the shooting and Mesi's shoulder still caused her a lot of discomfort. She had been given a repeat prescription by the doctors when discharged but had thrown it out when she had noticed how much she was starting to rely on the painkillers. Without them, she had to get used to pain as a constant until she healed fully. Her movement was still restricted and she berated herself for not being as dutiful as she might have been in doing her rehab exercises. Going back to sitting at a desk wasn't going to help but she couldn't face another day at home with nothing to do.

She had watched in frustration as the investigation first failed to build on her discovery of Kates' involvement, and then ground to a complete stop. It had started only days into her hospital stay when they had been unable to locate Brewer. They had spent days just watching and waiting, not wanting to alert anyone to their interest, only to discover that Brewer's secretary had contacted the police about his absence, leading to a missing persons report being filed. Samuels' response had been to have a team of investigators enter Spartan's offices with questions for senior personnel. Her impression of Samuels' decision was that it had merely been an exercise in ass-covering. It would leave him free to say later that he had done everything that could be expected based on such limited evidence.

As things stood now, there hadn't been any attacks on drug-related targets for over a month and the prevalent view was that the conflict had run its course. Nice, neat and a result with which everyone could be happy. With the decline in violence, locating Brewer or explaining his disappearance had dropped down the list of priorities.

One of her DEA colleagues, known for his cynicism,

had confided in her that there was another reason why their superiors were eager to move on and forget the whole affair. The feud had brought about a radical shift in the balance of power in Colombia's drug scene. Not so much on the cartel side, although Madrigal's position was known to be shaky, but in who controlled the territories where the drugs were produced. Army forces and the right-wing paramilitaries had succeeded in driving both FARC and the ELN out of their historic strongholds. The cartel's difficulties had crippled the supply of funds and arms to the left-wing rebels. Without this support, their ideological rivals, unintentionally aided by Plan Coca, had been able to gain a decisive advantage. Continuing to focus on what may have caused the feud when it was clearly dissipating might turn the media's focus to areas best left untouched. Only a few years earlier, an ex-informer of the DEA in Colombia had publicly made claims that he had acted as a go-between for the Administration and a high-profile death squad leader. He had alleged that the DEA was willing to provide funding and arms to this individual if he helped them eliminate specific drug traffickers. Strong denials had been issued and a State Department investigation cleared the agents in question but sceptics remained. Was it possible, she wondered, that the DEA was being influenced by the new ascendants in Colombia, blackmailed into letting this particular dog sleep?

Despite her frustration at their eagerness to move on at any cost, she was not as angry as she might have expected a few months before. For the first time in a long while, she was gaining some perspective on the place her job should occupy in her life. While still undoubtedly very important, it was no longer an all-consuming obsession. It was strange that the competition for her attention had come about because of the job itself.

Tom had become a regular visitor during her convalescence. When others' support for her determination to pursue her investigation had first wavered and then completely disappeared, he had remained constant. Despite his other responsibilities, he had compiled a comprehensive dossier for her, listing as much of Brewer's career as he could disclose. It had been interesting reading and although neither Samuels nor Marshall seemed impressed by its contents, there were a number of lines of enquiry she intended following up now that she had returned to work.

The first sign of a relationship developing between her and Tom had been a gradual change in their conversations. From where the only topic had been the investigation, they started to wander into other areas. Initially, it would be the odd remark or observation, and then, without her noticing, Tom could visit for a couple of hours and the conflict would barely be mentioned. They discussed anything and everything, surprised to find how similarly they saw things. With an increasing level of comfort, the discussions moved naturally to their personal lives. They spoke frankly of their past and where they saw themselves going. Like her, he had found fulfilment elusive and believed now he might have been looking in the wrong place. She understood better now what her ex-husband Alan had meant when he had referred to there being an impression of Tom being ill-suited to his profession. He had real issues with some of the things expected of him and told her how frequently he had thought about quitting. She told him about switching careers to the DEA, the aspirations she had had and how a combination of circumstances, agendas and, she guessed, her own inability to compromise, had left her in limbo. She could see a situation developing where each might provide the other with the courage to make the change they were both hinting at.

The more they had revealed to one another, the more obvious the attraction became. What others saw as shortcomings, she saw as a quiet strength and deep-rooted morality. She had been less prone recently to get things out of perspective, which she put down to his calm spilling over into her life.

It had been so long since her last serious relationship. Between her career, friends and interests, she had considered her life set if not complete, but the change the last couple of months had brought, from the low-point immediately after the shooting to how she felt now, was too obvious to ignore. So far, they had both concentrated primarily on friendship, avoiding mention of the developing romance, but she was ready to take the next step, no longer fearing it would jeopardise what they already had. With that in mind, she had invited Tom over for dinner later that evening.

She looked at her watch and decided she had better stop daydreaming if she wanted to get anything out of her first day.

Diane pushed herself back gently from the table to get the coffee and suggested he go through to the living room. She returned from the kitchen carrying the tray as the opening strains from *La Boheme*'s fourth act began playing softly in the background. The wall light's soft illumination combined with the music gave the room a soothing atmosphere. Ignoring the armchair, Diane took the seat next to him on the small sofa. They sat so close to one another that their knees brushed when she faced him and poured the coffee. The slight touch sent a thrill of anticipation through her, and the beginnings of excitement brought on by their physical proximity was palpable.

"Thank you," she said softly, looking into his eyes.

"I should thank you," he replied. "I've had a lovely evening, the meal was beautiful."

"I wasn't talking about just tonight; I meant everything. I haven't been this happy in ages."

He reached out and held her hand. "Me too."

They sat like that together, for a while, neither speaking but both totally comfortable with the silence. She released her hand from his grip and put it to his face then leant in to kiss him. She held the kiss for a few seconds, feeling her passion mounting.

When they broke, he started to speak. "I've wanted to do that – have the guts to make the first move."

"Now you don't need to bother," she smiled.

"I wanted to say how sorry I am at how little I've done since the completing the dossier. I'm sorry things have been kind of crazy lately."

"Don't worry about it," she reassured him.

"I wanted to have more done by the time you started back …"

She placed her hands to his lips, silencing him. "Tomorrow's soon enough for that; my mind is on other things right now."

They kissed again, this time with no restraint. He leaned back, pulling her to him, his hands stroking her body through the thin material of her dress. She undid the top buttons of his shirt, kissing his chest as he tried to pull her closer. They were virtually lying along the sofa now and its small size was making things a little awkward. Finally, after they had struggled pleasurably for a little while to make the best of the cramped space, she pressed her hand against him, freeing herself to stand up on unsteady legs. He came forward to the edge of the sofa, his hands reaching for her but she took a step back, beyond his reach.

She stood there looking at him squarely and for a moment he wondered if he had done something to upset her. Then, she reached behind her neck, undid the clasp of her dress and unzipped it. The smooth, black material slid off her with only the slightest movement of her shoulders. She stepped out of the garment which had pooled at her feet and, reaching out for his hands, pulled him gently to his feet and led him into the bedroom.

The non-descript office-block was ideal for his purposes. It provided him with somewhere to wrap up the last weeks of the operation. The occupancy level in the building was so low he probably could have paid cash for the time he needed and left it at that. But he preferred professionalism in everything. He had constructed a fictitious identity, used it to correspond with the letting agent and completed a twelve-month lease agreement. He sat in the middle of the empty office surrounded by a job-lot of cheap office furniture, laptop out, reading the latest gratifying report.

They now controlled more than eighty-five per cent of Colombia's drug-producing territories. In addition to the large revenues this would secure, payment had also been lodged from a major oil company for allowing resumption of work on their pipeline. The rebels had been looking to extort the company but were now fully occupied with their futile battle for survival. Plan Coca had distracted them and everyone else long enough to allow him to organise an effective coalition to move against them. Weakened by the drying up of their cash-flow from the cartels, it had not taken much, simply a combination of co-operative elements within the Colombian military and a series of attacks by his co-opted paramilitaries working on commission. And that was only the start.

Looking to employ classic management practice of controlling outbound logistics when first developing his strategy, he had asked the question, why stop at controlling production? Why not retail and distribution as well? True, there had been a tolerable working relationship with Madrigal historically but as long as they had to deal through him there was a limit to what they could achieve. He had extended the strategy to not only target the rebels who competed with their interests for territory but to erode Madrigal's power-base into the bargain. A hand-picked candidate, waiting in the wings, would assume control any day now.

What had surprised even him was how easy it had proved to rein things in. He had successfully arranged for the Kosovars to back off and the Colombians had quickly fallen into line. Almost before anyone knew it, the conflict was over. He had worried that one of the agencies investigating the feud might uncover something, but the only one who had come close was the woman, Mesi, and, luckily, the lack of support she had received had addressed that worry. Every indicator was that she had resigned herself to letting her investigation die. Still, there was a contingency plan in place for her removal. Just in case.

The crucial development had been the elimination of

Larsen. None of the other players had the same potential to ruin things. Not even Mesi, for all her abilities and tenacity, could wreak as much damage were the Dane to discover the truth. He would not be bound by due process or any observance of law. He had worked with Larsen himself years before and despite his cultivated detachment, the mercenary had made an impression. Although he would not have admitted it at the time, he did not mind recognising, now that the reaction stirred was one of fear. Larsen's combination of ruthlessness and focus had been unsettling to observe at close quarters.

He remembered when Brewer had originally approached him with news of Wallace's proposal. He had seen the opportunity and interwoven it masterfully with his own objectives. The key thing, on which everything else hinged, had been to carry off the sequence of attacks on cartel resources without discovery. Larsen had been the only person he had ever considered and he had ensured Brewer's selection process singled him out. The way it had unfolded, while Larsen had been up to the assignment, inflicting damage and eliminating individuals effortlessly, he had never threatened the real objective. Ultimately, it had been child's play to arrange for the unwitting Madrigal to eliminate him.

The one blip had occurred when he had been compelled to kill Brewer. He had planned to have the arrogant CEO removed at some point in the future anyway, but his sloppiness had forced it to be moved up. When he had heard of the unsuccessful attack on Mesi by Brewer's Cuban hitman, he had briefly feared it might all fall apart. Luckily, prompt and decisive action had ensured the problem was nipped in the bud. At least Brewer had been right about one thing: Wallace had been happy to walk away. He had kept a close watch on the industrialist but it had proved unnecessary. Even if Wallace had any desire to try and restart his campaign – and it was clear he did not – his two conduits to the worlds of mercenaries and intelligence were dead and buried. Surveillance pictures of Wallace over the past year, and particularly the last three months, had shown a marked deterioration. He would not be surprised if the business pages soon carried details of the demise of the founder of Diversified Holdings.

Madrigal, Mesi, Larsen and Wallace; all successfully dealt with. It had been a long gambit, years in planning and execution and now the end was in sight.

Madrigal lifted the canteen to his lips and drank deeply, letting the tension of the day seep out of him. He relaxed down into the canvas chair and lit a cigar. The men were bustling around the camp, getting things ready for the evening meal. He looked up and away from the campfire through the thick canopy of the jungle at the richly coloured twilight sky. The jungle sounds began to change around this time of the evening as nocturnal creatures emerged from their slumber. He had always enjoyed visiting Putumayo and now, with all that was happening, he found himself wishing he could stay longer. That option did not exist, he knew. His nature dictated that he not run away from whatever fate had in store for him. It had not been a bad run, he consoled himself. Born in a slum, he had gone on to build an empire.

He had come south to Putumayo to negotiate the new production agreement with the commander of the paramilitary unit that now controlled most of the region.

The commander had let it be known that he would view having to deal through a subordinate as a calculated insult. The meeting had centred on the price that the commander would demand per unit of raw or refined heroin and coca. The negotiation itself was a farce; Madrigal needed to get the supply lines back operating at their optimum level. The entire apparatus he had built had been so badly hurt by the conflict that only a speedy resumption of former production levels could stop it disintegrating altogether. The commander was well aware of Madrigal's position and was quite prepared to stockpile his product if he was not happy with the price offered. To save Madrigal's pride, the commander threw him a bone towards the end of the bartering, lowering the price slightly, but they both knew the concession was marginal. The only bonus to the whole deal was the fact the commander's close ties to the Colombian Army meant he could guarantee they need never fear consignments being disrupted within Colombia's borders. Once the meeting was over, Madrigal could not get back to his camp quickly enough. Even having to sit and conduct business with such a man sickened him. Many of the paramilitaries came from backgrounds similar to Madrigal but instead of trying to exercise some self-determination, they were content to let their natural blood lust be used by others. He had killed countless people on his climb to the top and most had not been spared a second thought, but the tactics of the paramilitaries were something else. They were savages employed by the ruling class and the military, to do their dirty work. They had pressed hundreds of villagers into service by threat of death and occasionally wiped out entire settlements for no other reason than to provide an object lesson. Things must be getting bad, he thought wryly, when a drug lord could feel so superior.

The agreement he had reached was just the latest ammunition for his opponents within the Alliance to use in getting rid of him. Although he would continue to fight, he was a realist and knew that his days were numbered. A summit meeting between the main figures in the Alliance would happen in the next few weeks. It was at this meeting, he surmised, that he would be pushed aside. He tried to predict how it would unfold. He had realised only recently where the main danger lay; before then he had never seen Rodriguez as a threat. The Mexican's aggression and enmity towards Madrigal had been almost reassuring. No need to waste time wondering what he might be thinking when he told you to your face. There were other experienced men whose subtlety and outward goodwill masked their real nature. You shook their hand and returned their smile, the whole time waiting for the knife. Lately he had discerned the change, which when he thought back had been gradually occurring in Rodriguez over the last couple of years. Yes, he still occasionally went off on vitriolic outbursts but much less frequently, and even then never with the total abandon of the past. Then there was the matter of letting him assume control of Zaragosa's operations. He should have seen that he was helping a dangerous rival but he had been too pre-occupied with his other problems.

It was shortly after Zaragosa's assassination attempt on Madrigal that Rodriguez had begun to make his move: a series of tactful approaches to senior members of the organisation. Whenever he encountered unhappiness or dissatisfaction, he worked away at it. Instead of coming straight out and suggesting Madrigal's ousting, he would merely plant the seed. He would bring up recent reversals, regret their occurrence and wish they could have been avoided. Nothing more. He would let the other party point out decisions which should have been taken and then reluctantly agree. The memory of Rodriguez imploring Madrigal to strike hard at the Kosovars early on and his gracious unwillingness later to blame the Colombian made a powerful impression. Revenues had suffered enormously since the conflict began and history now vindicated Rodriguez's stance. The fact that the Kosovars had finally backed off in the face of their strong retaliation proved it had all been an opportunistic grab for power on their part.

Understanding the situation and knowing who presented the main threat had been enough for him to avoid disaster in the past but not this time. No matter how often he went over it, he could see no viable options open to him. He had considered trying to pre-empt events by breaking up the Alliance and pulling the Colombian element out, but his own success thwarted him there. People had seen how profitable a cohesive strategy could be and were not going to forfeit the astronomical rewards just because of some personal loyalty to him. He was fairly sure he knew the course events would take. A number of people, most likely the eldest members of their committee, would respectfully suggest he take things a little easier, share some of his duties with Rodriguez. If he refused, it would only speed up the process, but if he accepted, he would have to face his position being eroded over months until he was effectively only a figurehead. At some point, to consolidate his position and to remove the threat of a future challenge, Rodriguez would have him killed. No one would fault him for the decision.

He reprimanded himself for wallowing in self-pity and

walked over to the fire to remonstrate with the men over how long it was taking to prepare the food.

———

eleven

It was for the best. That was what Mesi kept telling herself as she prepared for the open-ended period of leave. Ostensibly, the reason was her continuing discomfort with her shoulder and the need for intensive rehabilitation to address the problem. Arthur Marshall had been the epitome of the concerned boss when she had brought it up. There was no problem taking as long as she needed. They both knew they were using her injury as a convenient excuse.

After only four weeks back, she had taken stock of her position. All pretence of backing for her investigation had been dropped. Her dogged insistence in trying to resurrect the subject had rendered her a pariah. Even Alan, her ex-husband, had called and advised her that she was ruffling too many feathers. That in itself had been illustrative. How had a political lobbyist who represented a range of causes and interest groups, none of which were connected with illegal narcotics, come to know what was happening within the DEA? Pressure was being brought to bear, too much to ignore. She had asked who had talked to him but could not get an answer – he simply reiterated the caution.

In the end, she decided to acquiesce. She had been doing a lot of thinking recently. Thinking about what her career was costing her, not only in terms of time, effort and stress, but in relation to what she had to sacrifice in other areas. Up to a few months ago, she had been willing to place the job before everything else, not even seeing it as an imposition, but now? Whether the uncertainty was due to the shooting, the enforced period of reflection recuperation had brought or the developing relationship with Tom, was not clear. She needed to figure it out, to get some perspective, and she rationalised, since the investigation was plainly over, it was not a difficult decision.

Tom had been brilliant throughout. He had offered to support her regardless of what she decided. If she wanted to persevere, he would back her, but at the same time he recognised how the investigation's momentum had been squandered during her convalescence. He was concerned that she could put her health at risk by fighting for a cause that might already be lost. They had agreed that he would take some vacation time he had coming and they discussed getting away to a far-flung sunny beach, where they would place a ban on all work-related discussion.

She had been requested to clear her work area so it could be used when she was away and had almost finished – only two more drawers to get through. She opened the first drawer and dragged two wastebaskets over, one for rubbish and one for material to be shredded. She followed the procedure she had perfected that morning, taking out documents, deciding their sensitivity and disposing of them appropriately. Occasionally, she came across a noteworthy item and put it to one side for a particular colleague. She had almost finished the first drawer, working faster, eager to finish the repetitive task, when she came across the report.

When she had originally discovered the connection to Brewer she had asked one of the junior agents if he could find out who the main corporate investors in Spartan were over the last five years. The results hadn't come back before her visit to Kates' and with everything that had happened in the meantime she had forgotten the request. The listing had been placed in the drawer and had remained there since. On a whim, she flicked through the first few pages. The area of military consultancy, contracting and arms provision had not experienced the downturn the rest of the market had seen. For that reason they represented a good investment for many corporate institutions. Her thinking when requesting the list had been that the threat of approaching these shareholders might have given the DEA some leverage with Brewer. The report contained a few surprises, including mentions of blue-chip companies she would not have readily associated with a company like Spartan. She had placed the file in the shredding basket and moved through another two documents when it struck her. Reaching into the basket, she retrieved the report and flipped to the next-to-last page. There it was: Diversified Holdings. She had almost missed it due to its position so near the end of the document. The report was sorted in reverse order and Diversified's involvement in Spartan had ceased more than three years ago. It wasn't long before then that she had first become acquainted with the corporate group.

She had been with the DEA four years when the organisation had entered one of its most challenging periods. Inexplicably, its performance became the hottest of political subjects. Representatives from both sides of the house began asking questions. Difficult questions, intelligent, well-thought-out, well-researched questions. And they had kept asking them. Senior people had been put under intense strain as planned strategies were scrutinised and either scrapped or radically redesigned. New committees had been put in place to monitor effectiveness. Extreme stress permeated every level of the DEA. Still relatively fresh at the time, Diane weathered it fairly well, but she was the exception. Morale plummeted; some people quit while many others reached the stage where they simply stopped trying.

And then, abruptly, it subsided. As if some huge object had moved into their orbit, wreaked havoc and then moved on. Some months later, she learnt the reality. The occasion was a retirement party for one of her bosses who had taken a shine to her. A combination of too much alcohol for the retiree and an attempt to impress had resulted in him sharing what he knew. That year, Carol Wallace and her daughter had been the victims of a drug-related killing. An addict seeking the means to satisfy his habit had sought to rob Carol and events had gotten out of hand. Tragic but unremarkable, except for who Carol's father happened to be. Lawrence Wallace, former chairman and founder of the Diversified Holdings group. Apparently Wallace had set politicians and Senate committees on the DEA like a man sets his dogs on an intruder. She had barely believed that one individual could wield so much power. No one knew why he had decided to back off. Nothing good had resulted from his meddling. She had wondered if he might have realised the damage he was doing but was not sure that someone so used to seeing his wishes made reality would have accepted failure so readily. Subsequently, she saw a small article mentioning how Wallace was ploughing money into a newly established foundation which aimed to pioneer the field of drug rehabilitation. She had taken it as a sign to avoid summary judgements of people. The man she had pegged as obsessed with personal vengeance and as being equipped with an unhealthy amount of influence had used both to create something positive.

She closed the report and wondered if her first instinct back then had been right. She stood up and wandered away from her desk, as if putting physical distance between her and the report would change the direction of her train of thought. She tried telling herself she was crazy. There was no reason to think that Diversified Holdings' stake in Spartan meant Wallace himself was linked to Brewer. Some part of her, though, the part which had persevered in the face of all the crap, would not let her avoid it. Almost reluctantly, she began to hypothesise.

What was it she was proposing?

Lawrence Wallace, using resources at his or his corporation's disposal, had caused two major drugs powers to concentrate all of their resources on destroying the other. Why?

Personal revenge; no need to just rage at the injustice of it all and feel helpless when you're a self-made billionaire.

How could he have thought he could pull it off? How could he have dared set it in motion?

What, building a global empire and amassing an eleven-figure fortune should have convinced him to think small?

The question was, what did she do now? Run this by Marshall or Samuels and she would either be laughed out of their office or carted off to a padded cell somewhere. It would certainly mark a nice way to complete her career in the DEA. While she had come to terms with the fact that her days there were numbered, she certainly did not want to be pushed. Was it an option to simply walk away, tell herself it no longer mattered?

Tom let the waitress refill his cup and move on to the next

table. The coffee shop was virtually empty this early in the afternoon, the only other occupants a few students and a couple of resting shoppers. But he still kept his voice low enough for only her to hear.

"I agree that there's no point in bringing this to Samuels or Marshall," he said. "If Wallace is involved ..."

"What do you think?" she asked anxiously.

He had sat quietly, hardly having said a word to this point. Was he going to tell her she was delusional?

"I think it's bordering on unbelievable." He held up a hand to prevent her interruption. "But let's think about it for a minute. You said Diversified Holdings started divesting themselves of Spartan stock over four years ago, well before any of the trouble started."

"Yes, but the feud would have taken time to plan and he would have wanted to remove any visible links between himself and Brewer. His daughter died before the Spartan stock was sold, which was after he'd failed to get the results he wanted from meddling with the DEA."

"When did Diversified first invest in Spartan?"

"I'm not sure," she answered hesitantly. "Why is that important?"

"Well, it was obviously before his daughter died. Can't that be used as an argument that his involvement was all above board? How did he know then that he'd need the expertise they could provide?"

"The initial investment was probably based on sound business reasons but it doesn't change the fact that it provided him with access to Brewer. The timing of their decision to sell their stock in Spartan is definitely suspicious."

"Why?"

"If they'd waited another six months they'd have

increased their return by more than a hundred per cent. Odd move unless Wallace instructed them to do it so there was no link between the two companies."

"I thought you said Wallace had stepped down as CEO a few months after his daughter's death?"

"He did but he still controlled a massive block of shares. Do you think the board would have refused him if he suggested they sell their interest in Spartan?"

"Did Diversified make a profit on their investment in Spartan?"

"Sure, Spartan's stock has risen steadily every year since its inception."

"So, the timing of the sale may not be strange at all, they'd made a profit and decided to sell rather than be greedy."

She felt herself losing faith in what she had been so confident of only minutes earlier. This morning, she had been happy to walk away and even excited about a new chapter; now, here she was again getting totally worked up.

"Are you saying I should drop it?"

He looked at her for a moment before responding.

"Absolutely not. All I'm trying to say is don't rush to conclusions. Look, you're committed to at least a couple of months' leave, right?"

"Starting three days from now, yes."

"Let's spend the next few days when I'm away trying to figure out how we could look into this. When I get back we'll compare notes and take it from there."

"You're going away?"

"Yeah, I'm sorry, I was just told this morning. I need to spend a week away, I'm not meant to say where but I'll tell you. Things down in Colombia are a total mess since the Plan's cessation. A lot of senior people are panicking, and in an effort to appear as if they're addressing matters, various delegations are being sent down. I happen to be a very junior member of one of those. I leave tonight. I'm sorry. I wanted to be here, especially on your last day."

"Don't worry. It's not a big deal. I'll see you when you get back."

She knew she didn't sound convincing.

"I know it's lousy timing but I think I might have something to cheer you up," he said. "I wasn't going to tell you yet, but in light of what you've learned concerning Diversified ..."

"What?"

"I'd given up hope of finding anything useful about Brewer weeks ago. If there was any dirt, I figured it was well hidden, but then something just dropped in my lap. I was in a briefing yesterday regarding this trip and the aftermath of Plan Coca. There are all kinds of criticisms and recriminations coming to light recently."

"Such as?"

"How the fumigation flights routinely went outside specified areas. How US contractors have been participating in unsanctioned incursions against the rebels. Anyway, one of the State Department people mentioned in passing that they bore remarkable similarities to accusations made against Spartan last year."

She looked at him uncomprehendingly, not seeing the relevance.

"If Brewer was involved in a strategy to cripple the Madrigal Alliance, wouldn't it be compatible with a policy of straying beyond Plan Coca's remit to attack the rebels more freely? Think about it, who supplies Madrigal's principle source of cocaine?"

"My God! You're saying Brewer interfered with an official foreign policy initiative to augment the effect of the feud on the Alliance."

"I'm saying he might have," he cautioned.

"How did these allegations against Spartan come to light?"

"They terminated a contractor who they'd used down there, saying he couldn't provide the skills they'd contracted for. He contended it was his refusal to participate in unsanctioned missions that led to his dismissal and threatened a breach-of-contract suit against them."

"So what happened?"

"Nothing as far as I could ascertain. The case was never brought. I'm going to try to track the contractor down when I get back."

"What's his name?"

"Will Pickroom. Look, I don't want you doing anything on your own, wait until I get back."

"I promise all I'll do is try to find an address. It makes sense. I'm not going to have anything to do my last few days and it saves us some time."

"Okay, fair enough." He glanced at his watch quickly and stood up. "I'd better get back, how about I drop in tonight on my way to the airport, about seven?"

"Great."

She pulled the car in and turned off the engine. There was time to spare before the meeting and this diversion had seemed appropriate. She could see the house, partially hidden by the row of mature trees lining the street. Even at night with driving rain obstructing her view, it was clear that this was an exclusive neighbourhood, with the kind of properties she would have expected someone like Lawrence Wallace to choose. She knew the odds of him being there were slim. He probably had countless properties scattered across the globe but this one was in DC and it was nice to think that he might be inside, unaware of her attention.

Who knows? If it goes well with Pickroom you could be paying a visit to that very house soon enough.

She had managed to find a Baltimore address and phone number for the ex-contractor easily enough and had tried to follow Tom's instruction to sit tight until he returned. But two nights after he had left, she had been sitting on the sofa at home, bored, fiddling with a note containing Pickroom's details. She lasted about half an hour.

A woman's voice had answered her and initially it had not looked promising. She said she was Pickroom's wife but he no longer lived there. She was clearly agitated and Diane sensed she would not react well to pressure. Identifying herself as a DEA agent, she had asked if she could simply leave her number, in case the woman talked to her husband. The woman said it was up to Diane if she wanted to waste her time.

A couple of hours later the call had come. When she picked the phone up and announced herself, all she had heard was someone breathing. "Mr Pickroom?"

"What is it you want?"

"To talk. About what happened in Colombia, the circumstances surrounding your departure."

"Departure, huh, why don't you call it what it was? I was hounded out."

"So you said, but you dropped the suit, the chance for

compensation?"

The line went quiet for so long she wondered whether he was still there.

"Money's no good if you're not around to spend it," came the reply at last.

"Are you saying you were threatened, Mr Pickroom?"

Another long pause.

"Forget it, it doesn't matter, it's all done with now. Why am I even bothering with this conversation? Adios."

"Wait, wait, don't hang up," she had pleaded, knowing if she was brushed off there might not be another chance. "Mr Pickroom, I don't know what happened to you but I can guess. I've heard a little about some of your grievances against Spartan and ... and I believe them. I think Spartan had their own agenda. Can't we just talk?"

"I know all about Spartan's agenda. Believe me, you can't guess the half of it but why should I talk to you? Where were you a year ago?"

"You were coerced into dropping your case for compensation?" she said, trying to coax him into opening up.

"They did more than coerce. Someone interfered with my aircraft in Colombia. I was lucky to survive. They tried a hit-and-run when I got back here before I dropped the suit. I haven't worked in a year; they've made sure of that. I'm a nervous wreck, waiting for them to come. Tell me, why should I talk to you? I may be in a world of shit but at least I'm alive. Why take the risk of talking to you?"

"I want to know about what happened down there and I think you want to tell someone, otherwise you wouldn't have called. After everything that's happened, you must want some kind of payback. Will you talk to me?"

"No," came the answer, followed by a dead line.

He had hung up and she had been convinced she had screwed it up. Maybe it was for the best. If there was any truth to Tom's speculation about a connection between what Pickroom alleged and the manufactured feud, she should not have been taking the risk. Pickroom's account of what had happened to him was unsettling but what he had hinted at, concerning Spartan in Colombia, was intriguing.

Five minutes later the phone had rung again.

"I'll meet you – tomorrow night, eleven o'clock."

That was after she would have officially started her period of leave. "Can't you talk now?"

"Take it or leave it."

"Alright. Somewhere in Baltimore?"

"You know Canton?"

"By reputation. You're not suggesting we meet there, at night?"

"I'm safe in Canton; I've got friends. Look, I'm ready to hang up and this time I'm not calling back. Yes or no?"

"Yes."

He watched the car park, and moments later a woman emerged. She hugged her jacket around herself to guard against the rain, and walked away from where he was parked, disappearing from sight. A few minutes later he caught sight of her again, approaching on the opposite side of the street. She gradually came back into clear view, passing directly in front of Wallace's house, making a surreptitious attempt to glance in as she came level. He knew she would see nothing; the main living area was raised eight steps above street level. She continued on about twenty paces and then scurried back through the downpour to her car.

———

She closed the door, happy to get in out of the rain. Hoping to catch a glimpse of Wallace, all she had accomplished was to get thoroughly soaked. She checked her watch again and decided it was time to leave.

He watched her pull out, waited ten seconds and then followed.

Canton was exactly what she had expected. None of the streetlights were working and many of the buildings' ground-floor windows were boarded up. Here and there groups of youths congregated, staring malevolently at anyone who passed by. She pushed back her feelings of unease, telling herself her nervousness was really just anticipation. Most of her time, since her conversation with Pickroom, had been spent trying, unsuccessfully, to avoid speculation on what Spartan had been up to during the Plan Coca campaign.

She found the address Pickroom specified and drove her car around to the lot behind the building, as directed. She parked the car, praying it would be there when she returned, and entered the building. Once inside, it became apparent that the place had seen better days. The lighting was barely sufficient to illuminate a few paces inside the doorway and all of the original mailboxes had been vandalised beyond repair. She could feel bits of plaster and other matter crunching under her shoes as she made her way haltingly down the hall. Pickroom had told her to go to apartment 502, on the fifth floor. The elevator was out of order, meaning the trek up was going to be even more unpleasant. She started up the first flight, trying to stick to the middle of the stairs and avoid putting her hands anywhere near the filth-covered banisters or walls. She thought she heard a door swinging shut below her as she passed the first landing halfway between the ground and first floor.

Between the poor light and filth-strewn stairs, her ascent was slow. There were two sets of stairs and a landing to climb for each storey. It was only when she was halfway there that she realised there was something peculiar. Pickroom had said this was an apartment block, but for somewhere supposedly occupied, it was eerily quiet. She stopped on the third floor, to check that she had not mistakenly entered the wrong building. It looked fine, the doors were all there, solid and locked, which would not have been the case if the building was derelict. She stepped close to one of the doors and a television was just audible. She was worrying about nothing. The lack of activity was probably due to the lateness of the hour, she decided, and she resumed her climb.

She reached the landing between the fourth and fifth floors and had turned to take the last series of stairs when a youth emerged on the fifth-floor corridor ahead of her. He looked like he was dressed in some kind of gang regalia and she panicked briefly before remembering Pickroom's reference to his friends.

"I'm here to meet someone."

Her question was still forming when the gun appeared. There was no doubting his intention. She threw herself backwards off the step she was on and felt the gunfire pass, missing her by inches. Falling back to the landing heavily, she scrambled up and ran down the next flight of stairs, taking them two and three at a time. Behind her, she heard the landing she had just been on being torn apart by the hail of bullets. She continued down, almost making it to the third floor when the gunfire ceased.

"Chop, you stupid mutha'fucka, I said to wait," a voice below called out.

Christ, how many of them were there?

She froze, unsure of what to do. Drawing her sidearm, she raced back up. If she could get to the fourth floor before the youth who had fired on her reached it, she might gain some time. As she reached the last couple of stairs, he came into view, only a few feet above her. His surprise at seeing her coming back towards him was evident and allowed her to open fire first. Ducking away, he scurried up to the cover of the landing above.

She crouched down in the corridor, only feet from the stairwell but out of the line of fire, and tried to regain her breath after the sprint. She could hear the youth on the landing above, cursing her.

"Dammit, Chop, what the fuck's going on?" came the same voice from below.

"Bitch's on four. She shot at me."

The alarm in his voice made her smile in satisfaction.

At least she had given them something to think about. Maybe it would convince them to forget about her. It dawned on her then that this was not random; they had been waiting for her. If that was the case, they were not going to be put off by her being armed. They would have been prepared for that. The most she had done was buy herself a little time.

A different voice rang out from below.

"You hit?"

"No but damn close. I thought you said this would be

easy, Derrell?"

"Shut the fuck up," came the angry retort.

So, there were at least two below her. She took out her cell phone and cursed the lack of signal. She looked around frantically. All the doors in this corridor remained firmly shut; no one was interested in seeing what was going on. She realised the probable futility of looking for help, but did not see many other options. If the youths decided to rush her she would have no chance of holding them off. She ran to a door and slammed her hand against it repeatedly, shouting loudly.

A hostile reply was enough to prompt her to move to the next door. A handful of rapid, similarly unsuccessful attempts confirmed her worst suspicions. There were few remaining options. Even if it was feasible to shoot her way into one of the apartments, all that would accomplish would be to endanger the occupants. In the course of trying the apartments she had moved down the corridor away from the stairwell, and while trying to decide on her next move, she spotted a door forty feet away at the end of the corridor. It could lead anywhere but she hoped there was a rear staircase behind it. Sprinting towards it, there was a moment of relief when she pushed the heavy door open to confirm her suspicions.

The door had not even swung shut behind her when her hopes plummeted. A barrage of fire strafed the wall to her left and bit into her arm. There was another one below her on this exit route. Not even bothering to attempt to return fire, she grabbed the door before it closed fully and retreated back into the corridor. She moved back along the passage until she was halfway between the two sets of stairs. A burst of sustained gunfire from the main stairwell froze her in her tracks. The entire stairwell was briefly lit up from the effects of their gunfire. She figured they were preparing themselves to rush her.

Diane pressed her back to the wall and slid down heavily, feeling herself starting to lose it. Her shoulders shook and, despite her best efforts, the tears began trickling down her face. Cornered by at least four of them, each more heavily armed than she. Her arm was beginning to hurt from where the bullet had grazed her, bringing back all the unpleasant memories from the last shooting and its aftermath. She tried her phone again but there was no change.

"Fuck!" she shouted in frustration, throwing it against the wall.

It was over, there was no way out of this. A wave of bitterness swept over her. After everything she had been through, this was not fair. How much was she expected to take?

Then, it passed.

Bitterness gave way to anger, anger that demanded action. It might be futile but she would not just curl up in a ball and make it easy for them. She resolved to take at least one of them with her. There was little chance of realising that goal on the main staircase – the odds were too stacked. But there was a chance that there was only the one pursuer on the rear staircase. With escape no longer the primary aim, she might last long enough to achieve her goal. Once more, she began edging toward the heavy door.

Before she had moved more than a few feet, a deafening crescendo of sound emanated from the main staircase. The sound pierced her ears to the point of causing physical pain. She clasped her hand to her head but it did little to soften the onslaught. It took a moment to realise it was emanating from some kind of weapon. Whatever it was, the source of the fire was as removed from the youths' sub-machine guns as they were from her pistol. Mercifully, it only lasted seconds but her ears were left aching in the aftermath.

"Derrell! Derrell!"

Even with her impaired hearing, the shrill voice of the first youth was audible. He was shouting nervously at the top of his voice and was clearly in a state of panic. Whatever had happened had originated below him on the staircase and had not been expected. There was no guarantee that whatever was unfolding would benefit her. She had the choice of sitting there and hoping for the best or taking action. Staying tight along the wall nearest the door hinges, she resumed her movement towards the door. When she reached it, she weighed up the possibilities. If the youth on the rear staircase was merely covering the exit then he might not have moved from where he had been before. She estimated that to be one floor down. Alternatively he could be advancing, he could be only a matter of feet away, on the other side of the door. Whichever it was, she decided what would give her the best hope was the thing he least expected. She needed to attack. That meant completing the dangerous manoeuvre of opening the door and getting through it. She needed to start firing as soon as the door had moved enough to squeeze through. If she did not manage this, his superior fire would cut her down immediately. She visualised the procedure over and over again. Pushing the door, shooting, the lines of fire she would need for the different locations he might be in. With a heavy exhalation, she launched herself off the wall.

A number of things happened on top of one another. She was vaguely aware, as her right shoulder hit the door, of a second explosion of sound beginning behind her. She felt the door start to give, slowly first then a sudden release and she was through. Hitting something heavy, she stumbled and fell down the first flight of stairs. During the tumble, she realised, in an almost detached fashion, that the other component of the tangle of arms and legs was her intended target. The fall took for ever as they rolled over and over. Through the descent, flashes of his panicked face appeared. They hit the next level, separating and slamming into different corners of the landing. Her head hit the wall heavily and the stairwell shifted in and out of focus. She could just make out a blurred image of him scrambling for his weapon, which had fallen a few feet away. Raising her gun, which she had miraculously managed to hold onto, she squeezed the trigger. Her first couple of shots struck wide of the mark and his hand grasped the gun. Her third shot struck him in the chest but seemed to have no effect other than a small tremor, almost as if his food was repeating on him. His gun cleared the floor. The edge of darkness closed in around her vision, obliterating everything but the eighteen inches from the middle of his chest to the top of his head. With one final effort, she squeezed the trigger, again and again before her eyes closed.

A strong grip took her under both arms and pulled her to her feet. She opened her eyes blearily, making out the vague outline of a man's face. She fell against him unsteadily, then her vision started to clear. Peering over his shoulder, she saw the bloody corpse of a child, no older than fifteen, lying on the landing.

"Come on," he said, leading her out.

They stopped at a late-night diner two hours' drive from

Baltimore. Her companion had cleaned the superficial wound on her arm and the pain was bearable. Her mind was still in a haze; she kept replaying the shootout mentally, the images of the dead teenager impossible to banish.

He did not rush her, patiently waiting while he sipped his coffee. Slowly, she gathered herself together and took a good look at him. He had thick closely cut dark hair, a slightly cruel face and Hispanic features. His complexion failed to mask a sickly pallor and, even from across the table, an odour of stale sweat added to an impression of ill-health. Then it clicked and she knew who he was.

"Lorcy."

Momentary surprise and then it was gone. "That'll do for now," he shrugged. "If you're okay to talk, let's start with what happened back there?"

"Okay."

She waited, and after a confused silence, saw that he expected her to begin.

"Why don't you tell me what you know and I'll fill in the blanks?" she tried.

"Okay," he shrugged. "I picked you up at Wallace's place and followed you from there."

He went back to sipping his coffee.

"That's it?"

"Yes."

"What about the … shooting?"

"You tell me."

"You're saying you just killed at least three children and you don't have the vaguest clue why?" she asked.

"I've never seen you before tonight. I followed you from Wallace's and saw you enter the building. Two of those 'children' followed you in, it looked like they were expecting you."

"So you came in guns blazing?"

"I was barely inside the door when the first shots were fired. It was evident that someone had set up an ambush."

"And why did you get involved?"

He sighed. "I need answers to important questions. I need them quickly and there was little prospect of me getting them the way things were looking. I took a gamble you might have them."

"You killed three children," she repeated.

"They were hardly children, besides their age was irrelevant; their capability was as clear as their intent. Try watching experienced soldiers getting gunned down by AK-47-wielding twelve year olds and see what it does for your perspective."

She searched his face for any trace of doubt or remorse but there was nothing. Something he had said earlier struck home.

"You know Wallace?" she asked.

He nodded.

"It's true then."

Her mind flooded with thoughts, like tumblers in a lock falling into place. Wallace's confirmed involvement caused her to reframe all of the events around the conflict.

"Why should I talk to you?"

"Based on tonight, I'd say you're in a pretty bad jam. Maybe we can help each other."

He began shovelling food into his mouth, eyeing her dispassionately.

"I was there to meet someone."

He stopped, fork halfway to his mouth. "No, you were there to die."

"I was there to meet a contractor who can expose what Spartan were doing for Wallace. Obviously, he set me up. For all I know, you're part of it."

"Does that sound plausible? Set up an ambush, kill the ambushers and then bring you to a diner?"

"Okay, you weren't involved in the ambush but you're still mixed up with Wallace. You need to find out how much I know and who I've spoken to."

"Considering what you've told me so far, it seems like I'm not the only one who needs answers. What is it you think is going on with Spartan?"

"You've as good as admitted to being Lorcy, or using the name at least; don't pretend you don't know about Spartan."

"Know what?"

"Are you trying to deny what you were doing for Wallace?"

He shuddered and a trickle of sweat wound down his forehead. He reached into his jacket, pulled out a small container and washed some pills back with a mouthful of coffee. After he swallowed, he rested his head against the back of the booth and closed his eyes.

"What's wrong with you?"

"Let's just say I'm not as fortunate as you when it comes to shoot-outs. Look, let's try again. Who are you?"

She considered simply getting up and walking out. He looked as if he was having trouble just staying conscious. What could he do to stop her? What he had said was true, though, she needed answers. She had thought tonight's meeting would bring some but all it had done was leave her more frightened and confused. Someone wanted her dead and was likely to try again. But why trust the man sitting across the table?

In the end it came down to the simple fact that she would be dead if it had not been for his intervention and that had to count for something, regardless of his motives.

"I'm Diane Mesi and I'm with the DEA. My appointment was with an ex-Spartan employee who had information about Spartan's illegal operations in Colombia. Operations I believe are linked to your attempts to drag the Alliance and Kosovars into a war."

"What are you talking about? Spartan isn't remotely connected with anything I might have done. Where did you get that idea?"

"You're denying Andrew Brewer was part of your operation?"

He started to speak and stopped himself a couple of times before he seemed happy with what he wanted to say.

"Let's say, for argument's sake, I did know Brewer and have had dealings with him. We wouldn't have been foolish enough to involve Spartan. Spartan is too many people; where could you possibly get the notion it was involved?"

"I was going to meet an ex-employee who –"

"Had information. You said! How did you come by this employee?"

"He was fired because he objected to what Spartan were asking him to do."

"They were asking him to do something illegal?"

"Yes."

The man laughed.

"What's so funny? Are you saying Spartan couldn't exceed the remit of Plan Coca?"

"No, not at all. For all I know, Spartan and all the other private contract firms in Colombia exceeded it on a daily basis but it doesn't mean a thing. It's nothing to do with the Kosovars."

"Will Pickroom left Spartan last year; I checked."

"Maybe he did. So what?"

"I checked." She stopped, no longer certain.

"Do you really think there'd be some ex-contractor from Spartan walking around blabbing to people like you?"

Everything he said made sense. She had wanted there to be a connection between Spartan and the feud so badly, something concrete after months of chasing shadows. She had not even stopped to question the logic. Why would a group of people go to the lengths they had on the Mexican operation and then do something as sloppy as involve such a high-profile company? That was what happened when you became that desperate, you didn't think things through. Still, there was some consolation in not being the only one to have grasped at straws. Tom had thought that there was a link as well.

Then it struck home and her whole world disintegrated.

"Oh my God!" she sobbed, a physical pain gripping her chest.

A couple of customers seated at the bar looked over at the commotion and her companion had to reach across and grab her arm tightly.

"Keep your voice down. What is it? What's wrong?"

"I was set up," she cried, her face in her hands.

"You knew that!"

She shook her head slowly, tears starting to appear.

"You don't understand, I was set up by someone I know, someone I trust, someone I … "

He waited for her to compose herself but she only got worse, seeming to turn more and more in on herself. This was no good. He had seen people fall apart before; if he did not get her talking soon she would be useless.

He squeezed her arm hard, increasing the pressure until the pain was enough to get a reaction. "Who? Who set you up?"

"Tom."

"Who's Tom?"

"My friend." She broke down again. The people at the counter looked around again. This time it required a vicious glare from the man to convince them to mind their own business. They could not stay here much longer but he needed to know who she was talking about.

"Besides supposedly being your friend, who is he? What does this Tom do?"

"He works for the CIA."

Hughes tapped his fingers impatiently, waiting for the call to be picked up.

"Hello?" the sleepy voice drawled.

"You were meant to call with a status."

"No, I said I'd call when I heard something. I haven't heard."

"Are you mocking me, Clarke?"

"No, no." All trace of sleep disappeared. "All I'm trying to say is that when we chose to go this route it wasn't with standard expectations of professionalism. The only thing these little bastards are good for is pulling a trigger."

"So what are they doing? Why haven't they called in?"

"Honestly? They're probably somewhere, sucking on a crack pipe. They're fifteen-, sixteen-year-old gang-bangers."

"They were your responsibility."

"I told them to call me after," he protested. "I warned

you there were drawbacks in using them."

"Why are you assuming it went without a hitch?"

"I should have said, they did call to say she had shown up and that they were going in. She was on her own; they confirmed that much. There were four of them, with enough firepower to take out a small village."

He considered what Clarke was saying. "She was definitely alone?"

"One hundred per cent. Look you said you needed distance, that it needed to look random. This was the best way."

There was no point in pursuing this. "Okay, call me the minute you hear."

"Yeah, alright, but I gotta warn you, if they've gone off on one of their binges, it could be a while."

"I said call!" He hung up before he had to listen to any more.

It was irritating having to put up with this kind of nonsense. The matter should have been closed tonight. He pictured Diane the last time he had seen her. She had been excited. Partly with his discovery about Pickroom but mostly at what they had discussed for their future. Again, he questioned his conclusion that she had to die.

If there could have been another way, he would have accepted it eagerly. If only she had not come to suspect Wallace. At the start, he had only wanted to get close to her to keep watch on how she was doing with her investigation. He could feed her a little misinformation, ensure she was steered away from anything too dangerous. Then that fool Brewer had fucked up by using Kates, and the shootout with Abeylan resulted. After that, he had to do something more to gain her confidence. Showing her some support when everyone else failed her seemed to be the obvious way.

But it had changed at some point. She had started to mean something to him. Or that's what he thought had happened. He had been leading this life for so long that sometimes even he wasn't sure where the charade ended and reality begun. He remonstrated with himself to be truthful. It had been clear that it might come to this. He had used all her vulnerabilities to ensure he was optimally positioned. He had tailored himself to fill all the gaps, every emotional weakness in her life. Part of him protested at the thought and the self-loathing that came with it. The same part that had vaguely imagined some future with her after the mission had come to a successful conclusion.

He snapped himself out of it, remembering there was still work to do. Difficult work, necessary work which he had to see to. Later there would be time enough for this self-indulgence.

He closed his mind to all thoughts of her and turned his attention to the matter of Madrigal's displacement.

twelve

They drove over 300 miles to make it by morning.

Between the long trek and the ordeal of the previous night, she should have been exhausted, but the reverberations of what had occurred had left her in a trance-like state. She had tried to pick holes in her conclusion that Tom had been the one who had intended her to be killed. She desperately wanted to believe she was wrong and that what they had shared had been real. In the end, though, she had accepted the truth. Each time she began the process of trying to construct a plausible alternative, she had revisited the intimacy they had shared and the pain grew. A small part of her, the rational part to which she was just barely holding on, appreciated how he had played on her weaknesses, how her desperate need for an ally had made it so easy for him.

Larsen, which she had learned was her companion's name at some point or other during the night, had insisted they needed to see Wallace as soon as possible. She had been so preoccupied that his explanation as to why this was necessary hardly registered. Wallace had been in Washington the previous night as it turned out and when Larsen contacted him, they had agreed to meet at a property he owned in Charleston. The location was close enough for them to drive and afforded more security than DC. When they had arrived at his estate, they were informed that he was expected presently and shown to a reception room to wait.

They both sank into deep armchairs and waited in silence.

When Wallace arrived forty minutes later, Mesi was taken aback. When she had been researching him, she had come across numerous archived photographs. The consistent impression had been of a man who still possessed an enormous amount of charisma and vitality despite his age. There had been a palpable sense of power emanating from the images and she had considered him some kind of latter-day Caesar. In the flesh, he was far thinner than even the most recent pictures and looked tired. He approached Larsen, who remained seated, then slowed and halted a few paces away, his awkwardness evident.

"Until yesterday, I'd thought you were dead."

"Almost."

He nodded.

"I had no way of finding you … Brewer …"

Wallace hesitated and looked at Mesi. Larsen had mentioned her when he had called and said they would be able to talk freely as she knew virtually everything anyway. It had occurred to him that the mercenary might have turned and needed him to incriminate himself but he had decided that if this was the case, it was nothing more than he deserved. The way he had deserted Larsen justified any subsequent betrayal.

"We need to discuss how we're going to fix things," Larsen said.

"In what way?" He spread his hands and Mesi could see he wasn't sure what Larsen meant.

"We were infiltrated, I suspect from the start," explained Larsen. "We'll probably never be able to ask him but I'm certain it was Brewer, there aren't really any other candidates."

Mesi watched Wallace struggle to digest what he was

being told. His lack of acknowledgement at her presence angered her. Thoughts of Tom receded for the moment. The man ultimately responsible for everything that had occupied her since Mexico was standing right in front of her.

"What are you talking about?" he asked Larsen.

"In the last few months, you'd started to worry about the knock-on effects of what we were doing. I dismissed them as the noises of someone losing their stomach for what was necessary," Larsen replied. "But since Cartagena, I've gone back over it. The longer I spent, the more I saw how valid your concerns were. What looked, at first, to be merely a coincidence or two, started to seem deliberate."

"No, you're wrong. We tried to do too much. It simply couldn't work. There were too many variables outside our control. There was no deliberate sabotage!"

She could see that despite his words he was experiencing the same mounting sense of apprehension she had gone through herself only the previous night.

"I'll explain the 'why' in a moment," Larsen continued, as if Wallace had not even spoken. "As far as 'how' goes, in hindsight, Brewer had too much influence, acting as he did as the conduit between us. I should've seen that."

"You're wrong; Brewer did precisely what he was told, no more, no less. He followed directions," Wallace protested.

"That's not so. He worked with you from the start, refining your original vision, and he collaborated with me on individual missions. He had a significant say in the methods we used and the schedule we followed. It's easy now to see how he used that to maximum effect; to subvert the entire project. I underestimated him." Larsen's annoyance with himself was evident. "Really, when you consider it, he had the most effective position – he was so involved, interacted so much with both of us, that we never thought to suspect him."

"How could he, the two of us were there every step of the way?"

"I was always primarily focused on the next task to hand and you were only too happy to defer to him because it gave you a comfortable distance. Think about it, how often would he suggest a small, plausible alteration which you just accepted?"

Wallace tried to interrupt but Larsen held up a hand cutting him off.

"If he had done anything drastic we'd have noticed, but he was careful. The cumulative effect of all his inputs, though, of all his minor suggestions, was to render it as much his creation as yours. Or rather that of whoever was pulling his strings."

"You're saying he was working for someone else?"

"Only because this goes way beyond Brewer's capabilities. I'd say he brought your proposal to someone almost as soon as you'd finished your initial approach."

"What do you base that on?"

"Hindsight. It was naive to believe he'd go along, considering his vested interests and allegiances in Latin America. What you were proposing would have shattered the status quo and thrown all that into jeopardy."

"You're sure about this?" was all Wallace could manage while he tried to keep up with what he was being told.

"I'm sure I was set up. Who else could it be? I did briefly consider the possibility that you might've sold me out, that you had asked for someone to help bail you out."

Wallace stared to protest.

"It's okay, I know that wasn't it. Wider events consistently fell a particular way, moving towards an outcome which you'd never have condoned. Of course, the smart thing to do, once I'd seen that, would have been to walk away, instead here we are. Stupid."

Mesi could see that Wallace was struggling with the same problems she and Larsen had. As difficult as it had been for her to get her head around the breadth of the impact of Hughes' subversion of Wallace's plan, it would be even more difficult for Wallace himself. As the initiator of the strategy and suspecting what she did of his motivation, the hardest part would surely have been the suffering the conflict had caused to innocents. Wallace must have expected some collateral damage but would he view these revelations as a way of trying to absolve himself of some of the responsibility?

"You know," the Dane continued. "It only occurred to me recently that the two of us watched one unintended legacy of the initiative. We even discussed it in passing but we never thought to question it."

Mesi could see Wallace trying to figure it out and Larsen deliberately letting the other man do the work himself. She guessed it would be easier to convince Wallace that way.

"Were we used to destabilise Plan Coca?" Wallace asked hesitatingly.

"Among other things."

"What other things?" he asked, his fear evident.

"The combined effect of the Plan and what we did was used to reconstruct the power structure within the Colombian drug industry. The ELN and FARC have been almost wiped out."

"That's hardly a travesty; it was one of the Plan's aims!"

Wallace interrupted, his voice strained.

"Plan Coca's official remit stated one of its main objectives as wresting control of the drug-producing territories from the Marxist rebels. Without these territories, the rebels would have found it impossible to survive," the Dane replied calmly.

"Precisely," Wallace shot back.

"But it wasn't intended for seventy per cent of the rebels to be murdered by death squads. And it certainly wasn't part of Plan Coca's remit for the territories to be then handed over to these same death squads, so that they could resume production."

"How could what we were doing have had any bearing on that?"

"We cut off the rebels' cash-flow. We hurt the cartels so badly that they couldn't or weren't willing to extend the money that the rebels needed to fight back effectively."

"So we helped replace one element with another? That's not something to be pleased about, but ultimately I can't feel too much grief for the rebels. They made a living off the drug crops for years, at innocent people's expense."

During the exchange Mesi's anger had been building and with Wallace's last rationalisation it skyrocketed. His conceit was beyond belief. Some of what Larsen was saying was new to her but she believed him. It all tied in and it was clear the mercenary derived no satisfaction from any of it. He was explaining what he believed to be the hard truth and all Wallace was concerned with was mitigating his own culpability.

"The territories were only the first part of a chain," Larsen continued. "The next objective was to seize control of the Alliance from an uncooperative leader. Everything else, from due process to straightforward assassination attempts, had failed, so, there was only one alternative left."

"Weaken the Alliance to the point where Madrigal is undermined," Mesi cut in, "to the point where he's ready to be forced out. Of course, it requires that a more suitable replacement be standing by."

"Considering everything else they've achieved, that's got to be comparatively easy," Larsen offered.

"You're crazy. No one could have arranged all that, tied it all together," Wallace argued.

Mesi guessed Wallace was starting to believe otherwise, despite his protestations.

"Someone could and someone did. Ask yourself why I'd lie. If I wanted something from you, there are easier ways."

The matter-of-fact tone of Larsen's declaration completed the process. Wallace sunk down slowly onto a couch. Mesi saw the progression from bewilderment to slow recognition and finally despair. He looked old and frail sitting there, trying to come to terms with it all.

"That's it," Larsen concluded. "Control of the crops, the apparatus to produce and ship the refined drugs, all combined with the elimination of any threat from further US military intervention. Get ready for a drugs boom that's going to make what went before pale in comparison."

"There might be one more thing," Mesi said.

Larsen turned to her. "What's that?"

"There are three oil pipelines in Colombia which FARC had been extorting. Lobbyists for the oil companies had complained and asked the administration for protection. Some ground forces were dispatched and it looked like they were getting the situation under control. Now they'll probably be pulled out along with Plan Coca."

"The pipelines. You're right, I never even considered those and it doesn't matter that the troops assigned aren't there under the Plan's aegis. US troop deployment in Colombia is too sensitive an issue right now," Larsen agreed. "So, the odds are that the oil companies will begin to have problems again. This time, though, they'll find themselves dealing with right-wing death squads who can operate with impunity. Quite a nice sideline, extorting multinationals."

He stared at the subdued Wallace then looked back to her.

"The question is, what are we going to do about it?"

Wallace remained motionless on the couch, giving no indication that he was ready to continue. After a little while, Mesi stood up and said she was going outside for some air. The atmosphere in the room was suffocating. Larsen remained slumped in his armchair and, taking the container from his jacket, popped a few more pills.

Larsen was feeling the strain of the last few days. It had been over three months since the ambush in Cartagena but he was nowhere near fully recovered. How he had managed to make it back to the marina was still something of a mystery to him. Through a combination of first floating and later crawling, it had taken most of the night. One agonising yard at a time. He had almost been discovered on more than one occasion, the closest call being when a couple of police officers patrolling the tourist area of the waterfront spotted his prone figure in the distance. They had satisfied themselves with shouting a few derisive remarks, dismissing him as another partier who had overindulged. If he had not been discovered on his boat by a member of the assault team who had arrived to link up with him, he would not have survived. The team arranged medical treatment for him and in return he ensured they were paid in full despite the aborted mission. During his recuperation he had puzzled over why Brewer would have gone ahead and arranged for the team to travel to Cartagena. It didn't make sense if he had intended for Larsen to be dead by that stage anyway. Was he covering himself in case Larsen evaded the ambush, building a plausible way to refute the accusation of betrayal? Or had someone else arranged for the ambush and been either unaware of their arrival or perhaps simply too complacent? He would probably never know.

He had been told that the physical effects of the ambush would take a long time to get over and that he must avoid stressing himself too soon. He had taken as much time as he could until, seeing where events in Colombia were headed, he had to move.

The vigil outside Wallace's house in DC illustrated how stumped he had been in relation to where he should start. He didn't know where Brewer was or who he was working with and he had no idea how he could go about finding out. He had hoped that somehow Wallace might provide the answers. He had only started his stakeout the previous night and luckily he was in time to see Mesi. More than once during the drive to Charleston he had considered what would have happened had he arrived even one day later. Mesi would be dead and they would have no clue of Hughes' involvement. Coincidence could be a powerful force.

Despite Mesi's certainty regarding Hughes' pre-eminence in the affair, Larsen was not so sure. Perhaps he was the man pulling all the strings, or he might just be a cog in a larger machine, nonetheless his existence and his manipulation of Mesi meant Larsen had a hook into the enemy. His rage was the only thing keeping him going. All he wanted to do was curl up and sleep for a year. He was done, drained physically and mentally, but rage transcended all of it. Whether Wallace's plan would have succeeded without outside interference was impossible to say; perhaps not but that was not the issue. Once again, his actions had been taken and used to fulfil an agenda he had no knowledge of. All he had wanted was one last opportunity, something to believe in, and they, whoever 'they' were, had perverted that. This time, they would be disabused of any notions that they were untouchable. One way or another, he was going to face them and make them answer. He wished there had been some way to thwart their plans regarding control of Colombia's drugs – that would have been satisfying – but it was surely too late.

He looked at the almost catatonic Wallace, sitting across from him. For a long time since their last meeting, he had been angry at Wallace for his apparent weakness. He couldn't understand how the billionaire could have countenanced just giving up. He really had wondered, while he was recovering, if the ambush had not been Wallace's attempt to rid himself of the irksome gun-for-hire but he saw things more clearly now. Wallace was never the man Larsen had wanted him to be and that was no one but the Dane's fault. He had wanted some paragon leading a righteous crusade which he would be able to enlist in. Instead Wallace was just as flawed as anyone else and when he had seen his plans go terribly awry he had, understandably, faltered.

Mesi walked back into the room fifteen minutes later, more animated.

"We can still stop him!" she stated.

Larsen looked at her questioningly.

"Hughes," she said. "We can still stop him getting what he wants."

The remark roused Wallace. "Who is this Hughes?"

"The person behind the attempt to oust Madrigal and seize the territories."

"We're not sure of that," Larsen corrected her. "He could know next to nothing. He might just be following orders."

"I don't think so." She shook her head. "But whether I'm right or not, it doesn't change what I'm saying. We can stop what's being attempted."

"What are you talking about?" Wallace asked. "It's already too late. What can any of us do to stop it?"

"We can do the one thing that'll jeopardise everything they're attempting. We can provide proof of what they've done to Madrigal. He may be weakened but I'd be willing to bet that he could still make a fight of it."

Wallace rose quickly from his seat, eyes wide. "I thought he was finished."

"Not quite. Given the right help, who knows?"

"You're suggesting we throw him a lifeline? The culmination to all this is to attempt to save the most successful drug lord the world's ever seen?"

"Actually, it's probably the best option available," Larsen interjected, clearly seeing the possibilities and warming to her proposal. "At least this way we ensure all the control doesn't reside with the same party. Yes, we know what Madrigal is but can you suggest another way?"

"No. No, no, no."

At first she thought briefly that Wallace was agreeing

that there was no other option, but as his voice rose and he became more agitated, she saw he was objecting to her suggestion. Mesi lost her temper. She had spent weeks in the hospital, her career was in tatters and her personal life in ruins. There had been two attempts on her life and, whatever Hughes had done, it was Wallace's vendetta that had been the root cause. "What makes you think you have the right to object?" she spat. "I'm not an advocate for Madrigal but you've certainly given up any right you have to judge him."

"That's not fair," Wallace protested. "Maybe what I did was misguided and I'll have to live with my mistakes but I was trying to do right. If there hadn't been interference it might have worked. You don't know."

"Spare me! You lost a daughter and granddaughter and took it as licence to incite a war. This is the way we're going to go. You don't have a choice, just a moral obligation to make up for some of what you've caused."

She did not even attempt to control the viciousness in her voice. Her hatred for him was absolute and her entire frame shook with it.

"My God, listen to what you're suggesting – prop up Madrigal! You're a DEA agent; how can you even suggest it?"

"Do you think it's easy? This is the best chance we have." She stepped closer, standing within inches of him while she continued, her voice harsh. "Don't try to rationalise or justify your actions to me. You murdered countless people and caused countless more to die. That would have happened with or without interference. You're not one of the victims. Your pride and self-indulgence have brought us here." She pointed over at Larsen who sat quietly, watching them argue. "If I had my way, you'd spend the rest of your life in an eight-by-six cell along with your attack dog over there. Madrigal and Hughes could join you."

"There has to be another way," Wallace persisted.

"Anything else risks giving Hughes, or whoever, the opportunity to stop us. They're helped by the fact that no one in authority will really want to pursue this, they'll try to pretend it never happened. We need Madrigal."

"We could approach someone else in the Alliance?" he protested; anything would be preferable to resurrecting the Colombian.

"Who? Who could we trust? No one else would care as long as profits are assured and Hughes' intention isn't to cut the Alliance out, only to ensure they behave. Madrigal's the only chance. They want him gone for a reason: he's too independent."

"How will his survival help?"

"What we tell him will encourage him to become even more entrenched, less cooperative with the factions who now control the territories. First, though, he needs to consolidate his power in the Alliance and to do that he needs our help."

It was clear that Wallace was furiously trying to come up with something to counter her arguments and equally clear that he was failing.

"You don't see any other way?" he asked Larsen.

"No."

"Okay, what is it you want from me?" Wallace asked Mesi wearily.

"To help Madrigal we need to move quickly; give him proof he can use," she replied. "Hughes may have some heavy hitters working with him but there are a lot more who had their hopes pinned on Plan Coca. Political, military and intelligence. They've been screwed. If they knew how Hughes had orchestrated their misery, they'd want to stop him."

"How would they do that?"

"If any hard evidence exists, some of the pro-Plan contingent would know where to look. The problem is access. I have a fair idea who to approach but I'm a lowly DEA agent with a questionable reputation. I wouldn't even get in the door; you would!"

"Why not just hand the matter over to these people and let them deal with it as they see fit?"

"From here on in, you take responsibility," she warned him. "If we don't drive this, if we leave it up to others, they'd either take too long to act or decide to cut a deal for a piece of the action."

"You think we can do this without alerting them?"

"That's what we're going to find out."

Madrigal put the document down and stretched out the knot of tension between his shoulders.

"Once more, please," he said to the anxious man who was standing in the middle of the room.

"I received a call yesterday, advising me that a package containing information essential to your future was waiting at the reception of La Casa Magnífica."

"So you went to the hotel?"

"Not immediately. At first I discounted the call as a hoax or some kind of foolish trap. But the more I thought about it …" The man began fidgeting, searching for the words. "If there was even a slight chance that it could benefit you then there was no other option. I had the package collected and checked for tracking devices and booby traps."

Madrigal nodded. Each page had been placed in a separate plastic cover to protect anyone handling them from chemical solutions which might be present.

"And the envelope?"

"Plain brown with my name and nothing else on it."

"Okay, you can go."

The man exhaled heavily in relief and left the room quickly. Madrigal picked up a small rubber ball and began idly throwing it into the air then catching it while swivelling in his chair. He tried to digest the document's contents and divine the sender's motivation. He had two days before he would have to face Rodriguez's challenge at a specially scheduled meeting. He had been determined to fight but had known that the odds were stacked against him. Did this represent a chance to shift those odds?

Most of the document was comprised of detailed reconnaissance reports which had been used for various attacks during the conflict. The specific attacks were discussed as part of a larger strategy. Among the main objectives listed was his removal. A handwritten note accompanied the report.

The contents of this document confirm the planning that has gone into creating the crisis you face. There is more you need to hear. Knowing the full facts will enable you to survive this challenge and purge the Alliance of dangerous elements. I will be in the lobby of the La Casa Magnífica at noon on Wednesday, alone and unarmed. I am willing to go through any security procedures you feel are necessary. The one stipulation is that we meet in person; no intermediaries can be trusted.

Michael Larsen's signature at the bottom brought a

rueful smile to his lips.

The blindfold was removed from Larsen's eyes and it took a few seconds for him to get used to the light and orient himself. He was standing beside a set of wooden table and chairs under a large parasol on a huge manicured lawn. To the right was a small bar where a man was squeezing orange juice and in the distance he could see the roof of a large house behind a group of trees. Beyond the house stood densely forested mountains, their peaks shrouded in mist.

"Sit," ordered one of the three armed guards who were watching him intently.

He pulled out the chair facing the house and sat back, trying to relax. Five minutes passed, then it stretched to ten before he lost track of time.

One of the guards stirred and he looked out to see Madrigal approaching, flanked by two more bodyguards. As he approached, Larsen glanced around at the guards – the reverence they had for Madrigal was obvious. Larsen had been around a lot of people over the years who fancied themselves as leaders and he knew how rare the genuine article was. The drug lord radiated an authority undiminished by his current problems.

Madrigal sat down across from Larsen, and the newly arrived bodyguards positioned themselves six feet back either side of his chair. The barman walked over to the table with a serving tray and placed a large jug of orange juice, two glasses and a bucket of ice on the table. He moved to pour a glass for the drug lord, who waved him away. Madrigal grabbed a handful of ice, dropped it in his glass and poured the drink himself.

"You?" he asked, gesturing with the jug.

Larsen shook his head, knowing Madrigal had to go through the motions. He was demonstrating that he was not so desperate to get on with it that he would compromise his dignity.

Madrigal took a sip from his glass and put it down, taking a moment to savour the freshness of the drink. He studied the mercenary who looked to be in less than perfect health.

"I suppose it's some small consolation that you didn't escape Cartagena totally unscathed. The file you sent contained incredible detail regarding the attacks against us and the Kosovars. Tell me how you came to possess this information?"

"The reconnaissance reports were delivered to me before the attacks. The status reports I wrote, after the individual operations," Larsen told him.

"After you'd participated in their execution?"

"Yes."

"And the rest of the report?"

"The part outlining the overall objectives comes from a separate source. I'd been working towards another goal and was unaware of them. We're meeting now because we each have an interest in seeing those objectives aren't realised."

Madrigal smiled. "Does your interest stem partially from what happened in Cartagena?"

"It's related, yes," Larsen answered honestly.

"Before we discuss the goals outlined in the document, you say you were working to other ends. What were they?"

"A significant drop for an extended period in the amount of illegal narcotics produced and distributed."

Madrigal laughed and then saw that Larsen was not

joking. "Why?"

"It hurts a lot of people. Limit it and you spare them."

"It was a humanitarian mission?" he asked incredulously.

"To a degree. I was contracted for a fee."

"This is preposterous."

"Maybe, but achievable. It was starting to work."

"In the short-term perhaps but the market would have recovered in the next few months regardless of what had happened between us and the Kosovars."

"I'm not sure I agree but we'll never know."

"And who funded your operation?"

"That's beyond the scope of our discussion. You'll have to accept my word that the people behind it won't be resuming their campaign. The price involved was too high."

Madrigal considered this for a moment. Larsen knew the drug lord could always return to the topic later if he wished. Madrigal had all of the power and Larsen's life was in his hands.

"Okay, the document mentioned seizing the territories, which has been accomplished, and my overthrow, which … has not yet been decided. Your note said there was more to tell?"

"One of the Alliance's inner circle knew about it. More than that, he participated in it for his own advancement."

Madrigal's surprise was visible as was the fury which very quickly followed when the full implications of Larsen's statement sank in. He might have suspected there were leaks but for them to be coming from the top level would be galling. It would mean that the person responsible would have been fully aware of the consequences of this campaign. All the hardship and setbacks that the Alliance had endured had been orchestrated with the help of one of their own.

Just as Larsen then Mesi and Wallace had reeled from the implications, Madrigal was now going through the same process.

"You have proof of this?"

"Transcripts of reports referring to someone using a codename and describing actions taken to further his ascent. I also have intelligence reports, attributed to the same individual, essentially him selling out his own associates."

"How extensive are these transcripts?"

"Enough to demonstrate a strong correlation between the person and the codename. The guard over there," he pointed to one of his escorts, "took the copies from me at the hotel."

Madrigal gestured and the guard placed a number of individually wrapped pages on the table in front of him. Madrigal read through them carefully, taking his time. When he had finished, he sat back.

"These are interesting."

Larsen nodded.

"But not enough," the Colombian said. "He could say it's all a clever concoction, I need something more. Something to clinch it."

"In one of the reports the attack on Francisco Zaragosa is discussed. In order to ensure the traitor was locked in, tapes were made of his discussions relating to the assassination. He details how and where Zaragosa could be most easily reached."

"And these tapes?"

"When we're finished, I'll make a phone call and they'll be delivered to you. He might be able to convince people that the documentation is fiction, but combined with the tapes ..."

"Okay, let's get down to the guts of it. You've spelt out what you can do to help me but what's in this for you?"

"I'm ensuring that the people behind this don't get what they want."

"You find their objectives that abhorrent, or is it injured pride?"

"I might not have cared what they were doing, if they hadn't involved me," he agreed, "but that's not my sole problem. They tried to have me killed. When it comes to their attention that I'm still alive, they'll try again."

Satisfied with Larsen's answer, Madrigal moved on.

"You've admitted your part in what I've had to endure, and while I may have other concerns, what you did is hardly insubstantial. Why should I let you walk away from here? Why not force you to turn over the tapes and even the score a little in the process?"

"I don't have the tapes and I don't know where they are. Only a call from me from a specific location a day's journey from Colombia can release them. You could gamble, torture me and have me beg on the end of a phone. But I should say that the others involved had reservations about my approaching you. If the procedure's deviated from, you risk not getting the tapes."

Larsen waited in silence while Madrigal deliberated. This was the moment in which it all hung in the balance. Madrigal might choose to try coercion or he might just kill Larsen and gamble that the material he had been given, incomplete as it was, would be enough for him to see off the threat.

Finally, after what seemed like minutes to Larsen, Madrigal said, "Okay, I'll accept that, but tell me, why do you think I won't come after you and your accomplices when I've dealt with my current situation?"

"Assuming your gratitude wasn't enough?"

"Assuming that."

"If it was me, I'd do a risk-reward analysis. You're going to have your hands full reasserting control and trying to restore some balance to the relationship with the growers. Maybe it's easy enough for you to get rid of us but why take the chance?"

"To prevent you relaunching your humanitarian mission?"

"The moment is gone. Besides, we've seen the alternative to you."

"You've only given me part of it, the objectives concerning the Alliance and the traitors in its midst. What about the identity of those who conceived this scheme to displace me?"

"They'll be dealt with."

"Some of them directly by you, no doubt."

Larsen shrugged his shoulders.

"I think that covers everything," Madrigal said. "Although there is something I'd like to ask you. It occurred to me when I was reading your file. I know how I got here but how does the son of a Portuguese fisherman from Northern Denmark, an affluent, comfortable country, wind up negotiating with the head of a Colombian drug cartel?"

"I've asked myself that. Whatever the answer is, I think I'll be taking the more-travelled road from now on."

"A shame considering your capabilities."

Larsen did not reply.

"Well, I think we're finished. My men have taken the liberty of packing your luggage. They'll escort you directly to the airport."

With that, the blindfold was placed back over Larsen's eyes.

———

thirteen

Rodriguez had arrived early and watched the men file in for the summit meeting. He couldn't remember a time when he had been happier. This was the day he had waited for and he intended to savour every minute. What was about to unfold would have been unthinkable only twelve months earlier. Everyone in Mexico now looked to him for leadership and Lora, the other Mexican at the meeting, was only here because it suited Rodriguez. Appearing too much like a solitary leader might create the wrong impression.

The meeting began with a review of how they had fared since the conflict with the Kosovars had ceased. It was reported that, while they were almost back to former levels of supply, there was now more competition in the markets where other players had exploited their difficulties and moved in. To combat this the cartel had taken a conscious decision to subsidise the product until they had reasserted their position as market leaders. One factor that was undermining this effort, however, was the greed of the middlemen who were not passing on the full benefit. It was decided to continue with the current distributors for one more month and then, if the matter had not been resolved, to evaluate other candidates. When the lengthy review of recent business had finished, the men broke briefly for refreshments before the second half of the meeting, which was traditionally a forum for individual members to raise specific issues.

Rodriguez enjoyed the opportunity to mingle. Influential men from all over South and Central America appreciated the shift that had occurred and greeted him with deference. When he looked across the room at Madrigal, the Colombian appeared relatively isolated. A few stalwarts still stuck close, showing their allegiance. He supposed their loyalty was to their credit but made it a point to memorise who they were.

The break finished up and they made their way back to their seats to resume the meeting. He watched with detachment as a number of minor items were discussed and put to a vote. The unspoken expectation in the room was palpable. When it reached the point where he felt it could not be dragged out any further he nodded across the table to Cabieses who stood up and requested the floor. The elderly Peruvian was one of the most respected members of the council. In the past he had often been the calming influence and had averted many potential disputes. Regardless of the issues, he could generally be counted on to find the reasonable middle ground. His sterling reputation and reluctance to become involved in personal agendas at the expense of the Alliance made him the perfect man for the job. There had been no bribery or blackmail involved; both would have been impossible. Once he had been convinced of what was in the best interests of the majority he had volunteered himself.

"Gentlemen, I wish to discuss a serious matter," he began. "I do not raise this lightly but only because I see it as essential to our future. Before the recent difficulties we enjoyed unparalleled prosperity under Luis's direction."

The old man turned and bowed his head slightly to Madrigal who gestured for him to continue.

"Luis formed the group which gathers here today, seeing what no one else could. By working together we increased our revenues many times over and with this came a period of great stability. Despite everything he achieved, he never sought to dictate to us. Instead, he brought us together, eager to hear our thoughts. We should never forget how much he has given us."

The old man paused, giving his tribute to Madrigal time to sink in, then he resumed. "But all things have their time, they grow, mature and ultimately wane. This is the way of the world, you only have to look at me to see the proof."

Some of the audience politely refuted his words but he held up his hand.

"No, it's true. When I was younger my energy was boundless but now I leave much of the decision-making to the trusted friends who share this table. Occasionally I offer advice when I feel it appropriate and this is enough to make me content. Everyone, regardless of former capabilities, reaches a stage when they have to hand over the reins to others. Times change and new challenges arise; a man can find himself out of step with events."

He looked around the table slowly before continuing.

"The recent troubles almost destroyed us. There were times when I feared we would not survive and only the character of the men here today averted this disaster. Together, you held your nerve and managed to come through. But the question has to be asked, could it have been avoided? I have asked myself this question countless times, trying to see it from all sides, and each time I come to the same conclusion. Had we followed a different strategy, we might have been spared much of the crisis. I think this is proven by how quickly the Kosovars agreed to end hostilities once we stepped up our retaliation. One person, more than anyone else, argued for this course of action from the earliest days." Cabieses looked to Rodriguez for a moment, drawing the gaze of the others.

"Initially he was dismissed as impetuous by many, myself included. In the past Luis had demonstrated how caution and forethought were invaluable qualities. So, not surprisingly, we resisted calls for action, hoping to learn more. Caesar argued that we were overthinking the problem, the simple explanation, that the Kosovars wanted to supplant us, was the correct one. With the passing of time we began to see the wisdom in his words. Luis's commendable trait of caution became entrenched stubbornness and inflexibility. At this point Caesar showed his true qualities. Rather than force the issue and cause an irreparable rift, he convinced us to give Luis the time he needed. In the end Luis did retaliate with all the necessary force but only after his closest friend had been brutally killed."

Once more he paused as if he was not sure how to phrase his next remark. After a heavy sigh, he resumed. "With all this in mind, I respectfully request that Luis steps down and Caesar assumes charge of our future direction. In this new more dangerous time, a fresh perspective is required. Hopefully my example can show Luis that there is still a contribution to be made in a less active role."

Other than Cabieses no one was willing to make eye contact with Madrigal, but the murmured assents around the table reflected their feelings. Rodriguez, for his part, was confident that regardless of how Madrigal reacted it would make no difference. If he argued against the proposal and painted it as a betrayal, he would only make himself look worse.

Madrigal cleared his throat and the room went still. "Tomas, I have no doubts about why you felt it necessary to speak today and I know that none of it was said lightly."

Cabieses nodded earnestly at this opening remark.

"It's true that while I argued for caution we suffered badly," Madrigal continued. "It's also true that the Kosovars quickly saw sense once we did act."

While Rodriguez was happy with what he took as a precursor to Madrigal's acquiescence, he was a little surprised at how graciously the Colombian was admitting his errors. He warned himself to watch for any attempt to mitigate the admission.

"I see the sense in what was said regarding the phases we must go through and if I can be half as productive as Tomas, I would welcome the new role. When I first brought us together I knew there was more to be done than one man could manage. There is no question of my ego standing in the way of the common good."

The apprehension in the room subsided noticeably.

"Once again," Cabieses said. "He shows us the true nature of greatness. No petty selfishness; those feelings are alien to him. We have been blessed."

Rodriguez was so surprised when Cabieses began to clap and when the others joined in enthusiastically, he almost forgot to go along. It was such a perfect moment that he could not spoil it by appearing less gracious than Madrigal. The outgoing leader held up his hands, gradually bringing the room to silence. "I would just like to speak briefly about the recent troubles and my hopes for our future recovery, regardless of who steers us through it."

He walked around the table to stand behind Rodriguez's chair and placed his hands on its back. Rodriguez was not comfortable having him standing there but it would be awkward to twist around and rude to stand. He could smell Madrigal's cologne and was sure he could feel the man's breath on the top of his head as he spoke.

"Tomas has suggested Caesar, pointing out how attuned he is to what is now required. We all know of his dramatic rise which has outstripped even that of Francisco Zaragosa before the unfortunate incident."

People around the room voiced their agreement. Rodriguez found himself wishing Madrigal would hurry up with his abdication speech.

"He has disproved those of us who doubted what he had to offer. It seems like we were thinking about another person entirely. The gulf between expectation and reality has become so wide. You must tell us who's been coaching you."

Everyone laughed in appreciation of Madrigal's good-natured admission of error in judgement.

"Caesar was the first to call for a strike against the Kosovars. He argued passionately for what he felt was necessary for our survival. Despite this, when Esteban Zaragosa took matters into his own hands and moved against me directly, he was never tempted. Indeed, he even warned me about the planned attempt on my life."

Rodriguez could see everyone looking at him, thoughts flickering behind their eyes. No one was comfortable discussing Zaragosa's actions but they were equally uncomfortable with the thought that he had been betrayed by his compatriot to the Colombian. It was not something that could be easily given a positive spin. Lora looked particularly pensive. Rodriguez made a note to deal with that as soon as possible. Jesus, he thought as Madrigal droned on, when is he going to sit down?

"Caesar, if I can offer you some advice?' He felt the hands come to rest on his shoulders and, despite the air-conditioning, he started to feel uncomfortably warm.

"The first thing I would do is deal with the matter of how the Kosovars had such good intelligence. They knew exactly when and where to attack. I'm sure we're all aware that some of our people must have sold information. I've been looking into this matter and recently made some progress. Would you mind if I shared my findings?"

Everyone looked at Rodriguez.

"Of cour –" His throat was so dry he had to stop and drink some water. "Of course, you must tell me everything but perhaps later. Rather than trouble everyone with the interim findings, I can give a more conclusive status report when the matter has been dealt with."

"Well, actually I think you'll agree when you hear what I've found that it's already possible to draw conclusions."

The grip on his shoulders tightened ever so slightly.

"The first thing that struck me is to never be surprised how far people will go to fulfil their ambition. Please, if you will all just bear with me for a moment."

Madrigal stepped away from the chair and gave an order to two attendants who stood near the door. They left and returned a few moments later, one carrying a remote control for the sound system and the other some files. They placed these at the head of the conference table and stood back.

"It's a very short tape," Madrigal said, pressing Play. Distorted electronic voices immediately filled the room.

"Yes, I've set up contact with the Mexican, codename Viper from now on. He's eager to work with us."

"You're certain he's the right man."

"Oh yes, clever enough but not too clever. He's as ambitious as we've been led to believe but still aware of his limitations."

"The reservations about his inclination for hotheadedness?"

"I've laid the groundwork and I'll drive it home over time that we decide when direct action is necessary and the appropriate scale."

"Okay. What's the first move?"

"We're going to help Viper look good, a few successful forays led by him against their competition."

"We don't want anything too risky, no point in losing him, considering how long it took for us to identify him."

"Don't worry. With the intelligence we're going to give him it should be impossible to screw it up."

Madrigal stopped the tape and Rodriguez saw an array of puzzled faces. Before he could speak Madrigal pressed Play again.

"… other business, Viper, how's he doing?"

"Excellently, we've provided him with enough help to kick-start his upward progress. He's now just below the senior level."

"Well done, and the schedule for the final push?"

"One of the senior figures, the Young Prince, whom we've identified as a threat, will have to be removed sooner or later. It may as well be sooner so as to benefit Viper."

"You're confident it can be done, we don't want anything too public, something which would attract too much attention."

"Viper himself has helped us enormously in that. He's managed to get detailed information on the Prince's security

arrangements. Actually, I'll send you the tape where Viper goes through them in detail, I think you'll be impressed with his professionalism, considering your initial reservations."

"Excellent, excellent."

Madrigal stopped the tape again. The blood had drained from Rodriguez's face and he started shaking ever so slightly.

"The tapes you've just heard were made by rogue elements within the US intelligence community. They were delivered to me at the eleventh hour and as such I had no opportunity to share them with anyone before this conference. They deal with an operation whose aim was to first infiltrate and compromise our Alliance and then displace everyone who sits here today."

The room erupted, shouts of consternation battling with one another to be heard. Madrigal gave them a few seconds, letting them get themselves worked up, each feeding the others' tension, before he gestured for quiet.

"Like me your immediate reaction might be one of disbelief. Unfortunately, the contents of the tape referred to in the last excerpt, which I'll play in a moment, puts it beyond doubt. The Young Prince referred to was Francisco Zaragosa. His security was lax as evidenced by the attack on his Californian residence. But Zaragosa's fate, as tragic as it was, is not the important issue."

Madrigal had walked back behind Rodriguez's chair.

"That, of course, is Viper's identity. Who he is and the damage he has done. Viper worked for these people over an extended period of time to destabilise the cartel and bring it perilously close to ruin. He did this for no other reason than to further himself."

Rodriguez tried to rise but the pressure from Madrigal's

hands pushed him back.

"I don't know if he was aware of his associates' larger plans, which included sabotaging official US foreign policy and crushing the rebellion, but that's hardly important. What is important and ultimately tragic is that Viper is one of us."

Madrigal looked to one of the attendants who began handing out the files to everybody around the table.

"That document gives an overview of everything I've told you about. A more comprehensive account will be given to you later, to absorb at your leisure." The man distributing the files passed by, not leaving one in front of Rodriguez. "You'll understand why some of the names have been omitted. I need to protect those loyal to me. The most important item is the identity of the traitor. I'm sure you'll have lots of questions and I'm equally sure I can answer them all with some help from Caesar, once we've heard the rest."

Madrigal pressed Play once more.

Larsen closed the car door and removed the wrapping from the prepaid phone. Once he had topped up the credit balance on the cell phone beyond the modest amount it had been issued with, he made his call.

"Canton?"

"Conchillo."

They had agreed to use this code to confirm they were each okay to talk.

"You made it back okay, then."

"Once I'd made the call to you and he'd presumably gotten the tapes, he called off his surveillance."

"Good. It's been three days; do you think he's moved?"

They had agreed that, despite the precautions of using only off-the-shelf, prepaid cell phones, they still needed to be as circumspect as possible.

"Definitely, he couldn't have afforded to delay. We'll have to wait for definitive confirmation but I'd say there won't be any more sightings of the heir apparent. What's the status on your end?"

When she and Larsen had last talked, Wallace was in the midst of negotiations.

She had managed to identify key individuals in the pro-Plan contingent whom they needed to enlist. Initially, Wallace had been greeted with scepticism. Faced with the circumstantial evidence he was able to furnish, however, along with details of specific attacks on the Alliance, they had revised their opinions. Once they were convinced of how they had been screwed over, investigations were set in motion. They needed to move stealthily lest Hughes learn of their efforts and take steps to obstruct them. Additionally, since the vast bulk of the operation had been carried out through Brewer, using Wallace's apparatus, virtually no official records existed. It had come together slowly – whispers and almost insignificant traces of what Hughes and his backers had been doing began to emerge. In the end, just enough traces existed to implement Mesi's plan.

Their real battle had occurred, as she had predicted, when Wallace tried to convince the powers they had approached to go along with her strategy. Wallace had been forced to threaten their reluctant allies that he was willing to go public with details of the entire affair. They had argued that he would be destroying his own reputation in the process and that he had little in the way of concrete evidence anyway. She had been sure they would call his bluff, especially in light of his shaky commitment to the idea of propping up Madrigal.

With less than an hour to go to his deadline, they had buckled and agreed to release the documentation Larsen had delivered to Madrigal.

The next bone of contention had been ensuring those responsible, all of them, were made pay and it was this Larsen wanted a status on.

"Negotiations are ongoing," she told him.

"They're insisting they'll deal with it themselves?" he guessed.

"Yes."

"That won't work," he said angrily.

"We're hanging in there but we don't have much bargaining power left."

"Can't our friend use the same threat as before?"

"They know we've already gotten a large part of what we wanted and I think they've figured out his heart isn't really in it."

"They'll take too long, try to limit the damage by cutting some agreement and he'll be gone," Larsen said wearily.

"Probably."

They knew a lot of influential people would be happy were Hughes to disappear, whether by his own volition or not.

He agreed to contact her later that evening and hung up.

After wiping the handset and placing it back in its wrapping, he stepped out of the car and threw it in a nearby dumpster.

The back wheel spun faster and faster, until its friction on the A-frame treadmill became a high-pitched whine drowning out the radio. The rider bent forward over the stationary front wheel of the racing bike and pumped his legs faster, causing the bike to wobble in its cradle. He always ended his circuit by attempting to better his previous best speed. It was difficult to continually improve but he was optimistic, having felt very good before training. He pushed himself on, ignoring the sweat running down his face and stinging his eyes. He watched the speedometer climb upwards, the back wheel speeding along, filling the room with noise. His previous best was seventy kilometres per hour and he was at sixty-six now but feeling the strain. He glimpsed quickly at the readout beside the speedometer and saw that his heartbeat was one-eighty a minute, far too high to sustain for long. One last push. Sixty-seven, he blinked rapidly to clear his eyes; sixty-eight, his muscles cried out for release. Suddenly, he lost his rhythm and felt his legs being dragged around by the pedals as his speed plummeted. So close. He admitted defeat and straightened up in the saddle, placing his hands on his hips.

Hughes unclipped his shoes from the pedals and wearily stepped down from the bike. He was annoyed at the way the workout had ended but there was always tomorrow. He turned off the radio and opened the window wider to air the room. The rain still beat down outside, validating his purchase of the treadmill a few months before. Regardless of the weather he need never miss a workout again. He half-heartedly stretched for a couple of minutes and went through to the shower. He closed his eyes and turned his face to the powerful jet of water, luxuriating in the simple pleasure. He was looking forward to the day and the good news it would bring.

The final act, Rodriguez's deposing of Madrigal, would have occurred some time the previous evening. That was it, all objectives realised.

The only small cloud on the horizon was Mesi. It had been more than two weeks since her attempted killing and there was still no trace of the DEA agent. Clarke, his resource within the Baltimore police department, had called him the day after the ambush. He had told Hughes how the gang members whom he had recruited had been found dead. How had she managed to kill four assailants who possessed such superior firepower? He remembered then how resilient she had proved in the earlier altercation with Abeylan and cursed himself for underestimating her. On hearing the bad news, he had briefly worried that she would threaten his strategy, before sense prevailed. All she had was an unsubstantiated suspicion regarding Wallace, a suspicion which no one in the DEA would even consider acting on. There had been no sign of her going back to her employers. The feelers he had put out confirmed no one had been in contact with her and they were quite happy with that state of affairs. Cut off as she was, ignorant of all that lay beyond Wallace and his vendetta, what danger did she pose? A physical threat perhaps but that was it, she might come gunning for him when she realised he had set her up. Hughes arranged for her apartment to be watched and an experienced security team to shadow him discreetly. As the days passed with no developments, he began to believe that, in fear of her life, she had fled. She had been fragile enough before the ambush, so perhaps it had been the proverbial last straw? Satisfied that he was doing everything possible to tie up the loose end, he had returned his focus to where it belonged.

Stepping out of the shower, he looked at his watch. The first item on his official schedule today was a typically boring meeting with Petersen and some of the other bureaucrats. The main item on the agenda dealt with the cost of external consultancy; specifically the contract firm which had been called in to eliminate wasteful expenditure. They had proceeded to run up a seven-figure bill with nothing to show for it other than proposals any clerical worker in the building could have made. He wondered yet again why he bothered to retain his position – most of his energy was spent on other projects, projects that mattered. After a quick calculation, he decided he had enough time to check for updates.

He dressed quickly and left the house. Using a combination of taxis and Metrorail, he made his way via a roundabout route to the office he had let. Once there, he activated the speakerphone and punched in a number derived from a formula based on a fixed prefix and the current date. He waited for the call to be relayed through multiple routers until it got a ringing tone. Once it was answered and the current codes had been exchanged, he asked for news of recent contacts.

"A routine status report from Buenos Aires, want me to give you a summary?" his operative asked.

"No. Anything from Viper?"

"Not since we last talked. Should I initiate contact?"

He had expected to hear from Rodriguez by now, but the last thing he wanted was to feed the Mexican's ego by running after him.

"No, leave it for now."

He put the phone down and felt his irritation grow.

Rodriguez had initially been difficult to work with. He had no understanding of procedures or schedules. Not that anything onerous was required; the demands were consistent with his lifestyle but at critical junctures he was expected to report. Junctures like this. If he was looking for ways to exercise his newfound power by ignoring deadlines, Hughes would have to put a quick end to it. A gentle reminder of his vulnerability was all that was required.

He exited the elevator and walked down the corridor towards his office. When he got there, he was surprised to see his secretary standing nervously outside his door.

"Morning, Margaret, everything okay?"

"I'm sorry, Mr Hughes. Mr Petersen told me to ensure that you went down to see him immediately on arrival."

"Okay," he replied, "let me get a cup of java and I'll head straight down. Want anything from the coffee station?"

"I'm sorry," she repeated, "but he was most insistent that I tell you to go see him before you did anything else."

Hughes could imagine the highly-strung Petersen getting worked up over some trivial administrative matter and taking it out on Margaret. "Okay, I'll head down now. When I come back we'll have that cup of coffee," he reassured her.

When he knocked on Petersen's door his broad smile gave no hint of his annoyance. The bureaucrat was much easier to deal with if you did not try to meet him head-on. "Edward, did I get the meeting time wrong? I'd pencilled in eleven fifteen."

The bookish, bespectacled Petersen stood up and walked past him to close the door, looking even more grim than usual. "Tom, I hate to have to do this. The director called me at five this morning from London. He instructed me to tell you when you arrived that you're to be suspended, effective immediately." He did not meet Hughes' gaze. "You're to give me your security pass. There are two agents waiting outside to escort you home. They require access to your apartment so that they can conduct a search. They'll need your agreement unless they secure a warrant, of course, but my recommendation would be to cooperate. You're to volunteer any work-related material you may have there. I'm sorry."

Hughes was rocked to his core by Petersen's announcement. There was nothing he was working on officially that could have resulted in this. Years of practising concealment of his true thoughts and feelings were all that prevented him betraying himself.

"What else did he say?" he asked calmly.

"Nothing, he wouldn't talk about it. When I pressed him, he came down on me like a ton of bricks, basically instructed me to do what I was told and not ask questions."

Petersen opened the door again, clearly eager to get it over with. Hughes handed his pass to Petersen and walked outside in a daze. He wondered if the director had learnt of the Colombian strategy. It didn't make sense. If he knew even part of what was involved, why was he not being detained?

Later, Hughes watched from the window as the agents drove away. There had been no danger of them finding anything incriminating in the house. He paced around his study, trying to figure out what his next move should be. Something had been brought to the director's attention to cause this sanction, but what? And who had been responsible? He needed to be careful of who he asked as someone could be monitoring him. The first option was to go through his official network. He knew enough people to hope one of them would speak to him off the record. He called a colleague whom he had helped on a number of occasions.

"Glenn, Tom here."

"I'm sorry Tom, I can't talk to you."

"Come on, I'm not asking you to do anything out of line. Petersen must have gotten his wires crossed. I just want to know what this misunderstanding is all about."

"We received a directive in the last hour stating that any interaction with you would result in a severe reprimand. I'm risking a lot just telling you that much, I've got to go."

"Glenn, come on, no one's told me anything. I've just been given an inexplicable suspension. Surely, if I was in serious trouble, I wouldn't have been left unaccompanied."

"Sorry, Tom, I'm hanging up now. I hope things work out."

The line went dead. When he tried calling him back he got an engaged signal. He went through half a dozen contacts, being hung up on each time he announced himself. Okay, he thought, no other option. Reaching for his raincoat, he headed out of the house.

He walked for half an hour, ensuring he was not being followed. A couple of times he cut through crowded eateries just to make it more difficult for any unwanted company. When he was satisfied that he had done as much as he could, he went to a public phone in the lobby of one of the large hotels. Using his body to shield the number pad, with the same formula as he had used earlier that morning he derived a new number and dialled it in. The call went through its long sequence of routing, seeming to take even longer than normal before connecting. He listened to it ring, becoming more unsettled as the seconds dragged into minutes. Up to now, he had been confident that whatever the problem was it could be dealt with, but the unanswered ringing tone meant the situation had taken on a new significance. This was part of his network; the phone should have been manned twenty-four hours a day without fail. He hung up and started walking again, thinking about his next step. Subconsciously he performed standard anti-surveillance manoeuvres while his thoughts were concentrated on how he could find out what had happened. He bought a ticket at a Metrorail station. On the train he forced himself to calm down and tried to think of plausible explanations for why his call had not been answered. After a few minutes he gave up; there were none. Contingencies had been designed for every eventuality. Either the network had been breached or abandoned. He got off the train at Union Station and walked over to a row of telephones. Not bothering with his earlier procedure, he dialled a direct number, one he had memorised a long time ago but never before had occasion to use.

"I've been expecting your call."

"What's going on, William? Has the network been shut down?"

"Yes and once we're finished here, this number will be taken out of service too."

"What's happening?" he asked, his anger building.

"What do you think? You've been rumbled, you and the whole Colombian operation."

"That's impossible."

"Is it? Then there's no need to be having this conversation. Goodbye."

"No, wait. Wait."

"I'm waiting."

"How?"

"Some very annoyed people, on the Hill and elsewhere, found out everything, chapter and verse."

Hughes felt his chest constricting and struggled to breathe. The voice on the other end continued.

"If it's any comfort to you I'm fairly optimistic the imminent purge that's on the way won't be fatal. It's useful knowing where the bodies are buried."

"So, there's a chance we can walk away from this?"

"No, my boy, I'm afraid you misunderstood. It will take everything we have for just a select few of us to survive. Lots of markers had to be cashed in and a lot of scrambling done. Please understand, the reason I'm telling you this is so that you're quite clear of the consequences if anything were to cause this considerable sacrifice to have been in vain."

He despised the speaker but was incapable for the moment of any action against him. "That's it then."

"A final word of advice. If I were you, I'd ditch any unwanted surveillance and start making relocation plans. It seems to me that you've been let roam free for a reason. It would be much easier for everyone if you just disappeared. You get to choose whether it's on your terms or someone else's. No doubt you've salted enough away in some grubby account to maintain a reasonable lifestyle in a far-flung locale. Goodbye Thomas."

Hughes could not believe it. All the time, effort and risk he had put in, only for it to finish like this. For a fleeting moment, the desolation he felt almost convinced him to throw himself off a bridge or in front of the traffic. Then he snapped out of it. The way he saw it there were only a few choices open to him. He could give up like a coward, he could waste valuable time trying to figure out what had gone wrong or he could choose to survive.

He decided he was going to get out of this nightmare, get to somewhere safe and from there he was going to marshal his forces. This was not the time to dwell on how he had been abandoned, how the years of selfless service, sacrifices, had been discounted without a second thought. There would be a reckoning down the line. Anyone who thought he would meekly slip away, happy to survive with his skin, was mistaken.

He returned to the Metrorail and caught the Red Line to Bethesda. From the station he flagged a cab and headed for a one-bedroom townhouse he maintained there under an assumed identity. He had three properties like this in Maryland and fifteen nationwide. They were particularly useful for storing sensitive information or to provide short-term accommodation for select people. He paid the driver, added a ten-dollar tip and asked him to wait. He went upstairs to the bedroom, pulled back a rug and removed a section of floorboard. He took out a small metal box, opened it and spread the contents on the floor. There were four sets of similar documentation each bundled with an elastic band. He chose one of the bundles and placed it in his coat. He then took out his wallet, removed all existing cards and identification and placed these with the three remaining bundles into the metal box, which he then replaced under the floor. He returned to the driver and asked him to head back to the Metrorail.

An hour and a half later the girl at the desk smiled at the handsome customer as she handed him his tickets. "There you go Mr McDermott, your ticket to New York. While you're waiting for your flight to depart you're welcome to use the executive lounge. Have a nice trip."

He smiled and thanked her.

Forty-four hours later he eased back in his chair, trying to get some sleep on the transatlantic flight from Chicago to Frankfurt. Since leaving Washington he had been moving non-stop and was exhausted. He had done his best to make it difficult for anyone who might be looking for him, regardless of how extensive their operation. He had activated a number of agents still under his control to initiate domestic and international travel with aliases he was known to have used in the past. Additionally, he had used contacts not affiliated to the Agency in any way to create yet another new identity for him. Combined with the subtle changes he had made to his appearance, it should be enough to avoid detection. In his hand luggage, he had six more new sets of identification, which he would use on the subsequent legs of his journey.

Finding that sleep eluded him, he considered what the longer term held. In a few months he would start rebuilding. There were resources, known only to him, which had no connection whatsoever to the Colombian operation. They functioned in isolation and only required the correct protocol to be activated. There were also a number of offshore accounts which, even individually, held substantial sums. When he had regrouped, priority would be given to figuring out what had gone wrong.

Despite the frantic running of the past two days there had been time to reflect. While he still had so much to figure out, one thing was clear; underestimating Mesi had been a grave mistake. She had been the one variable unaccounted for and must have been responsible for the dramatic turn in events. Somehow, she had managed to first unearth his strategy and then prevent it. But he couldn't figure out how, considering how little she had. She would have had to recruit support to bring about what she clearly had, but he had made sure she was marginalised so that the necessary support should have been impossible to rally. More practically, he was mystified as to how she could have set it all up so soon on the heels of the attempted ambush. None of these or the countless other questions which sprang to mind could be answered but he was confident that all he needed was time. Everyone who had contributed, either directly or by simply deserting him, would pay for everything he was suffering.

That he could never return to the US under his true identity was what hurt most. Twenty-odd years ago he had left college as an idealistic young man, eager to serve his country. And serve it he had. He had shown promise and advanced rapidly. From very early on, he had gained an appreciation for how fragile his nation and its way of life was. He understood what it took to protect them. Stability was paramount and, to achieve it, people like him needed to exert control. He had not always liked what he was called to do; some of it had tested his resolve to the limit. But he had persevered, taken the hard path because that was what duty dictated.

Colombia was the latest of a long line. It had not been an easy decision to authorise some of the strategies; the collateral damage was considerable but there had been no choice. They had needed to regain control of the situation there before it was too late. The drug economy was too powerful to eradicate, something the well-meaning optimists who had backed Plan Coca could just not understand. No matter how much they expended in terms of manpower or firepower, the resilient cartels would always bounce back. And while the distracting sideshow was being played out on that continent, escalations in production from other regions were being left virtually unchecked. The only viable choice was for them to seize control of the entire Latin American apparatus while it, crucially, still enjoyed market dominance. That would have enabled them to influence the global drug economy. Once they had achieved their objective, they would have ramped up production but maintained greater control over where the output went. They could have kept it out of decent neighbourhoods and schools, channelled it towards those destabilising elements within their own country. They could have put the vast revenues it brought to good use as well; his thoughts lately had been turning toward using Wallace's template to sow division amongst the extremist groups who had become prominent in recent years.

Wallace had come along at exactly the right time. Hughes had been refining other strategies, aimed at toppling Madrigal and taking over the territories, but none had looked especially promising. The Colombian had been too well positioned, too powerful, but what Wallace had proposed, if managed correctly, provided the solution. The most difficult part had been ensuring, with Brewer's help and his own network throughout the Alliance, that Wallace was not too successful. On more than one occasion he had almost failed and the feud had looked like it would consume the protagonists whole. The anarchy which would have resulted if that had happened did not bear thinking about. Despite the obstacles, everything had come together perfectly and only the formalities had remained.

Catching himself, he refused to wallow in self-pity; instead, after ordering a whisky from one of the stewardesses, he turned his thoughts to how he would engineer his revenge.

The concept was simple. Once a year the senior management selected people from all ranks of the organisation to accompany them on an excursion. The people could come from any of the disparate subsidiaries owned by the parent company but all of them had one thing in common: they had each excelled in their jobs during the previous twelve months. This was the company's way of recognising their contribution and thanking them. The activity changed each year. Last year it had been hot-air ballooning, another it had been a two-day trek in the mountains of British Colombia. This year, the company had chartered five Beneteau 40.7 sailboats out of Boston. After some practical yacht instruction they spent three days, under the watchful eye of instructors, crewing the individual boats, often racing against each other. On the fourth day they returned to shore, exhilarated and exhausted.

He was glad now that he had relented and agreed to come along. It had been one of the most enjoyable experiences he could remember having in a long time. At first he had refused when Philip Sims, the newly-appointed CEO of Diversified Holdings, had asked if he would attend the corporate function. Sims had been harder to dissuade than his predecessor and had insisted that Wallace at least go away and think about it. He had argued that it would be a great boost for the employees to spend time with the man who had founded the company, and the strong internal culture, of which everyone was so proud. Not just the employees lucky enough to have been chosen for the trip either. Everyone who worked for the organisation got a mail-shot updating them on that year's activities. Imagine the feeling of connectivity they would feel, the CEO had argued, when they saw that the man who had started the whole deal had attended. Wallace was not sure if he agreed with modern corporate theory, the psychology surrounding people's affiliation and motivational needs. In his day, you worked to put food on the table and a roof over your head, but he had come to the conclusion that he really ought to give the company some time. Returning Sims' call, he said that, while he was not sure how significant his presence would be, he was happy to attend.

It turned out that the change in focus had been exactly what he had needed. He found mucking in on the boat to be great fun. In addition to the professional crew there were eight people from the organisation on each boat. His companions included the manager of an electrical goods retail outlet, a fork-lift operator and a programmer. Once the initial shock of being paired with him wore off, they began to treat him like just another crew member. On one occasion, the retail manager, wanting them to be the first crew to reach that day's finishing point, had torn into him with a number of suggestions regarding his head and his ass when he had been slow to react to an order. He had surprised himself with how quickly he had replied in equally colourful terms. That evening they had laughed uproariously about it over dinner.

Now, after reaching the final destination and having had

a chance to rest for a few hours, the forty of them were spending their last evening together. The atmosphere was wonderful at the outdoor buffet laid on by the yacht club. With the three days of sun and sea, people positively glowed, not only from the sailing but also from the sense of camaraderie which had formed. He was surprised to realise that he had not thought about his recent troubles for even a fleeting moment over the past three days.

Things had worked out as well as he could have hoped. The thought of saving Madrigal had been abhorrent. They had effectively strengthened the drug lord's position immeasurably. In eliminating Rodriguez and uncovering the conspiracy against them, his reputation amongst the other cartel members had taken on legendary proportions. Whatever obstacles the Colombian would face in the future, internal challenges were not likely to be among them. The friction between him and the people who controlled the drug-producing territories was still there, but mutual greed was overcoming any philosophical differences.

Most of the intelligence people behind the plot to discredit Plan Coca and misuse his own campaign had been dealt with. Expulsions and demotions at the lower levels, for those who were unaware of the final objective, and, he had been informed, executions for others. Unfortunately, a few had escaped with nothing more than a reprimand. These were the people who knew too much, the ones who had to be handled carefully. He could not complain too much; he had also used the same threat of blowing the whistle on the whole sordid affair to ensure he went unpunished. The hope was that these figures in the upper echelons of the intelligence world would have learnt their lesson as well as he had. Somehow, he doubted it. According to Larsen,

Hughes had escaped through the ineptitude of his former employers. Warned that the net was closing, he had been given too much time. Despite the manpower supposedly committed to locating him, nothing had turned up. Wallace was cynical enough to appreciate how content many people were for it to remain that way.

He had not heard from Larsen in the four weeks since that last call and doubted he ever would again. He had no idea where the Dane had gone or what his plans were. It was uncomfortable for him to think too long about the mercenary, because inevitably that stirred memories of how disappointed Larsen had been in him at the end. Not that anything had ever been said, but Wallace knew.

He had, however, finally stopped torturing himself over the harm they had done. It would do no good for him to spend the rest of his life fretting over what had happened. It had never been his intention to hurt innocents and he had done his best to make up for any damage he might have caused. That had to count for something. Besides, a large part of him still believed that, without outside interference, they might have succeeded in crippling the drug trade and kept innocent casualties to a minimum. At least the clinics were recovering. Now that the crisis was well and truly past, he had been told they would be back on track within six months.

"Larry. Hey, Larry!"

His thoughts were disturbed by Sharon Murray, the programmer from his crew.

"Sorry, what?"

"Rob's going inside to get another beer; do you want one?"

"No, I'm fine, thanks." He spent the next couple of

hours enjoying himself immensely, even being dragged up to dance at one stage by some of his fellow crew members. When the party started to wind down, he sat down beside Sims, the CEO.

"Well, happy you changed your mind?"

"Absolutely. Being here's shown me how much I've been missing. I was thinking of talking to you about maybe taking a more active role than I have been recently."

"That'd be great. As long as you're not thinking of taking my job," Sims laughed.

"No, no, I was …"

"Mr Wallace?"

He looked up at the manager of the yacht club, who stood beside their table. "Yes?"

"I'm so sorry to disturb you but there's an urgent phone call for you inside."

He had deliberately not brought his cell phone, wanting to have a complete break from the stresses of the past few months. He smiled in apology to Sims and headed into the club-house.

"Hello, this is Lawrence Wallace," he said into the phone.

"Enjoying your little jaunt?" asked a man's voice.

"What? Who is this?"

"My name is Thomas Hughes and this is just a call to let you know that this isn't finished for you yet. You have no idea how much damage you've done, but I intend to show you. I'll let you get back to your friends now."

The line went dead but Wallace remained standing there listening to the dial tone. Everything started to fade and the sound of the party grew steadily more distant.

fourteen

THREE MONTHS LATER

Hughes settled into the comfortable kitchen chair and opened the tablet edition of the newspaper. He would read it in more detail when he returned from his run, but five or ten minutes scanning it, over a cup of coffee, would give him time to wake up. He liked the early mornings best, here in Gweedore, the small town near the most north-western corner of Ireland. Everything was so quiet and the air had a special quality to it. It was a magical time when the sun was just clearing the horizon after the pitch-black winter night and everything seemed freshly scrubbed. Winstone and Feeney were still in bed, sleeping off the effects of a substantial amount of Bushmills from the looks of the bottle on the kitchen table. It was difficult to justify having them here and he would probably let them go in the next week or two. He couldn't see them being too unhappy as he knew the solitude was starting to get to them. The ruggedness of the landscape and feeling of space had restored him, though, and even after his imposed exile was over he could see himself returning here at some point. Saying that, he certainly didn't envy the locals who battled to eke out a living here. Most of the land was shale-covered hills supporting nothing but hardy scrub grass on which only a few herds of sheep were able to subsist. The limited dealings he had with the people were friendly enough, and they respected his privacy.

A headline halfway down the page immediately caught his attention. It reported that Lawrence Wallace had died the previous night, after a steady decline in health over the last couple of months. He had mixed feelings about the news. There was no doubt that Wallace had been partly responsible for his current situation. It was one less item to attend to but also meant he would miss the pleasure of confronting the industrialist himself. He would just have to make do with the fact that his phone call may have played a part in the rapid deterioration.

Hughes had gone over and over what he knew about the days leading up to his forced flight. By the time he had reached Europe he knew Mesi must have enlisted Wallace's help to put it all together. Although how she could have been sure Wallace was not an ally of his was just another question he had no answer for. It tormented him that he had made a mistake he could not identify. Surveillance he had put in place informed him that, weeks after his departure, she had resurfaced. Since tendering her resignation from the DEA, she had become a virtual recluse, sticking mostly to her apartment and barely venturing out. The photos he had seen of her, long-lens shots, showed a moping, slovenly woman who was finding it difficult to cope with everyday life. Not at all like the assertive, ambitious Diane he remembered. He supposed that the brittle, vulnerable traits he had detected and exploited had been brought to the fore by recent events. Obviously, much the same as Wallace, she lacked the necessary fortitude. It would be fairly easy to have her lifted when he was ready. Once he had worked out her culpability in his downfall, all residual affection had fallen away. There would be no compunction in doing whatever was necessary.

It was painful thinking back to those first few weeks on the run. He had been so on-edge that, even in this obscure bolthole, he had contracted Winstone and Feeney, ex-Royal Marines, as security. It was embarrassing now, considering the precautions he had insisted they take. Regular patrols, alternate night watches, thorough vehicle checks. As the weeks had passed, he saw how unnecessary these were and relaxed the demands on the men. In the last couple of weeks their duties had been so minimal that it had become a well-paid holiday for them.

He put the tablet down and started a series of callisthenics as part of a dynamic warm up. Once he was happy that he was properly prepared, he set off for his daily exercise. Running here required a lot of concentration because of the uneven ground. He made good progress and was soon sweating freely, moving quickly along the route. At the fifty-five-minute mark, the hill came into sight. This was the last leg of the run; after this he only had an easy ten-minute jog back to the cottage to cool down. Gathering his breath, he started up the steep incline. By halfway, his lungs and throat were burning. Fifty or so paces from the top, he put his head down and pumped hard, focusing on one step at a time. He almost fell over when he reached the top, stumbling a few times before righting himself. Standing up straight, he looked out at the ocean. A few drops of rain fell and a quick glance skyward told him that he had better head for the cottage.

He took his first step down the hill and the shale exploded less than twelve inches from his foot.

He froze at the sound of the gunshot. Not sure where it had come from, he couldn't decide whether to continue down or run back over the brow. Another couple of shots slammed into the top of the hill and made the decision for him. He began scrambling down the dangerous terrain as quickly as he could. Near the bottom of the hill, more shots struck close and he fell. Rolling over and over, he gashed his knee deeply on the rocks before coming to a stop. Ignoring the pain, he dragged himself to his feet. The rain increased and quickly soaked him through. The now slippery scrub grass was treacherous underfoot and the bare patches of earth were deteriorating into a mire. He slipped countless times and was soon caked in mud, carrying a number of additional small scrapes. The more level ground, though, was easier on his legs and he felt himself recovering a little from his exertions. The cottage was close, less than half a mile; once he got there he would be safe. The ground erupted behind him as the sniper opened up. He tried to move faster but fell again and felt his ankle wrench. Another bullet slammed into the ground beside him and he pushed himself up. When he tried to stand the pain from the ankle was too much and he was forced to crawl on his hands and one good leg as best he could. He was the easiest of targets and he expected the fatal bullet any second. After heart-stopping minutes of crawling frantically through the downpour, he guessed the sniper must have either given up or become unsighted. Either way it did not matter, he had reached the cottage and was safe now.

"George, Charlie!"

The shouts died in his throat at the sight that greeted him. Feeney had been shot by something powerful, his bloodied body beside the overturned kitchen table and broken whisky bottle. He hobbled through to the sitting room to find an even worse sight. Winstone's body lay beside the sofa. His throat had been slashed and the white cloth on the back of the couch was stained with arterial spray. Hobbling over to the set of drawers, he pulled one open and reached for the handgun.

"You don't think it's still there, do you?"

He spun around, eyes wide. A woman dressed in blue jeans and black sweater stood looking at him. Her red hair was pulled back tightly and she looked more worn than the last time he had seen her.

"Diane?"

He started towards her but stopped when she raised the gun.

"Diane, what's going on?"

"What do you think?" she asked, almost conversationally.

"Why are you pointing that at me? Can you please put it down?"

"I don't think so."

"My God, Diane, it's me!"

He had to try and draw her out; if he could get her talking, an opportunity could present itself.

She continued to study him, her stare burning through him.

"Diane, please, I've been so worried about you. What have you been told?"

That seemed to get her interest.

"Told by who?"

"The same people I'm hiding from, obviously. The ones who've constructed a conspiracy against me. Diane, please, don't let them make you forget what we've shared."

"Pretty good, Tom," she said. "The mixture of outrage and appeal, the reference to that sick charade I believed in."

"Can't you see you've been lied to?" he pleaded. "That

I'm the perfect fall guy for them?"

"Fall guys don't usually have their own secret army and assortment of off-shore back accounts."

"My work requires me to have those." He tried to keep the panic from his voice, to inject a soothing tone. "It allows my superiors deniability, but you must see it also leaves me vulnerable to deceit."

"Deceit, there's an interesting word. I won't waste your time. The only reason I'm here is to tell you that you failed. In everything you tried, you failed."

He tried desperately to think. To stall her, he deliberately exaggerated the discomfort his ankle was causing and limped over to lean against the fireplace while she watched him like a hawk.

Was she alone? Unlikely; she couldn't possibly have fired those shots and made it back to the house. Besides, she was bone dry which would not have been the case had she been scrambling around the hills. So she had at least one accomplice.

When he looked up at her, he put everything he had into it, words, pitch of voice, posture, all of the auto-suggestive prompts he had perfected. "You were right about Wallace; I did know about it, but you have to believe me, we only let it run to bring about the Alliance's demise. I was misled. I'd told my superiors about you and they'd guaranteed you'd be picked up, protected. I didn't know –"

"Give it up."

The dismissive way she cut him off was too much. Who did she think she was? A lowly investigator who couldn't even hack it in her own pitiful organisation. After everything, he had been reduced to this, grovelling to her!

"You stupid, clueless little bitch. You stumble around

blindly like the rest, no idea of what's really required," he spat.

She smiled at his outburst. "Careful Tom, you don't want to drop the mask!" She lowered the gun.

"What are you going to do now?' He faced her defiantly. "You're not going to shoot me."

"Look at your bodyguard over there and tell me how you can be so confident? There might be ten of Madrigal's men outside, waiting to butcher you."

His eyes shot to the door then back to her. He knew it was a lie. She was bluffing him, eager to extract her pound of flesh.

"You're right, Madrigal doesn't know about your hideout," she said, reading his thoughts.

His spirits soared; someone had recognised that he was too valuable to simply discard.

She turned to leave the cottage.

"But I would take a closer look at the way your bodyguard died." She stepped outside, leaving him alone with Winstone's corpse.

What was the stupid bitch talking about? The way he died? Someone had slashed his throat with a knife, so what?

Then it dawned on him.

She deliberately trained her gaze out along the coastline. Even so, in her periphery she picked up a figure entering the house. Then, Hughes' screams began. He begged her at the top of his voice to return. She walked down the grass-covered path, away from the cottage. In the distance, sea birds drifted up on thermals along the cliffs and then spiralled back down towards the surf. The morning sun had cleared the horizon now and she welcomed its warmth.

author biography

—

David Graham has a background in telecommunications and IT. In addition to working throughout Europe, particularly in Scandinavia, he has travelled extensively.

He has a keen interest in history, economics and current affairs.

David lives with his wife and two young sons in Dublin. This is his first novel.

—